THE FIRST CASUALTY

ALSO BY GREGG LOOMIS

THE FIRST CASUALTY

GREGG LOOMIS

MYSTERIOUSPRESS.COM

OPEN ROAD
INTEGRATED MEDIA
NEW YORK

Cover design by Mauricio Díaz

ISBN 978-1-4804-2686-3

Published in 2013 by MysteriousPress.com/Open Road Integrated Media, Inc.
345 Hudson Street
New York, NY 10014
www.mysteriouspress.com
www.openroadmedia.com

This book is for Suzanne

THE FIRST CASUALTY

"In war, truth is the first casualty."
—Aeschylus

1

48 East Houston Street
New York, New York
July 1898

The tall man with the mustache parted his hair in the middle. He wore a bowler hat and a light coat over his suit despite the heat wave that had been ravaging the city for more than a week. Shutting the main door of the four-story brick building, he turned to lock it before proceeding south. He was tempted to ride the El, Broadway's elevated railway, but chose a more direct route. He took his time walking through the Bowery, looked in a few shop windows along Saint James and picked up his pace when he reached Pearl Street.

At no time did his hand come out of the left pocket of his coat.

He stopped when he reached the steel skeleton of a building under construction on Wall Street. He had observed the project for a week, the only one suitable for the experiment. Finding a spot across the street shaded from the afternoon sun, he watched workers swarm over the structure like ants, driving rivets, manning the crane, riding the hydraulic lift up and down, until he was certain no one had noticed him. As calmly as though he owned the property, he sauntered over to the spot where one of the girders met the earth before it sank into the foundations.

He withdrew a metal cylinder from his left pocket, a device that closely resembled the battery-powered electrical hand torches that had just come on the market a few months earlier. He froze as a streetcar clattered by, iron-shod hooves of the two horses ringing on the rails.

Ascertaining he was still unobserved, he bound the metal tube to the steel with a leather belt and retreated to his previous observation post in the shade.

Minutes passed as a mix of pedestrians, horse-drawn vehicles, and automobiles made their way down the narrow confines of the street. He checked his pocketwatch. Thirty-six minutes. He frowned. It should not take this long.

He took a step as though to inspect the device just as he detected the slightest movement of the steel. One girder visibly expanded and retracted, then another. Now all were beating as if a human heart lay within.

There was a shout of fright from above. Within seconds, workers were crowding the elevator. Some were sliding down ropes hastily tied to crossbars.

Ignoring the growing pandemonium, the man in the coat crossed the street, removed his device and returned it to his coat pocket before leisurely departing the scene. This time, he would treat himself to the luxury of the El, though somewhat out of the way back to East Houston Street. He stopped long enough to hear an excited exchange between a policeman and a construction worker with a palpable Irish brogue.

"I'm telling you as God is my witness, an earthquake it was!"

"But I was only blocks away and didn't feel a thing."

"Then maybe you can be telling me what made the very steel shake."

The man in the overcoat didn't wait to hear a response.

2

Mary Jurgens was pretty sure the old man on the bed had passed.

She had no idea how old he was, but he had been living in the two-room suite long before she had come to work at the hotel just after she and Joshua, her husband, had left Alabama four years ago. Moses, Joshua's brother, had made good on his promise of good, regular wages and union hours at the Brooklyn Navy Yard for Joshua. Better yet, the job was going to keep Joshua out of the draft.

But what was she going to do about the dead man on the bed?

Years in the South had taught her not to be in the neighborhood when something like this happened to a white man. The white folks claimed it was different in New York, but Mary had observed they liked to talk about equality but put it into practice rarely. In fact, she and Josh felt more isolated in their Harlem apartment than they ever had as sharecroppers in a shack at the edge of a cotton field. At least in Alabama, white or black, there was a commonality of cause: Get the crop in or everybody was looking at a pretty lean winter.

Still, she didn't feel she could just slip out into the hall and leave the doctor there. He'd been as much a friend to her as any white person, asking in that funny accent of his how her family was doing, leaving her a crisp ten-dollar bill every Christmas and birthday.

An hour later, she wished she had left.

Four men in three-piece suits and hats had appeared within minutes of her reporting to the front desk what she had found. She was pretty sure they weren't New York City policeman. One spoke with a southern accent. They had taken her into a vacant room and were asking her questions that made her uneasy, as if they thought she might have something to do with the doctor's death.

How well did Mary know him?

Not any more than she had learned cleaning his suite daily and exchanging the occasional "good morning" when he was in it.

Who were his friends?

She had no idea. She had never seen anyone else in the suite nor had she seen evidence of visitors.

Had he ever been on the telephone when she was in the suite?

She couldn't remember. But if she had, she certainly didn't pay any mind to what was said.

Things like that.

To Mary, the questions implied these men thought she had been something other than a maid working for the Hotel New Yorker. Plus, it was starting to get dark outside. She couldn't afford a watch, but she knew it was past six o'clock, when Joshua would expect supper to be on the table.

The thought of food made her wonder. Had the red stamps, the ones for January's meat ration, come in yet? What about the ones for sugar and butter? She couldn't remember. One thing was certain: Whether they had or not, it would never occur to Joshua to take them to the grocery store down the street and buy something he could prepare himself. She wished they had decided to spend the money on a telephone.

For one of the few times since leaving Alabama, she thought of it nostalgically. There wasn't rationing when you raised your own chickens, maybe a hog or two. Butter was a luxury anyway, and lard did just as good most of the time. And nobody she knew had a telephone, so it wasn't any use to even think about one there.

"Mrs. Jurgens, I asked you a question."

One of the men in suits brought her back to the hotel room.

"Yes, sir?"

"I asked you if the deceased ever left papers out."

"Papers?"

The man made no effort to hide the annoyance in his tone. "You know, *papers*."

"He read lots of papers: *The Times, Evening Sun, Herald Tribune . . .*"

"No, no. I mean things he had written. Did he ever leave something like that lying around?"

"Not that I know of."

"But, if he had, you would have seen them, right?"

"I suppose. I try and tidy up as well as clean. I know he asked me several times if I'd seen anyone in his rooms while he was gone, asked me to call the police if I did."

For some reason, the man asking the question didn't seem in the least surprised by the dead man's fears his suite might be entered in his absence. "You'll be here tomorrow?"

She bobbed her head, yes, sir. "Ever' day 'cept Sunday. Used to get Monday off instead, but I been here long enough now I gets to choose my day off."

She was thankful she was free to go until she thought maybe she wasn't as free as she had thought. There was a white man in a three-piece suit on the Harlem Line, something she had never seen north of 120th Street.

Later that night, after she and Joshua had turned off the lights in their third-floor walk-up, something made her go to the window and peek between the blinds. There, just across 141st Street, a Ford was parked, a 1942 model, she guessed, made before the production of civilian automobiles had been halted for the duration. Inside, she could see the glow of a cigarette. Car like that, new as cars were going to get for sometime, people didn't just park at the sidewalk. A fact she pondered as she went back to bed.

3

Hotel New Yorker
West 34th Street and Eighth Avenue
New York, New York
The Next Morning

He was waiting for Mary when she walked into the hotel's rear entrance ten minutes before she was due to report for work. Short, stocky man with a jowly face that reminded her of a bulldog.

"FBI," he said, peremptorily showing her a badge in a wallet as he took her by the arm.

"I needs to get to work," Mary protested. "'Sides, I answered questions yesterday."

"This won't take long." the man assured her, his grip on her arm tightening.

A few minutes later, they were back in the doctor's suite. For the hundredth time, Mary noted how bare it was of personal effects. No photographs, no framed certificates, nothing but furniture placed there by the hotel, furniture that definitely had become a little shabby. Thankfully, the bed was freshly made and empty.

A closer look around showed drawers pulled out, drawers of the bureau, drawers of the two bedside tables, drawers of the two side tables in the sitting room. A quick glance into the bath showed a yawning-open medicine cabinet. There was no trace of toilet articles, the safety razor, shaving brush and mug, toothbrush, or tube of toothpaste, all of which were usually aligned on a glass shelf under the mirror above the sink. The door of the closet also hung open. It was completely empty of the rows of suits with shoes lined up beneath.

There were two other men already in the sitting room, one of whom stood, offering one of the two club chairs to the jowly man. Mary sensed an air of deference toward him, like he was the boss. No one offered Mary a seat, so she remained standing.

The jowly man sat and removed his hat, placing it carefully on a table. His dark hair, brushed straight back, glistened with some sort of pomade.

"Mary," he said in a voice much more friendly than she had heard yesterday, "look around. You see anything different?"

She did as she was told. "Yes, sir. All his things are gone."

"All?"

"Far as I can see, yes, sir."

"Did he have any special place, a sort of hiding place?"

"Not that I know of, no, sir."

"Maybe a place to put documents, papers."

"I don' know nothing 'bout any missing papers."

He jumped to his feet so suddenly, Mary took a step back. "Aha!" he exclaimed, pointing an accusatory finger. "Who said anything about *missing* papers?"

Mary looked from the jowly man to the other two men and back again. "They weren't missing, you wouldn't be asking me 'bout them."

The man who had given up his chair made an unsuccessful attempt to hide a smile and drew a glare from Mary's interrogator.

The questions, most of which had been asked yesterday, lasted another fifteen minutes before the man looked at the other two. "Anything you can think of?"

As one, both shook their heads.

The man pointed to the door. "You can go for now, but we might want to talk to you again, so don't go anywhere. Understand?"

Mary nodded. "Yes, sir. I ain't going nowhere."

"Good."

As she took the elevator down to the basement to collect her cleaning supplies, a number of thoughts spun through her mind: She had become inured to the rudeness of some white people, like Mr. Bulldog back there. It no longer bothered her. But the doctor must have been somebody besides the quiet-voiced, meek, little man with a funny accent whom Mary had known. What kind of papers would he have that would interest the FBI? A spy for the Nazis? She smiled at the thought of the mousy little man carrying a gun and taking pictures of . . . what? The Brooklyn Navy Yard? But then, weren't spies supposed to look like something else?

Then a thought came out of the blue and popped into her head, a thought so engrossing she didn't hear the uniformed elevator operator the first time he announced the basement. He had to repeat himself before she remembered where she was.

The jowly man. She had seen his picture before, both in the papers and at the Apollo Theater when movies with newsreels replaced live entertainment. The blocky figure, the swept back hair. But most of all, the bulldog face. That was him, she was sure.

But why would the head of the FBI come all the way from Washington to question her?

4

Hill 3234
Khost Province, Afghanistan
February 23, 1988

Charlie Sherman had been with the mujahideen too long. He was beginning to hallucinate. Maybe it was the food. *Qabili palau*, a sort of
rice pilaf with caramelized vegetables, at every meal was enough to get
to men far saner than Charlie. It had been so long since he had tasted
meat, he had begun to fantasize about the scrawny goats that bleated
in every village. Maybe it was the cold. Maybe he had been insane to
begin with, volunteering to liaison between the CIA and the natives
resisting Russian invasion.

Whatever. He knew the facts: A month ago, a Russian force had
been defeated trying to open up the road winding through the valley below. There were still a number of what he guessed were Russian
bodies. Natural decomposition despite the near frigid weather made it
hard to tell. Decomposition, plus the quaint local custom of stripping
the dead of anything useful, including uniforms.

But that wasn't what had Charlie questioning his own sanity.

Charlie's Afghan guide and translator, Aarif, whose name meant "understanding," wasn't understandable at all. He had kept pointing to the rusting hulk of a T-72. Like most Russian tanks he saw these days, it had a couple of large holes in it, the result of multiple RPG hits. This one, though, didn't mount the usual turret gun. Instead, it had a blunt-nozzle sort of apparatus. Charlie had heard the Ruskies were experimenting with various gases, but there wasn't enough left of the seared interior to tell what sort of weapons it had carried.

Strange but not weird.

Then Aarif had led him into a cave cut into the rock of the hillside. The walls were easily one or two meters thick, far too thick to be penetrated by the 85-millimeter shells fired by Russian tanks. Charlie switched on his flashlight. The cave was full of dead people, mujahideen fighters. Not only did they look as though they had simply gone to sleep—no decomposition, no stench of rotting flesh—the bodies were barely over a meter in length. Unless the Afghans had enlisted a brigade of midgets, there was something really strange there.

Aarif's English left a lot to be desired, but if Charlie had understood him correctly, he said the tank had fired something that had come through the walls of the cave. But there was no damage Charlie could see.

"Gas," he said, "the tank fired gas into the entrance?"

The Afghan shook his head adamantly, no. "Came through!"

Weapons that break through solid rock leaving no hole, fighters the size of small children that don't deteriorate . . .

Yep, Charlie had been in Afghanistan too long. On the upside, once he reported all this, he wouldn't be there much longer.

5

Air France Flight 447
Rio de Janeiro, Brazil–Paris, France
29° N, 30.6° W
June 1, 2009

The giant Airbus A330's 216 passengers remained strapped tightly into their seats. The storms indigenous to this area had tossed the plane about as though it were a child's ball. Last night's native Brazilian dinner, perhaps too rich, had caused Captain Marc Duboise to temporarily turn the ship over to the first and second officers while he made a brief visit to the first-class head. On long international flights, it was not uncommon to share the duties even though the captain had far more hours of experience than the two younger men combined.

Within minutes, the plane would reach TASIL, a point existing only on aeronautical charts and defined by the aircraft's global-positioning system as 780 statute miles west of Dakar, Senegal. Its only real significance was that it marked the end of the "dead zone," the point at which there was no VHF radio communication. Though no one voiced the thought, the sound of another human voice would make the turbulence more bearable.

"Merde!" the first officer swore as a particularly violent down draft buffeted the plane, pushing the nose down. He was thrown painfully against his seat harness. The aircraft was bucking like one of those wild horses he had seen in films of American rodeos. Broncos, yes, that was what they were called, broncos. He kept his line of vision on the instrument panel below the windscreen, taking no chance of being temporarily blinded by the lightning outside, flashing with the frequency of a celestial disco. He could only hope the repeated strikes had not damaged the electronics.

The second officer pointed to the altimeter and shouted to be heard above the crash of thunder. "You're off your assigned altitude of thirty-five thousand feet." He put a finger on the weather radar, indicating a narrow streak of green between red and yellow blobs. "Try flying zero-seven-zero. That might get us around the worst of it."

For an instant, the first officer contemplated switching off the autopilot. Its immediate reactions to extreme turbulence could, possibly, damage the air frame. He discarded the idea. Even with hydraulically assisted controls, he would be unable to make all the corrections required by this line of storms. Instead, he thumbed the electric trim tab on the control yoke, elevating the aircraft's nose.

"That should help," he shouted above the clatter of hail against the plane's hull, the sound of a coven of demons demanding admittance.

Neither man noticed the air speed indicator remained steady, an inconsistent reading since airspeed should have decreased in direct proportion to the elevated angle of the aircraft's nose—one reason planes land in a nose-up configuration.

"The altimeter!" the second officer exclaimed. "It is not moving. Neither is the vertical speed indicator!"

That was the least of the immediate problems. The yoke in the first officer's hands was not only twisting with the aircraft's gyrations, but now it was pulsating, a phenomenon neither first nor second officer had ever experienced.

"What the . . ."

There was a tearing sound, the cry of distressed metal, followed by a crash from the left side of the plane. The second officer looked up as a bolt of lightning illuminated the left wing. The number-one engine was gone, a gaping hole in its place.

"Mon Dieu!"

The stricken aircraft rolled violently to its left, shuddering in its death throes just as the strange expansions and contractions increased in violence. Over the terrified shrieks of passengers and the bedlam of the storm, there was the sound of ripping metal. From its location, the first officer guessed the vertical stabilizer had torn free.

6

Bureau d'Enquêtes et d'Analyse (BEA)
Aéroport du Bourget
7 Kilometers North of Paris, France
May 6, 2011

It was, perhaps, fitting that the French BEA, the agency charged with examining and investigating crashes of French-operated aircraft, should be located on the site of the first successful solo transatlantic flight, a feat easily eclipsing an earlier duo flight by a pair of World War I pilots. It was there on May 21, 1927, Charles Lindbergh's *Spirit of St. Louis* touched down 3,500 miles and 33½ hours from Roosevelt Field, Long Island. It was an exploit of individual courage not to be equaled until man walked on the moon.

Almost 100 years later, the field's 8,000-foot runway, multiple terminals, and status as Europe's busiest general aviation airport in no way resembled the open pasture that greeted the young American. Among the buildings clustered around the aviation center was a three-quarter acre, two-story structure that housed France's equivalent of the U.S. National Transportation Safety Board.

Inside, two men stared at a computer monitor in a combination of disbelief and incomprehension. The orange boxes recovered from the ocean floor more than 3,000 meters below the surface must have been affected by the great pressure of such depths. But the flight and voice recorders had been specifically designed to exist in such a hostile environment indefinitely, long after the batteries no longer sent out signals as to their location.

"*Impossible!*" Patrick Guyot, PhD in physics, exclaimed with the buzz of lips peculiar to the French pronunciation of the word. He was scrolling down the computer screen for the third time.

Charles Patin, aeronautical engineer, stepped over to a counter where a beaker sat on a single-ring burner, noted it was empty of the coffee usually brewed in it, and said, "Unusual, I agree. But impossible? We have checked and rechecked the readings, and they are consistent: The pressure driven instruments failed, the pressure altimeter, the static pressure vertical speed indicator. And the airspeed indicator, which would indicate the pitot tube, the . . ."

"And what is the likelihood of redundant instruments failing simultaneously? Even so, instrument failure was not the cause of this crash." Guyot looked around and lowered his voice before continuing though he and Patin were the only two in the room. "The aircraft literally disintegrated in the air. I mean, parts of the tail assembly were found nearly twenty kilometers from the fuselage's pieces. The wings weren't even found in the search area at all. What are the odds of a storm causing that?"

Patin was looking for the small bag of ground coffee kept in a drawer. "Worse than you would get in the casino at Monte Carlo, I agree. But that doesn't mean it didn't happen. There is no known limit to the severity of weather in those latitudes."

Guyot held up a multipage document. "And this series of tests: There is no explanation as to how parts of the aircraft's aluminum seem to have simply melted. There is also evidence of high heat on surfaces."

"Odd, I agree. I wonder if somehow lightning . . ."

Guyot shook his head. "To burn like that, lightning would need to be grounded. There is no ground between an airplane at thirty thousand plus feet and the earth."

Patin eased into a wooden chair that was every bit as uncomfortable as it looked. "If not lightning, what?"

Guyot pulled over the mate to his companion's chair and plopped down into it so close that the two men's knees were nearly touching. He fished a blue box of cigarettes from a shirt pocket, Gitanes, with a picture of a wisp of smoke forming a dancer. "Surely, you don't think what I'm thinking."

He offered the box.

Patin shook his head. He was almost a year past his last cigarette. He gave a wan smile. "Unless I can read your mind . . ." He studied the other man's face. "No! You cannot be serious!" He ground a finger into his temple, the French gesture to show one was mentally unbalanced. "This is crazy! Without absolute proof, I would not sign any report that even hints at . . ."

Guyot leaned forward so that his face was closer to Patin's, his cigarette temporarily forgotten. "We are obligated to report what we find, not what we think. Our report will simply relate that certain instruments aboard the flight failed at or about the same time. Panic would be the likely result of publicly stating the aircraft literally shattered in flight. We will pass that information along in confidence. There is also the strange matter of the few bodies recovered, the ones no one wants to admit exist. Desiccated and shrunken like prunes. How does one explain that? The politicians are the ones paid to decide what to do with it. Then, I intend to report what we suspect to the appropriate persons, say the DGSE, informally. If we are right, national, if not international, security is at stake."

7

Oval Office
The White House
Washington, DC
January of the Present Year
1:25 p.m. EST

The president of the United States shifted the unlit cigar from one side of his mouth to the other, a good sign he was still indecisive on the issue. The damned doctors had sufficiently frightened him away from lighting up the things after a brief encounter with lip cancer ending in an operation his staff had somehow kept secret from the media. Denied his favorite vice, he was reduced to simply chewing them into stubs.

Oblivious to the seriousness of the occasion, his six-year-old twins, Ches and Wes, were noisily testing their balancing skills with a Wobble Deck in front of the Resolute desk. Ordinarily, the two would have been with their mother in the upstairs private apartments, but the First Lady was hosting a luncheon for some female poet whose verse was angry, rhymeless, and unintelligible. It was an argument even the president dared not renew: If a person couldn't sell their (choose one) poetry, play, sculpture, or painting on the open market, why should the taxpayers pick up the slack for the poet, artist, or playwright whose talents would be better utilized in, say, a car wash? The First Lady, however, felt strongly about public support for the arts.

She felt equally strongly about the "self-expression" of her sons, whose unfettered exuberance with crayons, fingerpaint, and water-color had necessitated serious restoration of the decor of both the Blue Room and the Lincoln Bedroom. Had the Secret Service not intercepted an anonymous gift of a twenty-five-piece Black & Decker Junior Tool Kit, it was quite possible the damage done to the building in 1814 by the British General Ross would have seemed minor in comparison. The Service volunteered to provide a babysitter, but the president was unwilling to subject some unfortunate agent to the twins' unpredictable behavior, conduct that had earned them the service's code names Rape and Pillage.

"One of these days, someone in the Press Corps is going to catch you with one of those things in your face," warned the only other occupant in the room.

The president shifted the cigar again. Aware that today's smokers had replaced yesterday's lepers as pariahs, he had been careful to restrain his limited use when anywhere near a camera.

He replied to Hodges, his chief of staff, principal adviser, former campaign manager, and general dog robber. "So what? We've got two years before I'm up for reelection, and the average voter wouldn't remember if I had dropped trou and mooned the TV cameras yesterday."

There was no point in debating the electorate's notoriously brief memory span. Hodges cleared his throat and raised his voice to be heard over the twins. "Back to the problem: The Froggie's DGSE says, confidentially, that the Air France crash was no accident. The CIA and MI6 don't dispute it."

The president put elbows on the desk, leaning forward. "They don't concur, either. I mean, let's face it: Death rays and the like play out great in sci-fi, but this is real life. If I cancel out because of some Darth Vader–type threats . . . That, the voters *will* recall. If not, my next opponent will remind them."

Hodges shrugged, he was a man who knew when he was beaten. "It's your ass, Mr. President. At least reconsider in a couple of days."

The president sat back in his chair. "Agreed. Think where we go if we even think of canceling a state visit because some camel-fucking sum'bitches make threats."

"Not just any camel-fucking sum'bitches. We're talking Al Qaeda here."

"Al Qaeda or the Boy Fucking Scouts of America, I'm going to look like a coward if I don't go."

8

Hotel Adler
Herrengasse 2
Vaduz, Liechtenstein
Two Days Later

The moment he exited the hotel, Jason Peters knew he was being watched. With snow falling through the mist like feathers from a torn pillow, there was no need for the sunglasses the man across the street was wearing as his breath came in steamy puffs in the frigid air. Not unless he considered himself a film star or sport celebrity. The monochromatic light leached color from the day as if the blood had been drained from it. Hardly a time to protect the eyes. Overcoat collar pulled up, brimmed hat pulled down, the man appeared to be studying the display in the window of a *Buchhandlung*, bookstore. But unless immune to the fingers of the probing cold, no one would stand outside instead of enjoying the shop's warmth. No one who was really interested in the store's wares, that is.

Jason declined the offer of help from the comic opera-uniformed bellhop as he tossed his single bag into the space behind the driver's seat of the turbo Porsche, space that only the elves in Stuttgart could describe, with a straight face, as a backseat. He had not rented the car for its meager comforts, but for its nimble handling and blinding acceleration, features he had enjoyed on the winding sixty-mile drive south from Zurich. Liechtenstein had no commercial airport of its own.

He pretended to fuss with the canvas suitcase as he watched through the car's rear window, now rapidly shrinking as snow covered the glass. The man was using the reflection in the store's window to monitor Jason's movements.

Jason gave a sigh of resignation. Whoever he was, whatever he wanted, Jason didn't need his shit. He was tired and glad to be going home. Two days dealing with bankers had been enough to wear down the hardiest of souls. In an age when no electronic communication was 100 percent secure, face-to-face was the only safe way to transact business best kept secret.

The town's dearth of nightlife had not improved his stay. The only after-hours entertainment was a slightly discordant band playing German beer-hall music in the hotel's uninspiring bar. Liechtenstein prevented Switzerland from being the world's most boring country.

But Jason had not come here to haunt nightclubs. With revenue-starved governments' ever-tightening pressure on banks worldwide, it was becoming increasingly difficult to maintain the anonymity large sums of ready cash demanded. That was why he had chosen Liechtenstein. Other than Alpine scenery and collectable stamps, bank secrecy was all the diminutive country had to offer.

Now this.

Jason was well aware there were a number of people in the world who not only would like to see him dead, but also had the means to bring his demise about, violently and painfully. That was why he had spent the last ten years living in remote places, places difficult to reach, where arrivals were easily noted.

It was a good bet the man across the street was not watching out of idle curiosity. The question was why the guy had been so easy to spot. Jason's years-ago training with the U.S. Army's elite Delta Force had made observation a sixth sense. Anomalies, like sunglasses on a dark day, were like a mis-struck key in the middle of a piano sonata, a false note in a symphony.

Jason handed the bellhop a wad of Swiss francs and thanked him for his attentiveness before turning the key in the ignition. The engine snarled alive as the instruments jolted to life. Jason made a show of setting the electronically operated side-view mirrors. The man in front of the bookstore was speaking into a cell phone as Jason shifted into first gear, easing out the heavy clutch.

He made a random turn. On his right, the rococo parliament house sat behind a plaza decorated with a bronze stature vaguely resembling a horse, the falling snow on the metal turning the creature piebald. A picture-postcard moment, had he time to snap a shot. White-crested Alps, their peaks lost in the dove-colored eastern sky.

A Mercedes sedan followed. Black-tinted windows. Could not have been more obvious had it been pulled by eight tiny reindeer. Whoever was inside was a rank amateur—or damn sure of himself.

Jason slowed and gaped at the town hall, a tourist blithely unaware of potential danger. He turned onto Fürst-Franz-Josef Strasse. Ahead, he could see Vaduz Castle's gray Romanesque shape on its plateau above the town. Its distinctive single round tower stabbed the sky's sagging belly.

If whoever was in the Mercedes was knowledgeable, he would be aware the seven-century-old castle was the residence of the prince of Liechtenstein and his family, and not open to the public. If he had done his homework, he would know Jason was flying out of Zurich, which was in the opposite direction. If Jason could not tour the castle, then why would he be headed toward it?

If he were lucky, his pursuers wouldn't figure that out until it was too late.

A narrow road, Bergstrasse, split off to the left, snaking uphill until it was swallowed by low clouds. Without signaling, Jason peeled off. As expected, so did the Mercedes.

Jason resisted the urge to floorboard the accelerator. A sudden burst of power on the powder-covered road would spin his wheels at best. The deepening chasm along the left side of the pavement presented the worst. Stay cool; stay alive. He gradually applied power. The Mercedes showed no difficulty in keeping up. Despite its bulk, it successfully navigated the first two hairpin turns without any great speed loss.

An AMG-engineered S65, Jason thought. The car lumbered on the highway but had agility that belied its bulk. An elephant with the nimbleness and speed of a big cat.

As Jason climbed, he made mental note of details, a dead tree, a rock protruding from the hillside. Another bit of Delta Force training: If you don't memorize what you see on the way in, you're asking to get lost on the way out.

When the Porsche's tachometer hit 6500, the turbo kicked in at the same time the rpm's were "on the cam." In layman's terms, a mule kicked the car in the ass. Jason could spare only the briefest of glances at the rearview mirrors as he tried to hold the fishtailing vehicle onto the snow-slick pavement. The Mercedes was fading.

Jason was thankful he had insisted the Europcar rental place in Zurich replace the Porsche's normal, art-gum-eraser soft tires designed to give the car adhesion against pavement, tires that would be roller skates on glass in these conditions. At least the Michelin Latitude Alpin HPs gave the car an even chance to maintain a semblance of traction.

The snow had become BBs in a tin can, tiny pellets that rattled against the windshield. On an unfamiliar road that twisted like—as one of Jason's old army buddies used to say—a worm in a hot frying pan, a surface literally slick in some spots and iced over in others, with visibility quickly fading into clouds the color of dirty rags, there was no chance Jason could sustain the speeds of which the car was capable.

But he didn't intend to.

Instead, he reduced speed and turned on his lights. The mist gave him back the glare with interest.

Downshifting, he slowed further, this time to a near crawl. With the visibility now measured in a few feet, he was navigating by the guardrail, the thin metal margin between him and roiling clouds that filled an abyss like tea in a cup. He could not see the details of the road that would serve as braking points on the way down.

The good news was the Mercedes had the same problem.

Minutes later, he found what he had hoped for: a place to pull off the road, a scenic overlook in better weather. A quick twist of the steering wheel and he was now headed downhill, lights out.

The visibility grudgingly improved as he descended. There was a patch in the pavement Jason remembered as being twenty, thirty feet from what would now be a left-hand sweeper, a dent in the guardrail just shy of a hairpin around which he could only creep.

He met the Mercedes just past the hairpin.

The big car made an effort to swerve, to block the road just as Jason downshifted and hit the gas. The Porsche's rear tires shrieked against the icy pavement, slid.

Time came to a stop, milliseconds expanding into lifetimes. Jason felt the car in a four-wheel drift, the side of the Mercedes closer. The normal reaction would be to slam on the brakes; the normal reaction would kill him. Instead, Jason punched it out, stood on the accelerator. Protesting rubber found traction and the car lunged forward like a rodeo bull released from the chute.

There was an impact that threw Jason against his shoulder harness to the sound of distressed sheet metal screeching. And then he was clear.

As he descended, the mist grew thinner, shredded like rotten fabric by a light breeze. Fat bugs of snowflakes splattered against the glass, wipers tamping their remains into icy piles at the edges of the windshield. He could see his markers clearly, allowing him to brake and then accelerate through the line of each turn. He ignored the temptation to stop and inspect whatever damage the car had sustained. The steering wheel was steady in his hands, the suspension compliant with his demands. Superficial bodywork only. The Europcar people in Zurich might not be happy with the car's appearance, but Jason could not be more pleased with its performance.

By the time the Mercedes got turned around and tiptoed out of the clouds, he would be well on the road to Zurich, winding but comparatively flat as it followed the course of the Rhine. Almost as an afterthought, he took out his iPad, called the airline's reservation center, and changed flights and destinations. A precaution the availability of airlines' passenger manifests to even amateur hackers made almost obsolete. He might never know who those people were. As long as he never saw them again, that was okay with him.

Not likely, his inner voice whispered. *If they traced you to Vaduz, Liechtenstein, they'll find you again.*

Jason turned on the radio, hoping to drown the voice out. He didn't want to listen to it. What it said was all too true.

9

Maseline Harbour
Sark, Channel Islands
The Next Day

A slate sky was spitting snow into a gusting channel gale, the tiny white flakes bobbing like popcorn in the popper. The wind frosted the gray water with white caps that chewed hungrily at the concrete pier as the Sark Shipping Company ferry rounded the brake water. Eddies of the breeze played through the ship's rigging, an irregular beat of metal on metal. The meteorological maps in European papers had uniformly depicted a huge arctic depression of low pressure resting indefinitely between the Irish Sea and somewhere west of the Urals. That explained the unusual weather—the island's average temperature this time of year hovered in the high forties—but did little to make it more bearable.

Weather notwithstanding, Jason was glad to get home. He watched from the deck as the ship eased her way to its berth in the little L-shaped harbor. There was no room for a ninety-meter motor yacht anchored outside the breakwater, dancing at the end of her anchor line in the rough seas. Italian made, judging by the sharpness of her bow and the rakish slant of her superstructure. In addition to the complementary Union Jack, she flew the Panamanian flag. Normal enough. The super wealthy would hardly register their ship where they might be inconvenienced by safety regulations, minimum wage, and environmental concerns.

What was not normal was that she was here. None other than masochists went pleasure sailing in the cold, stormy waters of the English Chanel this time of year. The ship would have been more at home in the Caribbean's sunny climes. Or, at least, the Costa del Sol or the Balearic Islands. Sark had nothing to offer besides near-arctic winds, the surrounding gray cliffs, rocky beaches, and more cows than people.

The island was hardly for the glitterati. With only about 500 permanent residents, most of whom farmed, a new pair of Wellies was likely to draw more attention than a diamond the size of the native potatoes. No place to show off a Ferrari or Bentley, either. Tractors were the only motorized vehicles allowed on the three-by-three-and-a-half-mile island.

No, that yacht was definitely out of place and out of season. Jason's innate paranoia demanded an explanation. He could well be the reason. Why it was there was a mystery Jason intended to solve. He would inquire of the harbor master, a man happy to receive the small monthly stipend Jason paid for information as to arrivals on the island.

There were no accidental ones.

To reach Sark, one had to get to Guernsey, usually by a Channel Express Fokker F-27 Friendship, a twin turbo prop, departing any number of British airports. Then onto the ferry for the fifty-minute voyage, the sole means to or from the island available to the public.

The last of only half a dozen passengers disembarking the ferry, Jason made his way across the concrete pier to a small, one-window structure at the end. He set his single suitcase down in front of the wooden door and knocked.

A whiff of stale tobacco stung his nose and disappeared in the wind as the door opened. Before him stood a diminutive man whose navy-style pea jacket reached the patched knees of his khaki pants. A walrus mustache twitched like a living creature above a clay pipe smoldering like a subterranean fire, the source of the malodorous smell. Eyes the color of a summer sky twinkled under an unruly thatch of silver, on which rested a faded and rather ragged British Warrant Officer's cap.

Jason was looking at Sark's harbor master, Andrew MaCleod.

MaCleod stepped back from the door, making room for Jason to enter. "Mr. Peters! Welcome home! I ken you've been gone a spell."

Jason stepped in, shutting the door behind him. Hobson's choice: Stand in the cold or endure the smell of the pipe. The single room contained a table on which a computer rested and two swivel chairs with cushions long since flat, but displaying faded embroidered birds. The sports section of yesterday's *Daily Telegraph* partially covered a ship-to-shore radio as though the device had snuggled under a blanket to supplement the meager comfort of the electric coil heater that buzzed feebly in a corner.

"Wretched weather!" Jason commented, noting the room was cold enough to see his breath.

MaCleod gave the window a glance as though to confirm or deny the statement. "Aye, but it'd be like spring in Aberdeen."

Only a Scot would prefer the Channel's winters to those of his native land.

Jason hugged himself seeking warmth. "That yacht out there, what do you know about it and its passengers?"

MaCleod removed the pipe from his mouth and dug in it with a nail-like instrument. The excavation continued in silence for several seconds. Then, "Not much. The *Allegro*. She was here when I arrived this morning. No request for customs, no yellow flag, so I assumed she had sailed from either another island or one of the Channel ports."

Yellow flag, representing the letter Q in the international alphabet. Q for quarantine. Historically, a message there was no disease aboard. Currently, a request for customs service, something a ship arriving from a British or European Union port would not require.

Jason went to the window for another look. The falling snow gave him a view as though through gauze. "There's a davit on the foredeck but no boat."

There was wet sucking sound and the hiss of a struck match. Jason turned to see the harbor master staring disappointedly into the smokeless bowl of the pipe. "I dinna ken where on this island would be more comfortable than that ship," he observed. "But someone must have come ashore last night."

The same conclusion had already occurred to Jason. He reached for the doorknob. "Thanks for your help."

The pipe was now issuing a slender tendril of blue smoke. "Anytime, laddie."

Outside, wind rattled metal rigging against steel masts. The little harbor's small boats were rolling from gunwale to gunwale at their moorings, tethered animals trying to break free.

Jason squinted in a futile effort to keep the blowing snow out of his eyes. Through the white curtain, he saw movement on the land side of the harbor. A second's concentration and he recognized Mr. Frache and his two-wheel wagon. When he was not tending to his dairy cows, the man earned a few pounds acting as the island's taxi service, meeting the ferry and picking up fares to one of the half dozen hotels and numerous guest houses.

Jason waved his arms, yelling. At first, he thought the elderly farmer couldn't hear over the wind. But then the single horse turned toward Jason and the wagon lumbered over.

"G'day, Mr. Peters." Frache was looking down at Jason and his suitcase from the driver's perch. "You'll be needing transportation?"

Jason tossed his bag into the cart and climbed in behind it. "Sure do. Stocks."

If Frache thought the request to be taken to the island's finest hotel instead of Jason's home was strange, he didn't show it. It offered what little luxury the island could boast. The beamed dining room's fare—though modest when compared to Le Havre, an hour by hydrofoil from Guernsey—was the best on Sark. Even so, everyone on the island knew the place was closed from New Year's Eve to mid-February. Frache didn't question this, either.

Stocks was also about a quarter of a mile closer to the harbor than the 300-year-old stone Norman cottage Jason currently called home. Approaching the house on foot would give Jason a number of tactical options not available to an arrival by road. If Jason was the reason the people aboard the *Allegro* were here, surprise seemed a sensible precaution.

The two rode in relative silence, the only sounds being the horse's hooves crackling through the patina of ice that had formed on the dirt road. Sights were no longer familiar in their winter costumes. The fields were a pristine white, their undulating slopes marked only by tracks of animals seeking forage under the white blanket. Snow coated the upper surface of branches of wind-stunted trees as though they had donned starched shirts.

Only the wind, though far colder than usual, was the same. On Sark, the wind hummed, sang, or screamed. It was rarely silent. Today, it spoke with a white-tinted voice as puffs of talcum whirled across the ground.

It was a time to marvel.

And a time to think.

Jason had come here, what, a year or so ago? It had been what he guessed was an intermediate step in an endless journey that had begun on the darkest day of his life and of his country, a late summer day, September 11.

The morning had begun like any other. Having announced his retirement from Delta Force, Captain Peters, J., had drawn Pentagon duty for the balance of his enlistment. In less than two weeks, he would permanently exchange his spotless, razor-creased uniform for an artist's smock. His paintings, acrylic on canvas, were selling very well not only in a gallery in Georgetown, but in New York and Los Angles as well.

No longer would his wife, Laurin, worry about his frequently unannounced absences to places he could not mention and from which he stood a good chance of not returning. If his artistic success continued—and the galleries in the aforesaid cities had no reason to think it would not—Laurin would soon retire from her Washington lobbying firm. Her largest client was the U.S. Army, whom she represented before the various Congressional committees in the ongoing interservice rivalry for funds.

It was tragic but not accidental she was in the Pentagon that morning. She had just stuck her head into the cubicle that served as Jason's office.

"Hi, soldier! Buy a girl a cup of coffee?"

Jason glanced at the coffeepot behind his desk, a device that produced a viscous fluid more akin to motor oil than a drinkable beverage. "Sure. Let me finish up here a minute. Go on down to the canteen and I'll meet you there."

"Better yet, I'll step and fetch. Be back in a minute."

He watched her turn around. His interest in what he described as the world's most beautiful ass had not diminished in the six years of marriage. He wondered sometimes if birth of the child she was carrying—but not yet showing—would change that.

He never saw her again.

Almost as bad—they never identified her body.

Unlike most 9/11 families, he had no grave to visit, only the very contemporary memorial erected on the west side of the Pentagon. Whenever he was in Washington, he took time to visit, leave flowers with a card bearing her name, knowing they would be collected and discarded by the grounds crew at the end of the day. It was the only way he had of giving Laurin back her identity, if not her life.

The gaping hole in his soul filled with a burning hatred of terrorists of any stripe and a mounting frustration of his inability to strike back. That opportunity came out of the blue a month or so later when he was invited to visit the Maryland offices of Narcom, a secretive company whose sole client was the U.S. intelligence community. Narcom took on jobs too politically sensitive, too dangerous, or those requiring plausible deniability.

The assignments paid obscenely well. Better yet, all Narcom's fees, and hence Jason's, were, by special agreement, tax-free. Aware of the suddenness with which political winds shifted and bearing a healthy distrust of government in general and the IRS in particular, Jason had made his accumulation of wealth as hard to find as possible.

The best part of the job, though, had been the work. Assassination, kidnapping, any sort of dirty trick devised by the warped minds in Washington. Most directed at the same ragheads responsible for Laurin's death, those who violently mindlessly perverted a religion and culture that was perfecting algebra when Europe was still burning heretics.

Job satisfaction indeed.

But the work hadn't exactly made friends. Revenging honor was a driving force among friends, associates, and relatives of those Jason had dispatched to their reward of seventy-two virgins. Although he no longer worked for Narcom, extremist nut bags had long memories.

From time to time, he had taken the occasional assignment, more out of boredom than need. That had caused problems with Maria, the Italian volcanologist and ardent pacifist, who, from time to time, shared his life. Now, as was frequently the case, she was on an expedition, this time to study an eruption in Indonesia, leaving Jason to the care of Mrs. Abigail Prince, his grandmotherly housekeeper.

Mrs. Prince had a genuine fondness for Maria, although her Anglican background viewed the relationship as sinful. Hardly a day passed some reference was not made to marriage, in spite of both Jason's and Maria's clear disinclinations to commit matrimony at this point. Though she scolded constantly, the woman also held an affection for Pangloss, a large, shaggy, and nondescript dog Laurin had rescued from the pound. Jason suspected she had chosen him because, ugly as he was, adoption by someone else was unlikely. Finally, there was Robespierre, a one-eared tomcat that simply appeared one day after being the obvious loser in some feline dispute. Since no one owns a cat, Jason had been at a loss as to where he might return the animal.

Jason was looking forward to the dog's eager greeting, even the disdain with which cats view the world. For that matter, he had been looking forward to giving his iPod a rest while he enjoyed his favorite Italian Baroque composers, Vivaldi, Corelli, Bononcini, Albinoni.

All of this he had eagerly anticipated on two different airlines and a ferryboat. Now his homecoming would have to wait. Or at least the one he planned, wait until the question of that yacht was resolved. He doubted anyone intending him harm would have arrived in such an ostentatious manner, but the man in the Mercedes hadn't been exactly covert, either. He hadn't lived this long without being cautious.

He—

"Looks like we're here!"

The wagon was stopped in front of the three buildings in a *U*, made up of twenty-three rooms in what had been a sixteenth-century farmhouse and outbuildings.

Mr. Frache had his hand out. "That'll be two pounds, three."

Jason instantly regretted jumping to the ground. His shoes were now full of very wet snow. He reached into his pocket, produced a clip of bills, and peeled off a five. "Keep it. Thanks for the lift."

The driver's smile spread across the weathered face as he touched the bill of his cap with one hand and shook the reins with the other. "Thank *you*, Mr. Peters!"

Jason took in his surroundings.

A place he had passed or visited hundreds of time now might as well have been on the backside of the moon. The white stone facade, moistened by snow, had become a dirty gray. The five windows across the front were blind eyes staring not onto a manicured sweep of lawn but an arctic plane. The lush, green trees on the hills visible behind the hotel were a hostile thicket of sharp black daggers sheathed in snow. There was no ambiance of the rustic chic hospitality for which the hotel was known. The scene suggested harsh indifference.

Jason picked up his bag and went around to the rear where the swimming pool was like a thermal spring, leaking steam around the edges of a canvas cover. Chairs, recliners, and tables, misshapen with lumpy snow, reminded him of animals gathered around some African watering hole. Low hummocks indicated where summer's rosebushes were hiding.

He took a step, his socks squishing with melted snow from his ill-advised leap from the wagon. He toyed with the idea of stopping to ring them out. Frostbite was the last thing he needed. No, it would take him less than twenty minutes to reach his house from there.

What exactly he was going to do once he got there? Well, that depended on what a reconnaissance turned up. At the moment there was something he missed even more than Pangloss and Robespierre: His .40-caliber Glock.

10

Stocks Hotel
Sark, Channel Islands

Should Jason take the road? Though a mixture of ice and slush, the snow was not as deep, the going would be easier. So would spotting him were someone looking for his arrival. If trouble was waiting for him, he'd be an easy target. By the time the track reached his house, though, it was sunken, not visible from his windows. Bag in hand, he set out down the shallow Dixcart Valley that pointed to his home like a gun barrel.

The volume of both fog and snow increased, reducing the landscape to little more than gray blurs, an old black-and-white photograph with the picture just becoming visible in the developing solution. If this kept up, he would not need to worry about being seen. Still, he had rather approach from this angle. The house faced the hill split by the road. The rear opened onto almost a full hectare of apple orchard, which ended at a cliff jutting over Derrible Bay.

The rocky teeth below gnashing at the white water was one of his most frequently painted scenes. He was particularly fond of one that depicted a fog bank creeping across the water like a predator stealthily approaching its prey. The crash of waves as the wind bashed them against the shore had, in Jason's mind, become a symphony. Today, the sound, the wind, the fog would mask his arrival. Unfortunately, they would also make it difficult to observe the house.

The wet snow was over his ankles as he trudged through it, filling the cuffs of his trousers and adding to the misery of his soaking socks. The wind was becoming a firm opponent, slowing his progress and filling his eyes with white flakes. Was it really true, he wondered, that no two of the trillions of snowflakes were exactly alike, that each had a unique symmetry? IF so, and if any higher power existed, He surely had far too much time on His hands.

Navigating the rock-strewn fields in this world of whites and grays wasn't easy, even if Jason had come this way dozens of times in better weather. Twice he stumbled over boulders that had become one with the shadows creeping from their lairs as the afternoon aged. In winter at these latitudes, darkness came early. It did not fall but seeped out of the lower parts of the valley like liquid from a sponge.

Though an inconvenience, possibly a hazard if he took a bad fall, darkness was an ally. It would provide Jason with a cloak of invisibility as effective as Harry Potter's. On the other hand, the cottage, if he could see it at all in these conditions, should be a lighted beacon unless Mrs. Prince had been derelict in her duties.

Or had been prevented from performing them.

Upon his initial arrival at Sark, Jason had worked industriously and secretly, journeying to the mainland to buy weight-detecting plates wired to a silent alarm system which he buried randomly around the cottage. Although, abstractly, he had known cows, in general, weighed more than humans, he had not considered that fact or the liberty to roam granted the local bovines. Within a week, he removed those plates not already destroyed by hoofs. Motion detectors, infrared cameras, some of the most sophisticated security equipment available, all defeated by the island's dairy herd.

At least his arrival would not be electronically announced.

He stopped suddenly, listening. There was the wind, now reduced to a sigh, the gentle sound of the flakes as they kissed his clothes. The fresh snow crunched underfoot. But he had heard something else, something that was not of the wind and snow. He turned his head slowly as if directing an antenna to track the source of the sound.

There!

Definite footsteps ahead. Or were they? They came too quickly to be human and there was a chuffing sound, an animal breathing heavily. As far as he knew, there were no wolves or bears on Sark. He could distinguish a shape now, gray with snow-covered fur, moving quickly toward him.

He recognized the form just an instant before the valley rang with joyous barking. Jason stooped to bring his face even with the big dog's and rub the muzzle grayed with snowflakes.

"Pangloss! What in the hell are you doing out here?"

His answer was a loving tongue across the face.

Jason scratched under the hairy chin. "What did you do to get Mrs. Prince to let you out so late?"

This time the reply was a series of snorts as the dog backed away, started barking. Pangloss was like that: Rarely gave a direct answer. Jason knew, anyway. Pangloss was anything but modest in letting his needs be known. If he wanted outside at times other than those scheduled, a raking of those big paws across the cottage's front door served notice.

Had he known Jason was nearby with that near-supernatural ability dogs have of sensing things and people far out of eyesight? Or was he on his perpetual hunt for moles? Targets for Pangloss, more than once at the expense of a neighbor's garden.

A click of tongue against teeth and the animal fell in beside him. Like the old friends they were, the two set off up a slight rise that marked the end of the valley. They were on the verge of the apple orchard. Trees stood in military ranks, arthritic limbs covered in uniforms of white. Though he could not see it, the sea announced its presence with its unabated assault on the rocks below the cliff. The house was somewhere down a sloping field less than 300 meters distant but as unseeable in the wintry mist as the future.

Jason wished his canine companion had a different disposition. It would be helpful if Pangloss could differentiate between good and bad guys, or at least approach the house and growl if strangers were present. But that wasn't in the dog's DNA. He didn't know a stranger.

Everybody was Pangloss's potential new best friend. Had he been human, he would have been a maître d' in an expensive restaurant. Or a politician.

At the moment, Jason would have cheerfully traded Pangloss for a pit bull or Rottweiler.

Moving from one apple tree to the next, Jason edged toward the place he knew the cottage was. The scant cover was unnecessary in the icy mist that was now beginning to freeze on his jacket.

At the last row of trees, he could see a diffused light, no doubt from the cottage's windows. He could smell the acrid odor of the stone fireplace, but the smoke itself was lost in clouds low enough to caress the roof top.

He got down on all fours, making sure his head was below what he remembered as the height of windows. His ungloved hands numbed in the snow. In a minute, he could see the house. Or, at least part of it. Still creeping, he reached the near wall, stood just beside a window.

Pangloss thought this was great fun, some sort of new game. He was barking appreciatively. Jason shot a nervous glance in the direction of the front door. If the dog's racket drew curiosity, Jason would be caught in the open, unarmed with no place to hide.

Movement on the other side of the window drew his eye. A tall man with skin the color of charcoal, suit the same. Though he could not see the face from this angle, Jason knew it featured lifeless eyes the color of steel ball bearings. The man's name was Samedi and he would not be here alone.

Jason's concern was replaced by an anger that made his lips curl. Once again, she had found him, invaded his space.

Whoa, the voice inside his head protested. *You may get pissed every time she finds you—and she always does—but why do you think she keeps doing it? Maybe because you have a hard time saying "no"?*

I've said "no" plenty of times, Jason retorted, feeling slightly silly arguing with himself.

But only before saying "yes."

Inner voices were a pain in the ass.

Resigned to having to deal with a problem, Jason turned and trudged to the door. Ice on the walkway crunched beneath his feet like dry twigs.

Delightfully warm air and the aroma of tea kissed his face the instant he opened it. He set down his suitcase as he surveyed the scene. Seated in front of the fireplace was Mrs. Prince and a huge black woman wearing a mumu, its bright colors screaming in discord with the earth tones of the cottage. Jason marveled the rustic bentwood chair had not been reduced to kindling by her three hundred plus pounds. Between the two women was a tea trolley on which sat the tea caddy and the only tea set in the house that had all its pieces—cups, saucers, pot, creamer, sugar bowl—matched, and not chipped or cracked.

For an instant, the two women stared in surprise at Jason as Pangloss wriggled his way past and into the house.

"Pangloss!"

Too late.

The dog gave a massive shake, spraying the room with water and melting snow.

"A trick I taught him," Jason said, his eyes leveled at Mrs. Prince. "He only does it in front of uninvited company."

Indifferent to the puddle on the gray stone floor, Pangloss crossed the room to sit beside the visitor's chair, lavishing her with adoring eyes.

"I'm sorry if I done wrong," Mrs. Prince said, rising from her chair. "But this lady here said as how you was old friends an' bein' as how it were snowin' outside . . ."

Her voice trailed off as though fully aware her employer was not as angry as he sounded.

"I understand," Jason said. "Our guest here has the ability to charm the meanest of spirits." He pointed to the ball of fur in the massive lap. "When is the last time you saw Robespierre do that?"

The cat, normally scornful of affection, turned yellow eyes on Jason at the mention of his name, a possessive look that clearly said he and the woman had formed some sort of bond.

The woman stood, placing the resentful cat on the floor. "Now admit it, Jason, you be glad to see Momma."

Momma, the only name Jason knew for the woman who owned and operated the secretive Narcom. With a quickness that belied her bulk, she grasped him in a near suffocating bear hug that smelled of tropical flowers and charcoal, the odors Jason associated with her native Haiti. There, she had been the second in command of the dreaded Tonon Macoute, the Duvalier secret police whose record for brutality put Hitler's Gestapo in a favorable light by comparison.

Jason managed to free himself. "I suppose the yacht outside the harbor is yours."

"Not mine. Belongs to a friend."

The first indication Jason ever had that she had one.

"Not using it right now," she continued as she looked around as though seeing the cottage's interior for the first time. "You sure manage to find hard-to-get-to places."

"It keeps away people I don't want to see. Doesn't always work."

Mrs. Prince's hands were clasping and unclasping, a pair of birds mating in midair. Her eyes flicked from one to the other, a spectator in a verbal tennis match. "With your permission, Mr. Peters, I'll be putting the tea things away, make your supper. Will our guests be joining us?"

"Definitely not."

Without waiting for further response, Mrs. Prince fled to the kitchen, pushing the trolley ahead of her. Jason was sure she intended the clatter of crockery to curtain her from further conversation.

Momma resumed her seat, motioning Jason to the one vacated by Mrs. Prince. Like she was a hostess in her own house. In a single leap, Robespierre was back in her lap, eyes on Jason, daring him to take the territory away.

"Older you get, Jason, the less hospitable you become," she said amiably. "Almost give me the impression you don't 'preciate all I done for you."

"Like damn near getting me killed?"

"You ain't dead, but you sure rich."

There was no arguing with that. "You didn't come all the way to Sark to discuss either status."

Momma gave a single nod of the head, her turn to concede a point. "That pretty little gal of yours, Dr. Bergenghetti, she not here."

A statement, not a question.

"Why do I think you knew that before you came?"

"She's over in . . ."

"Indonesia."

"Indonesia, checking out one of them volcanoes she like so much. I had to guess, I'd say she be there 'nother couple months at least."

"That was what she said in the e-mail I got a few hours ago. So now you're reading my mail, too."

Momma shrugged her shoulders, an earthquake of mountains. "She stayin' 'cause she got an additional grant, one over what the Italian government willing to pay."

"I can't imagine where that came from."

Momma ignored the sarcasm. "So, I figured since you'll be leaving this here island . . ."

Jason held up a hand, stop. "Leaving? Who says?"

Momma crossed arms the size of legs of mutton. "Well, I just thought . . ."

"Thought what?"

"You just now coming back from that little country . . ."

"Liechtenstein."

Momma knew his every move. Annoying as it was, what could he do? Devices that tracked cell phones, spy satellites, hacking into airline reservations. Privacy was as obsolete as the buggy whip.

"Yeah," Momma nodded, seeming to relish the name, "Liechtenstein. Little bird tell me you got into trouble."

"Your little bird must be a dodo. Trip went smooth as glass."

Momma pursed her lips, an expression almost coquettish. "You weren't running that Porsche up them hills for the fun of it."

She pronounced the marque without the *uh* sound for the final *e*.

How the hell could she have known about that? Must have a really good observation team for him not to have noticed. Either that or there really was substance to her claim of being a *Hounan*, a voodoo priestess.

Damned if he was going to give her the satisfaction of asking. "I don't see the correlation between what *might* have been trouble and leaving Sark."

Actually, he saw it with the clarity of a photograph, a very ugly photograph.

"Don' much think them fellows in the other car were chasing you for your autograph. They know you in Liechtenstein; they sure know you here. Just a matter of time."

He watched her for a moment as she used one massive hand to scratch Pangloss between the ears, the other to rub Robespierre's belly. The domesticity of the tableau would make it difficult for a stranger to believe this woman ran what was probably the most efficient covert organization in the world, undoubtedly the most efficient in private hands.

He was tired from travel, his stomach sounded like there was a really unhappy animal inside, his feet were wet and cold, and his immediate future included going to bed alone. He was in no mood for Momma's games. "Let me guess: Since I may be in some danger here, I need to leave. Since I need to leave anyway, you just happen to have a little job that needs tending to."

At first, Momma didn't reply. Instead, she gently placed the cat on the floor and stood, to Pangloss's evident disappointment. Stepping across the room, she stopped before a pair of Jason's paintings.

"Sunset and sunrise from the same vantage point. I like the way the reddish tones of morning and late afternoon contrast with the gray of the ocean, particularly the reflection on the water and the wet rocks."

Jason felt his anger seep away like water from a cracked cup. It's hard to be mad at someone who both admires and understands your work.

But he said, "I'm retired, remember?"

"That's what you said last time. You was bored to death with your woman gone then and you're bored to death with her gone now."

Not only did Momma keep track of his whereabouts, she read his mind, too.

Momma glanced at the gold Cartier on her wrist, a tiny button attached to the trunk of a mighty oak. "Tell you what: It's late. We can carry this on in the morning."

"Nothing to 'carry on.'" Jason made quote marks with his fingers.

Momma made a motion with one catcher's mitt-size hand, and Samedi soundlessly stepped from the shadows. The man creeped Jason out with his dead, corpselike eyes and the way he had of simply appearing like a spirit summoned from Hades. Jason couldn't remember him ever speaking, either. There was something in his hand . . . a book.

Momma took it and held it out toward Jason. "Take a look through this and we'll talk."

Hands behind his back as though afraid to touch the proffered book, Jason retreated a step. "No thanks. I'm behind in my reading as it is. My Kindle is loaded up. Besides, we really don't have anything to talk about. I'm retired. I mean it this time."

Undeterred, Momma laid the volume in the seat of the chair she had occupied. "Take it as a gift. Retired, you got plenty of time before Dr. Bergenghetti—Maria—comes back, certainly enough to at least look through it." She glanced around the room, taking mental inventory. "Not like you got anything else to do. You don't even have a TV."

True. The European Yagi aerial got blown off the roof in the first week of Jason's residency, ending what fuzzy reception it provided. He detested the ugly mushroom-on-steroids dishes required for satellite, which provided equally poor service during the six-month rainy season. And, even when functioning, the viewing menu might as well have consisted of events on Mars: soccer, foreign language reruns of American sit-coms and films, and news from world capitals on CNN Europe. TV on Sark was a classic example of something not worth the effort.

"That's a blessing, not a hardship."

Momma pointed to the book as Samedi opened the door. The howl of the wind all but drowned her out. "At least take a look."

Jason started to reply, but she was gone.

11

Excerpts from Nikola Tesla: Genius or Mad Scientist
by Robert Hastings, PhD

Nikola Tesla was born in humble circumstances in Smiljan, Lika, then part of the Austro-Hungarian Empire, now Croatia, on July 10, 1856. His father, Milutin, was an Orthodox priest and his mother, Djuka Mandic, an inventor in her own right of household appliances. Young Nikola attended the Polytechnic Institute in Graz, Austria, and the University of Prague, where he became fascinated with electricity. He was working for a telephone company in Budapest when he conceived the idea of a rotary magnetic field, an idea that would play a significant role in his later life.

Having been employed by the Continental Edison Company in Paris, he emigrated to the United States in 1884 to work with the great American inventor. It was during this association that a divergence of opinion began. Edison had invested millions in producing direct current (DC). The alternating current (AC) invented by Tesla obviated the need for power stations every two miles. Alternating current, by its very nature, moves back and forth, needing little of the "boost" required by direct current.

Edison refused to pay the bonus he had promised should his young protégé be able to improve Edison's system. Outraged, Tesla quit. Recognizing genius, George Westinghouse hired the young émigré and the "Battle of the Currents" was on.

Edison's propaganda described direct current as flowing "smoothly, like a river while alternating current runs roughly like rapids," although this simile's influence on the public is unclear. To make his point, Edison even arranged the first execution by electricity, having the warden of a prison employ alternating current instead of hanging before a horrified press corps. The anticipated national revulsion against alternating current did not occur.

Propaganda or not, alternating current was selected to illuminate the World Columbian Exposition in Chicago in 1893, and, subsequently, streets and homes across the country.

The battle was over.

12

Derrible Bay
Sark, Channel Islands
Two Hours Later

Recently published novel in hand, Jason was swaddled in a comforter, a mummy wrapped in eiderdown, stretched out on the bed that occupied the sole room of the cottage's upstairs. Corelli's Concerto Grosso No. 4 in D Major filled the room, violins punctuated with occasional brass. Fundamental order, yet tuneful, sometimes exuberant. The sound came from a turntable playing a 33⅓ LP vinyl record. CDs were digital, records analog. Since actual sound is analog, digital reproduction is like comparing a photograph to the real thing. Jason's ear could distinguish between the two.

The kitchen downstairs had been quiet for some time now. Mrs. Prince had done the supper dishes and gone home for the night. The snow had turned to sleet, now clicking against the window panes in the language of winter. The room's gas heater whispered in conversation with Pangloss's rhythmic snores from his hooked rug in a corner. There was an occasional low growl as the dog stretched, pursuing a mole through doggy dreamland. Robespierre was somewhere in the house, conducting his solitary nocturnal patrol.

Jason surprised himself by not nodding off within minutes after a day of travel followed by his hike through the snow. He put down the book and looked around the room. Whether it was Momma's observation about being bored in Maria's absence; the span of empty, cold sheet beside him; or his rare feeling of loneliness, he couldn't concentrate on the book's plot line.

His eyes went to the pine table that served as a desk and the volume on one corner, the book Momma had left. Maybe . . . Nah, no reason to even think about getting involved in whatever problem Narcom was handling.

Momma had charmed Maria at their first and only meeting; but, then, Maria had no idea of what Momma and her company did. If she had an inkling of the mayhem caused by the woman with the radiant smile, knew of the volume of blood on those huge hands that had given Maria's arms a friendly squeeze, heard the death sentences uttered in the same mellifluous voice that had made small talk, Jason's mere association with Momma would be grounds for Maria's final and permanent departure. She had all but left him a year or two ago when an unfortunately placed TV camera had implicated Jason in the assassination of an African dictator. That and nearly getting her killed in Sardinia within the early months of their relationship.

Maria believed that there was always a peaceful solution no matter how many times she was proved wrong. An English language bumper sticker on the Fiat she owned when they first met proclaimed WAR IS NOT THE ANSWER. That, of course, depended on the question. Like so many who believed in ideals rather than reality, she insisted if one side to a dispute simply refused to resort to violence, the other would follow suit. Violence, no matter the justification, was simply evil, brutish, and unacceptable. Jason supposed that, at some time in his life, he might have held views equally idealistic. He just couldn't remember when or what they were.

No doubt about it: Any further involvement with Narcom that Maria discovered would be his third and final strike.

Wait a minute.

It was the ever-annoying voice inside his head again.

On the average of every couple of months, Maria takes off to some place to observe a volcanic eruption.

"So? That's what volcanologists do," Jason retorted, unaware he was speaking out loud.

In his corner, Pangloss opened one eye, assured himself nothing requiring action was taking place, and resumed his snoring.

So, what do you do? the voice persisted.

"In case you hadn't noticed, I paint. Make almost enough selling in the galleries in Guernsey and Jersey to pay the rent here."

Swell. Maria studied, became a volcanologist, has a job with the Italian government, doing . . . ?

"Like most people in the field, she hopes by studying eruptions, they might find some way to predict them. You can see why that might be of interest to the Italians."

And you were trained . . . ?

Jason saw where this was going. "I've retired from what I was trained to do. Now I paint."

How wonderful and fulfilling daubing pigment on canvas must be. Particularly, in view of your former occupation.

Jason wasn't sure how a person could be sarcastic with himself, but the damn voice was a master at it.

You're telling me that the life of a painter on a remote island is as exciting as what you used to do, that you enjoy it as much? C'mon! Kidding yourself isn't good mental hygiene.

"So, OK, the old life had its moments, but all good things . . ."

Come to an end? Like you and Maria?

"Make your point."

Simple enough: You're bored out of your gourd when a trip to Liechtenstein to see your bankers is the highlight of your winter. Maria is doing what she loves. And whoever she loves, for all you know. The two of you never discuss what happens when you're apart. She does what she wants; you paint.

"What if painting is what I want to do?"

If it were, we wouldn't be having this conversation, would we?

Jason disentangled himself from the comforter. He was staring at the book on the table as though it might exhibit some paranormal qualities, levitate, disappear, spontaneously erupt in flames, something like that. His feet appeared from under the covers like early spring flowers through the snow. Groping blindly with his toes, he located first one then the other fur-lined moccasins that served as bedroom slippers. His breath emitted a cloud of steam despite the efforts of the heater. Jason took the two or three steps required to cross the room.

Pangloss raised his head, an inquiry as to what was going on. He started to lower it again and stopped halfway. From somewhere deep in his throat came a low growl, a most un-Pangloss noise. Whether it was the unusual sound or long-ago Delta Force training-become-instinct, Jason hit the light switch, flattening himself against the wall next to a window. Slowly, he extended his neck to see through the pane. He used a circular motion of a hand to make a peep hole through the glass slick with translucent frost.

The wet glass gave him back only his reflection. Beyond, the night was as dark as the stomach of any Jonah-swallowing whale. Other than the absence of sound, Jason couldn't even tell if the snow/sleet had stopped. He sat, his eyes just above the sill. Unless someone out there had night-vision equipment, he doubted he could be seen from the yard. The cold of the glass would defeat infrared, and he guessed light enhancement would have little to work with, with the darkened room as backdrop.

He waited a full five minutes by the luminescent dial of his Rolex, the watch he removed only in the shower. Pangloss was growling, whining and, from the sound of nails clicking on the wooden floor, pacing. Dark nothingness on the other side of the glass was the only reward for Jason's patient vigil.

He stood, snorting at the dog, "Alarmist! There's nothing out there but . . ."

Before the sentence was complete, a red dot of light, perhaps the size of a dime, danced across the window's glass.

Jason threw himself aside, away from the window, just as the glass shattered inward.

On his belly, Jason crawled quickly back toward the bed. Small shards of the window glass pricked at his bare hands like insect stings. Beside the bed was another hooked rug similar to the one on which Pangloss slept. With one hand, Jason lifted the near edge, using the other to grope underneath. His fingers closed around a metal ring sunk into the floorboards, and he heaved upward. Blindly in the dark, his hands explored the hidden compartment until they touched what he was searching for: The American version of the South African Armsel Striker, a twelve-gauge shotgun mounted over a twelve-round revolving magazine.

Grabbing the rear pistol grip, Jason dragged the eighteen-inch barrel free of its hiding place at the same time pulling into place the top-mounted folding stock. Again, commando fashion, he crawled across the floor, this time to the open well of stairs leading below. His progress was heralded by the crackling of glass particles under his weight.

His back pressed against the wall, he put an exploratory foot on the top stair. He was well aware of which steps tended to creak or groan underfoot and where, but weather and age moved these locations with exasperating unpredictability. He reluctantly trusted to luck the ancient wood would bear his weight silently.

He was fairly certain whoever had taken the shot had not entered the house. Redundant indoor alarm systems out of reach of local cattle would have alerted him to an entry. Unless the shooter had found a way to disarm them. Although that was unlikely, Jason had more than one former comrade who had suffered the consequences of ignoring all possibilities.

In the seventh of well-memorized fourteen steps, he stopped, listening. Other than Pangloss somewhere behind him, the night gave him only an ear-ringing silence in which he imagined he could hear his own breathing. There were the phantom footsteps of old wooden beams expanding or contracting, the low moan of the endless breeze caressing the shingle roof.

By that intuition common to nature's predators and learned by their human counterparts, Jason sensed emptiness. Nonetheless, he waited another full five minutes before completing his descent. Aware as any blind person of the exact location of furniture in his home, he crossed the small room to a chest, opened a drawer, and produced Night Optics night-vision goggles, a bulky apparatus that resembled something NASA might have invented more than something worn by a pilot.

The room came to visual life, furniture black shapes in a green murk. Cradling the shotgun, Jason stepped to the window that framed the orchard, the place from which the shot had come. The familiar trees in their shrouds of snow were huge, green vegetables, the snow, greener than fresh grass, shifted in the wind like a restless tide.

There was no sign of human life. Jason might as well have been viewing some long-dead planet on which restless emerald sands blurred objects as through a photographer's Vaseline lens. Edges of trees and rocks were particularly hard to distinguish, but close scrutiny revealed two sets of dark marks in the snow.

Tracks?

Human tracks?

Hard to tell from the indistinct images of the NVGs. Possible tracks left by wandering cows, although the thrifty farmers of Sark would probably house their livestock in this weather rather than risk loss by freezing. For sure, Jason had no intent of going outside for a closer inspection. It took little imagination to visualize a rifleman, his night scope zeroed in on the door, as he waited for such a move.

13

Jason made a circuit of the cottage's great room and bath before entering the kitchen and testing the lock on the back door. Not substantial enough to resist a determined assault but sturdy enough to cause a racket before yielding. Satisfied he had done everything he could, he was returning to the stairs when he stepped on something soft, something that emitted a hair-raising yowl loud enough to send Jason staggering backward in astonishment.

"Goddammit, Robespierre!" he muttered, "Why can't you stay put at night like the rest of us? I could have shot you by mistake."

From wherever he had taken refuge in the dark, Robespierre maintained an unrepentant silence.

Still grumbling about the perverse nature of cats in general, and this one in particular, Jason sat, shivering in the cold invading the space that had been heated by the stone fireplace. Relighting the fire was a temptation, but one easily dismissed by the necessity of a visit to the woodpile behind the house. Instead, he moved quickly upstairs, snatched the eiderdown comforter from the bed, and wrapped himself in it so that only his eyes and the hand holding the Striker were uncovered. He returned to his vigil, this time the same bent wood chair Momma had occupied. Its hard back and seat would diminish the chances of falling asleep.

Not that there was any great chance of that. Nothing like being shot at to get the old adrenaline flowing.

From upstairs, he could hear Pangloss's resumed snoring. Having done his duty in detecting the intruder, the dog had obviously washed his paws of the matter, leaving Jason to deal with the problem. Whose best friend? For that matter, a fine pair, Robespierre and Pangloss. At this moment, had there been a public animal shelter or a pound on Sark, both might have been in jeopardy of having to find new homes.

He moved his thoughts to a potentially more useful purpose. Who had taken the shot, or, more realistically, who had sent the man who had taken the shot? Elementary logic suggested whoever sent the man in the Mercedes to Liechtenstein. But elementary logic didn't name him. Or them.

Jason's first guess would be the followers of Mullah Mahomet Moustaph, one of the 9/11 plotters, and the only man Jason blamed for Laurin's death. He was, of course, no more responsible than his co-conspirators, but he was the only one free and still alive. Maybe. Jason had been largely involved in the terrorist's capture and transport to an interrogation site someplace where due process was usually administered with hard objects and car batteries. The thought of the mullah's discomfort was as pleasing as the idea of his followers finding Jason's hideaway was disturbing.

Of course, the mullah's cadre of crazies weren't the only people who would not mourn Jason's passing and would be happy to expedite it. Most in that category were dead, but the number of those surviving made it difficult to be certain of the source of the would-be assassin.

Whoever, Jason had been found here on Sark, and the island was no longer sanctuary. The first step in terminating someone was to locate them, and that step had obviously been completed. No matter his martial skills, it was only a matter of time till the next attempt, or the one after that, succeeded. He had to leave Sark.

Jason gave a sigh of frustration. He had been forced to vacate a beachfront home in the Turks and Caicos Islands, then a house on a cliff on Ischia, overlooking the Tyrrhenian Sea. And now Sark. All since he had initially quit Narcom.

Some retirement benefits, spending your golden years as a fugitive. If you lived that long.

So much spilled milk. Time to think of where next. It was a decision that would take time he might not have. He needed to disappear right now. How . . . ?

Momma, of course. Take up whatever task she had for him, that would provide an escape. All he had to do was finish the job in the month or so before Maria was to rejoin him and find a new residence.

Somehow the hours passed, the darkness lightening like coffee as cream is added. Trained to lie in waiting for days at a time if necessary, Jason remained motionless in the chair. One part of his mind was thousands of miles and a dozen years away. He and Laurin, laughing in the spray over the bow of the small Super Snark as she came about, sail luffing, in the choppy winter waters of the Potomac. Firm breasts pressed into his back, arms around his waist, as the artist's palette of the Blue Ridge Mountains' autumn foliage sped by a in blur of color to the tune of the BMW 1000's exhaust. Laurin, her swimsuit barely adequate to cover the strategic places . . .

His reverie shattered like fine crystal dropped on a stone floor as another part of his mind took command, cruelly depriving him of what came next. He was surprised to note his cheeks were wet with tears, but he had no time to consider. Something had drawn him back to the present.

He stood, the eiderdown comforter slithering to the floor with a whisper. He was both resentful of the interruption and careful the chair made no sound as it was relived of its burden. Dawn's gray veil covered the windows and he could see it had stopped snowing. Upstairs, Pangloss stirred. Robespierre eyed Jason curiously from the top of a pine china cabinet as though wondering if his altitude alone would insure no further encounters such as last night's.

All normal here. But what . . . ?

Then he heard it, the crunch of footsteps on the crust of ice that had formed on the front walkway. Jason had noticed it last night when he arrived. He stood back from the door, the collapsible stock of the Striker pressed into the hollow of his shoulder.

Hold it, he told himself. *What kind of an enemy announces himself with noisily crushed ice and an arrival at your front door?* He risked a side on glance from one of the front windows. Just above the edge of the road cut, a dapple gray horse's head shook, nostrils expelling jets of steam quickly swallowed by the crisp morning air.

Old Bess, the horse that had been bringing Jason's twice-a-week delivery of milk and butter for over a year now. Not that Jason needed the dairy product. Indeed, Maria eschewed butter as though it were a magic potion sure to add inches to her slim waist and hips. But Jason knew the value of blending into a community, particularly one as small as Sark. He not only subscribed to milk and butter, but fresh eggs and, in the summer, vegetables as well. A good customer was a good neighbor. And a good neighbor was someone you watched out for.

There was a barely audible thump as the milk came to rest just outside the door. Jason watched the retreating back of Mr. Dunn, on his way to more deliveries. Jason cracked the door and extended an arm to blindly grope for the bottle. Suddenly, beside him was a warm furry body, purring loudly. Jason had not heard Robespierre pounce from the cabinet to the floor. But then, he rarely did. Jason had no problem imagining some ancient feline relative, lost in history, depending on stealth to seek out a living between saber tooth tigers and cave bears.

A product of evolution or not, Robespierre was now the picture of a docile, human loving house cat. The animal knew milk had been delivered and milk meant cream.

Make that stealth *and* deception.

14

Creux Harbour
Sark, Channel Islands
Twenty-Five Minutes Later

Puddles of melting slush along the dock were tiny lakes in some arctic tundra. Jason hardly noticed. He was intent on the yacht slowly tugging at her mooring outside the harbor, as subtle among the working craft as a moose in rut. Although the temperature was struggling toward Sark's comparatively moderate maritime climate, there was no one in sight. The half dozen fishing boats, the ones that would be full of sport anglers in summer, had left at sunup in pursuit of the mullet, sole, and mackerel that haunted the rocky shores. The fishing was actually better in fall and winter, sufficient reason for professionals to brave the churning, angry Channel waters.

So, how was he going to contact Momma? The president's cell phone number was a less tightly guarded secret than hers, and Narcom existed in no directory, telephone or otherwise.

Overhead, a gannet cried out as it cut circles in an empty blue sky. With nothing better to do, Jason watched the bird peel off into a dive that would have done credit to a fighter. Its bill barely rippling the water, the fowl struggled back to altitude, a shiny silver morsel in its beak. Jason wondered why the bird didn't rest in the swells to enjoy its catch.

A sound of an outboard motor distracted him. A launch was departing the yacht. He was chagrined to realize she had been expecting him.

Once aboard, Samedi, still clad all in black, conducted him across a shiny teak deck to a pair of French doors of the same wood with brilliantly shined brass handles. Opening one, Samedi ushered him inside, closed the door, and disappeared on silent feet.

Jason was in the ship's grand salon, standing on what he guessed was an Oushak carpet that was worth more than most houses on the island. The bulkheads were of dark wood and hung with oils, two of which were either by seventeenth-century Bolognese painter Guido Reni or damn good copies. Two near-life-size gilt Nubians guarded the far door, possibly as expensive as they were tacky.

The light came not from windows—there were none—but from an indirect source in the deck above. It shone down on a Boulle desk, lined in bronze and inlaid with fruitwood. Momma sat behind it.

She displayed her usual dental brilliance. "Mornin', Jason." One massive hand indicated a pair of equally ornate wing chairs upholstered in red velvet. "Have a seat. Had breakfast yet? This boat has a full kitchen. Or should I say 'galley' "?

Jason sat carefully, uncertain if he was lowering himself into a priceless, if gaudy, antique or a reproduction. "Coffee would be nice." He gazed around the room. "Must be good to have friends with nice toys."

With this degree of opulence, must be a very successful Mafia don. Or head of a medium-size oil sheikdom, someone more prone to extravagance than taste.

"Convenient, anyway. You have a chance to read the book I left with you?"

"I, ah, got interrupted."

Momma's eyebrows arched. "On this island? By what, an escaped cow?"

Jason was spared the necessity of an answer by the arrival through the far door of a man in a white jacket. He carried a silver tray bearing a steaming Meissen pot with matching sugar bowl, cream pitcher, cups, and saucers. Jason had no idea how he had been summoned.

Momma waited until he had set the tray down on the desk and departed before she began to pour a stream of fragrant black coffee. "You showed up, I figured you'd read the book."

He stood to take the cup she was offering him. "Maybe you can just tell me about it?"

She did.

Jason was uncomfortable balancing his cup and saucer on a knee, wishing there was a table nearby to set it on. "Sounds more like sci-fi."

"A lot of people wish."

Jason took a long sip of the coffee. There was something in it. Chicory, perhaps? "And you really believe this, this force, whatever it is, took down the Air France Airbus. That there was some kind of directed weapon, like a laser beam? We're talking a death ray, like out of the comic books?"

"The people at both Le Bourget and Toulon don't see anything comical about it. Some bunch call theyselves the Islamic Maghreb claim credit for it."

"I didn't see that in the news."

"You won't. No point in starting a world panic."

"Then how do we know they really are responsible?"

"We don't. But we may be fixin' to find out in the next ten days."

"How's that?" Jason asked, skeptical.

"Last week, they broadcast a demand over Al Jazeera, say we got two weeks to release every prisoner at Guantanamo or they going to shoot down another airliner."

"You believe that?"

Momma shrugged. "There's them what don't want to find out. You got ten days left."

"The BEA and the manufacturer believe." It was a statement, not a question.

Momma refilled her cup. "From the voice and flight recorders, as well as the parts of the plane the French were able to retrieve, the U.S. National Transportation Safety Board is of the opinion there is no known force in nature that could twist and bend metal like that, nor any that could have caused the readings on the flight recorder."

Jason stood to place his empty cup on the desk, shaking his head no as she held up the coffeepot. "So what makes them so sure of the source?"

"If you'd read the book, you'd know."

"You tell me."

Momma lifted an arm to consult a diamond-encrusted antique Girard-Perregaux that Jason knew had at one time belonged to Elisabeth, wife of Austro-Hungarian Emperor Franz Joseph. The empress had been considered one of the most beautiful women in Europe, even by 1898, at age sixty, when she was stabbed on the streets of Geneva. Her assassin, an Italian anarchist, supposedly snatched the watch as he plunged his homemade dagger into her chest. He still had it when arrested. How its present owner came by it was a subject upon which Jason could only speculate.

The watch was a shiny mole on an arm larger than a leg of lamb. "Ain' got time to go into all that." She produced a manila envelope, handing it cross the desk. "It's all in there."

Jason took the envelope. "You in a hurry?"

"Nope. You are. You got a flight outta Guernsey into Heathrow in a couple of hours. Only ten days left, remember?"

Jason was suddenly aware his mouth was open. This was the height of presumption even for Momma. "Oh? And just where am I going?"

"You decide once you read what I just gave you, that and the book. The job pays one million, no taxes. You're going to want to put together a team. I'll cover those expenses."

"And just what, may I ask, makes you think I want the job?"

"Among other things, your old pal, Mahomet Moustaph, is involved."

Jason ignored the sound of grinding of his own teeth.

"Last I heard, he was in some CIA hellhole of an interrogation center off the map."

"He escaped."

"But how . . . ?"

"Not like them spooks over to Langley going to hand out press releases ever time they screw up. What I hear, though, is some of Moustaph's throat-cutting buddies bribed the native guards."

That was the problem with detention and interrogation centers located in places too remote to come to the attention of U.S. official-dom: The incentive to the locals in allowing such a place to exist was purely financial, not patriotic. Consequently, the natives were often for sale to the highest bidder.

Momma continued, "Thought of you the minute I heard."

Well she might. Jason made no secret of the fact he viewed Mou-staph as his own personal quarry. If there had been any doubt he would take the assignment, it vanished with the possibility he might be able to track down the man responsible for his wife's death. Still, he wasn't going to let Momma think she could evoke a Pavlovian response every time the man's name came up.

"9/11 was a long time ago. Other than Moustaph, what makes you think I want the job?"

Momma's brow furrowed as though she were in deep thought. "Well, first, you're bored."

"You're guessing."

"And you need to leave the island."

"I can make my own arrangements."

"And you came here."

For that, he had no answer.

He turned to leave, stopped, and turned again. "If the location of this, this . . . *thing* is known, there are any number of ways to take it out without putting boots on the ground."

Mamma nodded her agreement. "True. But a drone carrying a bomb can't sift through the wreckage to make sure the machine is destroyed. Since it's inside, the drone can't confirm even if it's there, for that matter."

"No, but a team of Marine Force Recon, SEALs, or Delta Force could if confirmation is essential."

"That would be putting those boots on the ground, wouldn't it? No, way it is, the country has enough enemies in that part of the world to be sending in troops to blow up a mosque."

"A mosque?"

Momma pointed to the envelope in his hand. "Jason, you really need to read this stuff yourself, 'stead of wasting time and maybe miss-ing your plane. We know the area from which the weapon came. Some kind of triangulation I don't pretend to understand. We have an idea of the size of a machine that could strike from that distance. Only building big enough to hold it around there is a mosque, a rather famous one as it turns out."

A job too dangerous for uniformed professionals in a hostile and volatile area. Sometimes Jason wished he had a higher boredom threshold.

15

Federal Bureau of Investigation
Re: Nikola Tesla
File No. 2121-70
TOP SECRET

Date: October 21, 1941
To: J. Edgar Hoover, Director
From: Tim O'Flaherty, Director, Manhattan
Field Office

Interception of subject's mail at the request
of British Secret Service Bureau and authorized
by secret Presidential Directive 42 indicate
frequent mail contact with family members in
the Independent State of Croatia. The director will recall this small country became a
signatory to the Triparte Pact on 6 June of
this year, thereby becoming a formal ally of
Nazi Germany and Fascist Italy as well as Impe-
rial Japan and a number of smaller countries,
although Croatia has been considered a Nazi
puppet state under the N.D.H. since the Axis
invasion of Yugoslavia in April of this year.

Since subject holds a number of patents of a scientific nature with possible military implications, the possibility exists of his family being used as hostages by the country's pro-Nazi government in an effort to obtain access to subject's inventions for use as potential weapons. Subject's nephew, Dari, has volunteered to join the 369 Reinforced Croatian Infantry, the troops Ante Pavelić, Croatia's "leader," has promised to send to aid in the German invasion of Russia. Whether this young man has done so out of a love of the Nazis or the long-lived Croatian hatred of Russia is unknown.

The director will recall subject attempted to sell some sort of ray to the British military and succeeded in doing so to the U.S.S.R. for a reputed $25,000.

So far, there is no evidence subject's communications contain anything more significant than family news. Surveillance will continue.

16

Excerpts from Nikola Tesla: Genius or Mad Scientist by Robert Hastings, PhD

Tesla liked to retell the story of how, as a young man, he was taken ill at school in Carlsbad and hospitalized. The physicians, according to Tesla, were unable to cure his mysterious ailment. One day, a nurse handed him several publications, including several articles by the American writer and humorist Mark Twain. Tesla so enjoyed them that he effected a miraculous recovery. From that day forward, Mark Twain became someone Tesla wanted to meet. The fact that, historically, Twain had written little of note and nothing worth translating at the time of Tesla's supposed illness never dissuaded him of his claim the writer had saved his life.

In 1884, the scientist succeeded in meeting Twain through mutual acquaintances who were members of Manhattan's Players Club. Though the two were never close friends, Twain was a frequent visitor to the lab at 48 East Houston Street, where the writer once observed, upon watching an experiment that involved twenty-foot electrical arcs and bolts of homemade lightning, "Thunder is impressive, but it's lightning that does the work."

Later, Twain was to praise Tesla's AC polyphase system as "the most valuable patent since the telephone."

Twain took great pleasure in standing on a platform above one of Tesla's inventions, the mechanical oscillator, feeling it sway back and forth in response to electrical impulses. On the first such experience, Tesla suggested his guest had ridden long enough and he should come down. Twain declined, saying he found the motion "invigorating" and "healthful."

Minutes later, he scrambled down, shouting, "Tesla, where is it?"

He meant the toilet, of course, having learned what Tesla's lab assistants had already painfully experienced: Riding the machine too long had a definite effect on the bowels.

In 1896, Twain was traveling in Europe, keeping up a sporadic correspondence with the scientist. From Austria, he wrote a letter, which, in part, read, "Have you Austrian and English patents on that destructive terror you are inventing?" Twain had his own ideas as to peace and disarmament: ". . . invite the great inventors to construct something against which fleets and armies would be helpless and thus make war thenceforth impossible."

Twain went on to offer his services in marketing the patents to European powers and rulers he had met in his travels, including Emperor Wilhelm II of Germany, presumably on the theory that if all nations possessed such a weapon, war would be impossible. Exactly what the nature of this "destructive terror" was is not mentioned, nor is the method by which Twain learned of it.

A final and rather sad note to the relationship between scientist and writer: In 1942, shortly before his death, Tesla summoned a messenger, giving him a packet to be delivered to a Mr. Samuel Clemens at an address in Manhattan. When the messenger returned, unable to find either address or addressee (the street had changed names), Tesla flew into a rage.

"Mr. Clemens is a famous writer," he howled. "He writes

under the name Mark Twain. Someone will know where to find him!"

The frustrated messenger returned a second time, informing Tesla that Mr. Clemens had been dead some time.

"Impossible!" the scientist protested. "He was here last night." He pointed. "He sat in that very chair! He is need of money, and I am sending it to him!"

The author relates the above anecdote as possible evidence Nikola Tesla was ever delusional, or, at his age in 1943, suffering dementia. He was dead weeks later.

17

Guernsey Airport
Guernsey, Channel Islands
The Same Day
Day 1

Jason knew the good people of the island were proud of their small airport. The terminal, a glass toadstool, had won a number of architectural awards upon its opening in 2004. Meaning, in that year, there had been a paucity of avant-garde or just plain ugly new buildings.

But aesthetics were not his mind at the moment. He had barely had enough time to put funds in Mrs. Princes's house account—to run the cottage; take care of Pangloss and Robespierre; and pay her wages for the next two weeks—and still have Momma and her borrowed yacht make the crossing from Sark to catch his flight to Heathrow. The BA CityFlyer Embraer 170 that would take him there was the only plane on the tarmac. At this time of year, the small but comfortable terminal was empty of tourists made cheerfully boisterous by the prospect of a fortnight of holidays on one of the islands. Instead, there was a handful of men, most in suits, whose interest in their watches and cell phones made Jason guess they were on various business missions.

Arriving just in time to clear security and board the plane, he shoved his single bag into an overhead bin and squeezed himself into one of a pair of empty seats. Of the seventy-six available, barely half were occupied. Although he had seen it dozens of times, he watched the winter-browned grass along the pavement move in the wind, waving a final farewell as the aircraft trundled out to Runway 32. This departure was different; Jason had no plans to return.

Now Sark, with its wind-bent fruit trees, rocky shores, and hardy cattle, was his most-recent former address. Maybe next time Jason would try a place on some mainland, someplace out of the way but not so remote as to make him conspicuous; someplace removed from civilization, but not too far removed; someplace that had nothing to attract anyone other than the residents.

Kansas suggested itself.

Thoughts for another day. He reached into a coat pocket and produced the book and envelope Momma had given him and began to read. He wouldn't get a lot read in the eighteen-minute flight, but it was a start.

He came awake with a start, unaware he had drifted off to sleep, as the aircraft lurched forward, its twin General Electric engines screaming in reverse thrust. The short duration of the trip had obviated any in-flight service that might have disturbed his brief nap. He barely had time to reflect that this was the first time in memory he had actually slept on an airplane. He normally suffered in-flight insomnia, involuntarily attuned to every sound, every change in pitch of the engines. He knew it was absurd—what could he do if things went south at 35,000 feet—but some obscure, atavistic sense of self-preservation kept him awake anyway.

As he liberated himself from the seat belt, he glanced out of the window where the much-heralded Terminal 5 was suckling a litter of Airbus 300 series and Boeing 700s: 80,000 tons of steel, 36,000 square yards of glass for a giant rabbit hutch. He had no idea why the numbers stuck in his mind other than the persistence of the British press in featuring every phase of its construction. There had to be a rule, known for certain only to the cognoscenti, that airport terminals, unlike the older, eye-teasing train stations of a century ago, must be either modern beyond attractive or tediously utilitarian.

He stood and removed his bag from the overhead as the plane

docked at a somewhat less lionized, if equally unattractive, terminal and, like cattle to the slaughter, shuffled his place in line down the aisle to the exit into Terminal 1. Duty-free shops opposite departure/arrival gates lined the left side of the walkway, windows gleaming with expensive luxury watches, the latest in electronics, and other high end goods. Airport retailers are not known for bargain prices.

Jason's passing stare into the glass was rewarded by the reflection of a man as he stood up from one of the lounge chairs that lined the center of the concourse. He would have gone unnoticed had he not taken something from a jacket and folded it into the newspaper he held in the other hand. Gloved hand, Jason noticed. Most people who wear gloves indoors usually have a purpose other than keeping their hands warm. The guy wasn't Ronald McDonald. He maneuvered around a woman pulling a pair of roller boards to fall in behind Jason at a slightly faster pace. Alarm bells were clanging in Jason's mind, but he maintained the exterior of one fascinated by the gaudy retail display.

He picked his spot in front of a display of Rolex watches. Arms akimbo, he leaned forward as though to better see the timepieces. In reality, he was carefully watching the approach of the man with the rolled newspaper. Jason waited until the stranger was only a step away, reaching into the paper.

Jason took a step back. It was the move of a man suddenly tired of what he was viewing, or, perhaps, remembering something he had to do. The heel of his shoe came down on the stranger's instep hard enough to elicit a yelp of pain. At the same instant, Jason's elbow hit the wrist of the hand with the paper, knocking it loose.

"How clumsy of me!" Jason said, stooping. "Here, let me . . ."

Before the astonished man could protest, Jason shook the pages of the newspaper. A syringe rolled onto the tiles.

Jason snatched it up before the other man could close his fingers around it. The man bolted, shoving surprised passengers aside.

Jason's impulse was to give chase, but he held up. Like mice, the presence of one assassin meant there was a good chance more were around. He gently pushed the syringe's plunger, bringing a few drops to the hole in the needle and sniffed. No odor. Jason would have bet is was also tasteless. The really nasty stuff usually was.

Only then did he notice a small crowd of curious onlookers.

"My physician," he explained with a forced smile. "He has his own way of delivering my annual flu shot."

18

Terminal 4

London Heathrow Airport, United Kingdom

An Hour and a Half Later

Jason waited as long as possible before paying cash for his ticket, reluctantly showing his passport for identification. Absent false ID, there was no way he could keep his name off the passenger manifest, a document any moderately talented teenage hacker could get. His hope was that by the time his name was added, the flight would have departed.

In the waiting area, he selected a seat with a wall at its back. The thought of how easily the syringe's needle could have slipped through the fabric of the seat or those on an aircraft made him squirm. Easy, quiet, undetectable. Undetectable until one of the plane's flight crew discovered the passenger in 14F was dead, not sleeping, by which time the killer would be long gone. Equally disquieting was the certainty the attempt had been perpetrated by professionals, not one of Moustaph's disciples, filled more with religious zeal and hatred than talent. Not that the Al Qaeda leader didn't have capable killers available.

Another disturbing thought was the question of whether the men in Liechtenstein were connected to the shot fired through the bedroom window. Jason was fairly certain they were. Both the lack of subtlety and the blind shot through the window had an amateurish quality. Not like the would-be attack with the syringe.

The more he thought about it, the more uncomfortable he became. Two sets of assassins? One, the amateurs, acting out of revenge at the command of Moustaph, the other, the paid professionals with ready access to poison syringes and an arsenal of equally deadly weapons.

Not much he could do about it now other than to e-mail Momma and Narcom a list of what he needed so far. He had just finished when his flight was called.

Moments later, he was seated, iPod earbuds inserted as the violins of Scarlatti, the greatest of the Neapolitan Baroque composers, danced through his head. He ignored the scientifically dubious claim of possible interference with the aircraft's navigational system and began to read the material Momma had given him further.

19

Excerpts from *Nikola Tesla: Genius or Mad Scientist*
by Robert Hastings, PhD

From letters preserved by present-day relatives of Tesla and shared with the author by surviving members of Tesla's family in Croatia, it becomes clear he was concerned about the welfare of his family there under Nazi rule. He was particularly distressed by the service of his young nephew, Darf, in a regiment of Croatian infantry fighting the Russians, along with the Germans at Stalingrad. His unhappiness came not from a political point of view, but from a fear of harm to Darf, harm suffered on behalf of the Germans whom he trusted no more than the Russians.

In September 1942, when the Stalingrad offensive had just begun, he wrote his sister, Ljerka, Darf's mother.

> I fear for Darf. He is young, impetuous, and likely to take unnecessary chances on behalf of the country's current masters who care nothing for Croatia nor the fate of its youth. Besides, the lad suffers from asthma

and may perish without his family to care for him.
It is possible I may be able to help secure his release
from the military.
If so, it is my intent to do so.

Thereafter, Tesla corresponded with the U.S. Department of State, seeking to have the U.S. government intervene in some manner. Since America was already at war with Germany and its allies by this time, there was little the government could do. Tesla then contacted the embassies of neutrals Switzerland, Sweden, Spain, and Portugal as well as the representative of the Holy See in New York (exchanges of ambassadors between the United States and the Vatican were not established until 1984). As an internationally known scientist whose inventions "benefitted all mankind," he asked each, in the "name of humanity" to intercede with the Croatian pro-Nazi regime to free his nephew from military service.

As naive as his efforts may seem, Darf's children in Croatia today relate the story their late father told of his sudden release from the army just as the November 1942 Russian counter-offensive began in some of the worst weather conditions known to modern warfare. He was flown home and given a job in his country's small war-production office. We may only speculate which neutral country succeeded in fulfilling Tesla's requests. Or, more puzzling, why the German army, desperate for every man it could muster, would acquiesce.

20

Last night's train ride to Paris, a stay in a nameless airport hotel, and the early flight from the madness that was Charles de Gaulle was a blur. During it, though, Jason had finished both the book and material Momma had furnished. If he had entertained any doubts as to the urgency of his mission, he did so no longer.

But, before he could complete the task, there were a number of questions that needed answering, questions that were a stream of consciousness as he walked along one of the dozen new concourses added to what had been a Russian-built terminal, the massive, ugly, if utilitarian, architecture common to most former Soviet states. Communist Gothic, Jason called it. Other Russian influence also lingered: The escalator from the second to bottom floor was out of service.

Setting down his only bag in front of the Air France counter, he waited while the single clerk listened to a stocky, elderly woman. Head covered by a scarf, her tone was angry, a complaint even if Jason couldn't understand the language, though it sounded like Russian.

From her gestures, it became clear her luggage had taken an excursion of its own. Despite the clerk's polite replies, frustration was in her tone as she tried to point the angry woman to wherever victims of misdirected baggage went.

Jason checked his watch. He had been standing here nearly five minutes. Not a great deal of time, but more than enough to give a potential attacker an opportunity to set a trap. Not having to wait at baggage carousels was the reason he never checked a bag.

Finally, the old woman either understood that lost luggage was not to be found at the ticket counter, gave up, or decided to vent her anger elsewhere. The clerk, a young woman with blunt-cut dark hair, gave Jason a radiant smile.

"Thank you for your patience," she said in accented English. "It was the *babuška*'s first flight, bags not arrive." She shrugged. "Or, more likely, her *kutija*," She made a rectangle with her hands. "What is the English?"

"Box?"

"Yes, box. Many Russians come here because is little cost, particularly the older ones, never travel more than a few kilometers from their village. Now that they are retiring from government . . . how you say?'

"Government work? Government service?"

"Yes. They have retire and now are no government restriction on travel like when Communist rule. They come, but do not own such thing as real suitbox."

"Suitcase?"

"Yes, suitcase. They never own, put clothes in cardboard box, tie with string. Sometimes not so good, string break. Plane land, baggage hold full of loose clothes."

"I can see that might be a problem," Jason said, turning to scan the area for anything out of the ordinary, anything suspicious. "I'm Jason Peters. I think you have a package for me."

Her face clouded in confusion for an instant, then brightened, "Yes! A man . . . what is the English?"

"Courier?"

She shook her head. "DHL delivery."

"OK, DHL. There's something here for me?"

She disappeared behind the counter, returning with the bright red-and-yellow package of the delivery company. After he produced his passport for inspection, she handed it across the counter.

"It is heavy!" she observed.

"Books," Jason explained as he lifted the parcel.

He assumed the *"Dobro jutro!"* she called after him as he headed toward the mens' room was Croatian for something akin to "have a good day."

Regrettably, he had made other plans.

Inside a stall, he tore open the cardboard. Momma had fulfilled his wish list: Passport bearing an unflattering picture, American Express and Capitol One Visa cards, all bearing the name of one George R. Simmons. A driver's license gave Mr. Simmons's address as P Street in the Georgetown section of Washington, DC. Three wallet-size photos of two chubby cheeked children filled out the identity packet. A .40-caliber Glock with two fully loaded clips and belt holster were next. Jason pressed the magazine release, slid it from the butt of the pistol, and noted with approval it was also full. Cocking the pistol, he slipped it into the holster and clipped the holster to his belt at the small of his back before he dropped the extra clips into his pocket. Next, he removed a knife, one he had designed himself. He took it from its scabbard to check the titanium blade. Ten inches in length, it was only half an inch wide with a razor-sharp edge on both sides. Ideal for stabbing or slashing with minimum risk of getting entangled in bone or entrails. He returned it to its scabbard, strapped it onto his right calf, and pulled his trouser leg over it. He turned the open end of the package downward and shook it. An enveloped floated to the stall's floor, the last of the box's contents.

Inside was a single piece of paper on which were Momma's neat block letters:

Herka Kerjck
Budačka ulica 16
Gospić, **Lika**
She has been contacted and is expecting you.

He memorized the name and address and consigned the shredded paper to the toilet.

He then went to a booth to exchange his euros for kuna, the local currency. Seven and a half was a slightly better exchange rate than he had expected. Once again, he took careful stock of his surroundings as he pretended to focus on counting the money before exiting the terminal to join a line of people waiting for cabs. What was it about the town that made waiting for a taxi at the airport make a similar wait at, say, La Guardia, seem nonexistent? Nearly twenty minutes later, he was in a cab, riding the ten kilometers into the city. He gave the cabby the rail station as his destination and sat back to enjoy the view.

Zagreb could have been any Eastern European city—Prague, Vienna—with its white stone buildings and red tile roofs. Bright blue trams clattered along tracks in the middle of main streets. Like those other cities, it, too, was in the plain of a river, the Sava. The cab darted from a very modern highway into narrow cobblestone streets. Shops and eating establishments dominated the first floors with living quarters upstairs. Ahead, the twin towers of the fourteenth-century Cathedral of the Assumption and its colorful mosaic roof, depicting the coats of arms of two of the church's early patrons, dominated the skyline.

The curbs of the street were lined with cars, mostly of the claustrophobically small European variety. But the streets were filled with more economic transportation, bicycles and scooters. Jason knew Americans liked to whine about high gas prices, but they paid roughly a third of what their European cousins did.

The cab emerged onto a large, grassy square, Tomislavov Trg, where a statue of Croatia's first king showed his back to a large, Greek revival building with rococo ornamentation below a widow's walk at the top of its peaked roof. The rail station, obviously predating the featureless, massive Communist buildings. Kiosks selling food, cigarettes, magazines, and other items that might be of interest to train passengers ringed the entrance.

Unsure if his driver spoke English since, unlike Western Europe, many cabbies there did not, Jason pointed to an open spot at the curb just vacated by another cab. "There."

His guess had been correct. The driver said something Jason didn't understand and pointed to the meter mounted on the dash: 16.90. Jason reached over the seat to hand him a twenty. The reaction, a smile like a picket fence missing a few palings, told him he had been overgenerous.

If the outside of the station had been busy, the inside was chaos. Gypsy women, many suckling babies as they sat on the floor, beseeched passersby for money with raucous cries. Men and women in farm clothes clutched tickets as they formed lines for no reason Jason could discern. A group of perhaps a half dozen women in hijabs and head scarves reminded Jason that this part of the Balkans had been part of the Ottoman Empire and that Moslems, though now a small number, were a recognized minority. Part of the reason for the "ethnic cleansing" that had taken place in November 1992 when Bosnia and Croatia had become civil war battlefields. Orthodox Serbs had attacked Roman Catholic Serbs with both attacking the Moslems. Centuries of ethnic suspicion, hatred, and jealousy, suppressed by Communism's iron fist, had boiled over. Had it not been for intervention by the United Nations, with strong U.S. support, the countryside would have been littered with dead men, women, and children. Although subsequent war-crime trials revealed thousands killed, most defenseless citizens, the true number would never be known.

Thankful that the signs above the ticket windows were in Roman as well as Cyrillic letters, Jason edged his way through the mob to stand in line in front of the one reading GOSPIĆ, LIKA, his destination.

The train could have been any of the electric variety common in Europe. But there was nothing common about the scheduled arrival time posted in electric lights above the track: four hours plus. Jason rechecked his iPod. Sure enough, the distance was only 185 kilometers.

"But it's two hundred and thirty-two by rail because of the turns going through the mountains," a feminine voice informed him.

He whirled around to look into a pair of laughing blue eyes in a round face. A knit cap covered the rest of her head, other than a renegade strand of blonde hair that reached the collar of her suede overcoat.

She slipped off a glove and extended the hand. "Natalia Čupić, frequent rail rider."

Jason returned the iPod to his coat pocket and shook. "And mind reader."

She tinkled a laugh, showing nothing of the poor dentistry for which Eastern Europe was infamous. "Not really. I couldn't help but notice your iPod. Then, I saw what was on the screen. Did you know you make a grunting sound when you are disappointed? Or is it when you are surprised?"

Jason climbed the three steps up into the railcar, pulling himself up with one hand on one of the vertical chrome rails beside the door installed for just that the purpose. Without them, boarding the train would have been difficult for someone burdened with heavy baggage. He extended a hand to help her manage her one bag. "Do you make a practice of reading other people's screens?"

She swung up into the car, the move of an athlete, holding on to his hand a full second longer than necessary. "Only those of interesting-looking men, and only when I am faced with a long, boring journey. And that is the last bit of information you get until I know your name. I do not have conversations with strange men."

He was in front of her as they walked past groups of seating, two facing two with a small fixed table between. "Even interesting ones on long boring trips?"

"A girl has to have some sort of rules."

Jason shoved his bag in the overhead. "Seat twenty-three, that's me." It took a split second to remember who he was. "George Simmons."

She tossed her bag next to his and sat. "I'm right across the table, number twenty-five. Now that we are properly introduced, might I ask what an American is doing traveling to such an out-of-the-way place as that to which this train is going?"

Jason was instantly on guard but kept his tone jocular. "The train makes a dozen stops. Just how did you know where I'm going?"

She looked up at one of the several signs depicting a smoking cigarette in a circle with a line drawn through it. "That's new, that NO SMOKING sign. Croatia is following the West in getting into the health police business. Bad idea, don't you think?"

Jason sat, his knees nearly touching hers. "I think you ought to answer the question I just asked: If you're not a mind reader, how did you know where I was going?"

She gave that musical laugh again as she swept off her cap, freeing a cascades of golden hair, "I didn't."

"But you said . . ."

"I said you were going to an out-of-the-way place. Take a look at the train's route. There's not a stop on it that has ten thousand people living there. So, what is an American doing in places like that?"

Jason relaxed. "Visiting relatives, actually. Or, rather searching for them. My mother came from the town of Gospić. As long as I was in the country on business, I thought I'd spend a little time seeing if can find a cousin or two."

"More like five or six. Families in the mountains are large. There is not much else to do. What sort of business?"

Jason held up a hand, palm out, stop. "Whoa, Natalia! You've just about heard my life story and all I know is your name. For starters, how did you learn such good English?"

The car clanked forward with a jolt and trains on adjacent tracks seemed to slide by with increasing speed.

"I was fortunate to have an excellent teacher in school, an American. My parents paid her for four years of extra tutoring. Satisfied?"

Not entirely.

Natalia was thirty, perhaps thirty-five. Her schoolgirl days would have been, when, in the late '70s, early '80s? Tito, the Communist dictator of Yugoslavia, of which Croatia had been a part, died in 1980, and the Communists remained in power until 1990, when the country fragmented like a hand grenade, creating not only Croatia but Slovenia, Serbia, Macedonia, Bosnia, Herzegovina, Montenegro, and one or two countries that might include Disney World for all Jason could recall. It was doubtful an American, particularly one teaching English, would have been hired in the state-run schools of a Communist country. At least, not the schools open to children of ordinary people. Possible, but not probable.

The train was reaching speed now, accelerating smoothly.

Jason stood. "Don't go away. I'll be right back."

Heading toward the end of the car where the toilets were located, he turned back to watch her as she looked out of the window. When he was fairly certain she wouldn't turn away, he took his iPhone from his pocket and snapped her picture. He would have preferred a full, rather than partial, face shot, but this was the best he was going to get without alerting her.

Once in the tiny toilet, reminiscent of those aboard aircraft, he locked the door, pulled down the seat, and held the iPhone in one hand while the fingers of the other typed a text message. Then he sent Natalia's picture.

21

Excerpts from *Nikola Tesla: Genius or Mad Scientist*
by Robert Hastings, PhD

Nikola Tesla was eccentric. Like Howard Hughes, he had an obsession with germs, washing his hands constantly. He could be easily identified in a restaurant by the stack of eighteen napkins upon which he insisted so he would not have to use the same one twice. He meticulously calculated the volume of each dish he ate and consumed only food that had been boiled. He was fascinated with numerology, demanding that the number of his hotel room be divisible by three.

He was particularly fond of the pigeons in Central Park, ordering special birdseed for them. One, a white female with gray-tipped wings, was his favorite. He told of her flying into his hotel room one night, her eyes "shining with a light the like of which I had never before seen" before she died in his hands. He took this as an omen of his own death.

As idiosyncratic as he might be, he was compelling when seeking investors for his inventions. J. P. Morgan put $250,000, a fortune by the standards of the day, into a scheme by which

Tesla would use the ionosphere and the earth's electromagnetic field as a giant transformer to power all forms of transportation worldwide. When he returned to the noted financier seeking additional money for the project, he made the mistake of telling the famously conservative banker how his invention would make the nations of the world one. Morgan was horrified and additional funding was not forthcoming.

Several of Tesla's inventions had a decided dark side. The electromechanical oscillator so enjoyed by Mark Twin could, according to its inventor, destroy the Brooklyn Bridge in a matter of minutes. Given several days, it could "split the earth in two like halves of an apple." When skeptics pointed out a number of flaws in his claim, Tesla replied he could at least "peel the surface of the earth away, which would serve to destroy mankind just as completely."

Another was his so-called "Death Ray," the stuff of which comic-book supervillains are made. In 1937, he described it thus to a *New York Times* reporter: "It will send a concentrated beam of particles: through the free air of such tremendous energy that they will bring down a fleet of 10,000 airplanes at a distance of 250 miles from the defending nation and will cause enemy millions to drop dead in their tracks."

Since light trends to diffuse over distance and the concentrated beam of the laser was still in the future, the "ray" was to consist of tiny particles of mercury charged with more than one million volts of electricity sprayed into the air from towers by means of a special nozzle that resealed itself to maintain the vacuum necessary to eject the mercury particles. This device was never patented, if indeed it ever existed, so we do not know how the nozzle both sprayed particulate matter and maintained a vacuum. We do know that both the U.S. military and Great Britain declined to purchase the device. The Soviet Union paid Tesla $25,000 for the plans. Had the Soviets succeeded in manufacturing the machine, World War II would have come to an earlier conclusion.

The author made considerable effort to find existing evidence of the "Death Ray," if it existed, including reviewing the microfiche documents in the Tesla Museum in Belgrade, Serbia, some 155,000 in all, including almost 70,000 bits of correspondence both personal and business and more than 45,000 papers of scientific content. The Nikola Tesla Museum of Science in Colorado Springs, Colorado, contains re-creations of a number of the man's inventions, including the oscillator. It also has copies of his journals, which are infuriatingly incomplete. No mention of the "Death Ray" was found.

22

Somewhere in the Croatian Countryside
Sixty-Two Minutes Later

Natalia had been right: It seemed to Jason the train stopped almost before it got going from the last stop. From what he could see, it stopped at groupings of a few wooden houses or in empty country. He rarely saw passengers get on or off, but he did note livestock—sheep, horses, goats—seemed to grow more numerous as the train progressed ever upward. He was certain the animals' interest in the train increased in direct proportion to the steepness of the grade. It was as if they were curious as to whether the engine would make it to the top of the next hill.

At first, he noticed snow in patches, most in the shade of groves of trees. Then there was more white than the brown winter grass. Within minutes, they were crossing a white mountain meadow, the bottom of a bowl created by the snowcapped Dinaric Alps. Jason wondered if he could capture the subtle shades of white on a canvas. The tones varied only from the gray shadow of passing clouds to a blinding white that gave back the glare of the sun. Far different from the seascapes of Isola d'Ischia and the Channel Islands that had occupied his brush for the last few years. Probably wouldn't work, he decided. The acrylics with which he painted gave depth to colors of the sea and land, the greens, the blues. A nearly monochromatic scene such as that outside the window would suggest a medium such as watercolor.

Natalia pressed a gloved finger against the window, pointing. "You have heard of Medvednica?"

Jason admitted he had not.

"Very famous ski resort, one of the best in the world. It is on the other side of that mountain range there."

Jason doubted Med . . . Med-whatever . . . He doubted it was either famous or competed easily with Saint-Moritz or Garmisch-Partenkirchen or Kitzbühel or, for that matter, Aspen. He also knew better than to question a matter of national pride.

She took his silence as assent. "Do you ski?"

The question brought of a picture of Laurin sluicing between moguls, her laughter echoing through the snow-burdened trees along Jackson Hole's black diamond slopes. Snow like he was looking at frequently recalled the memory. "Not in a long time."

She seemed to consider this for a moment. "The family you are looking for, what is their name?"

He almost blurted it out before, "Name?"

He was stalling, trying to think of a common Balkan name. He had known a number of them during the 1992–1995 Operation Deliberate Force in which U.S. military joined the United Nations in ending ethnic warfare. He certainly wasn't going to tell a near stranger where he was going. That was a mistake few people in this business had the chance to repeat.

"Name, you know, how is your relative called?"

"Dragan Horuat."

It was the name of a Serb Jason's Delta Force unit had captured and interrogated. The man was suspected of setting fire to Moslem homes with the occupants still inside. Jason recalled the man had both the face and the soul of a rat.

"Dragan Horuat," Natalia repeated as though tasting the sound. "I do not know the name."

"Should you?"

She shrugged. "In Croatia, as in many parts of what was Yugoslavia, the intermarriage of few families has led to many common names. I . . ."

She was interrupted by the conductor, a silver-haired man in a navy blue uniform with brilliantly polished brass buttons and that round pillbox with a brim, the cap peculiar to railroad conductors. After each stop, he had walked the aisle checking and punching tickets. Every time, he had carefully inspected Jason and Natalia's as if the destinations printed on them might have changed. This had to be the fourth or fifth time he had been by. But, as Jason well knew, whether in the United States, Croatia, or Outer Mongolia, nothing is more important to a functionary than his function.

Jason turned to watch the man walk the length of the car, now empty of other passengers. Inside his pocket, his iPhone vibrated.

He stood. "Excuse me . . ."

She gave him a bewildered look.

He shrugged "Too much coffee, waiting for the train, I guess."

She smiled indulgently. "The *ručak dama*, lunch lady, should be passing through. Should I get you something if you're not here to choose for yourself?"

Jason hadn't thought of food. He hadn't eaten since a quick, cold croissant washed down with bitter coffee at Charles de Gaulle. He was suddenly ravenous.

"Sure. What do they have, sandwiches and stuff?"

"Lunch is the main Croatian meal, so she should also be selling something more substantial, too, *sarma*, cabbage rolls stuffed with meat, *mlinci*, baked noodles, pizza, stuff like that."

He was edging toward the end of the car. "Whatever looks good."

Locking the door of the claustrophobic toilet, he again sat on the seat and read the text on the screen.

"The picture you sent could be Habiba. NLN. See attached photo. Habiba is believed to be a woman born in Spokane (Wash.) of an American mother of Bosnian descent and Saudi father. She gave her name in college as Abeer Al-Wafd and was active in radical, pro-Islamic causes. She was believed to have been active in the Balkan War 1990–1995 and was convicted in absentia in 1998 by the International Criminal Tribunal of the murder of Serb Catholics by Bosniaks (Bosnian Moslems). She is suspected of planning and participating in both the 2000 attack on the *Cole* and the 2002 bombing of the resort in Bali, Indonesia. Because of her European looks and fluency in both English and Farsi, Habiba, as she calls herself, passes easily from the Islamic world to the West without detention so far. The last-known contact was a security camera at Heathrow that photographed a physically similar woman disembarking from a flight from Sana'a, Yemen, a week ago today."

Jason called up the attachment, a fuzzy black-and-white snapshot of a woman in a hijab, the head scarf common to Bosnian Moslems, not the niqab, the full robe and veil revealing only the eyes, hands, and feet, common to Yemeni women as demonstrated by a woman to the left of the picture. The scarf, of course, concealed the hair; and, pulled tight around the face, could be distorting the features.

Could be Natalia. Could be the person he was going to see, this Herka Kerjck, had mentioned she was expecting him. Could be idle conversation had gotten to the wrong ears in time to set up an attempt to stop him. Could be. Jason wasn't sure; he didn't have to be. One of the many things he had learned working for Narcom was that suspicion and paranoia were good for the health.

As he walked back to his seat, a glimpse out of the windows told him the train was climbing a grade cut into the mountainside. To his right was sheer rock; to his left, empty space. Mountain roads have tunnels, he thought. He took his seat, giving Natalia a smile. And tunnels meant darkness. Maybe not. He could see lights recessed into the car's ceiling. He looked around, failing to see a switch.

"Looking for something?"

"Yeah." He pointed upward. "How do you turn those lights on?"

She put down the copy of the magazine she had gotten from somewhere, a magazine with a man in a suit on the cover along with Cyrillic letters. His practiced, sincere expression told Jason he probably was involved in politics.

"They come on automatically when it gets dark in the car, why? You will have arrived at Gospić, Lika, before sunset."

"Just curious."

She gave him a questioning look before returning to her magazine.

He was about to ask about the lunch lady when the car seemed to blink: It went ink dark for less than a second, then full light retuned. Before he could comment, it happened again.

Jason tensed, anticipating what he guessed was coming. He didn't have long to wait. The car plunged into midnight again, this time for longer than before. There were no lights from above. Quickly and silently, Jason jumped into the aisle, only a split second before he heard something rip the seat's fabric, something that he guessed would have stabbed into his chest had he not moved.

There was heavy breathing. He sensed movement from across the table. Jason froze, fearful any move would give away his location.

Then it was light again, a transition so sudden he was nearly blinded by it. But not so blind he could not see the sun's reflection shimmering along the six or more inches of steel embedded in the seat back where he had been sitting.

He didn't have long to look.

Natalia snatched the blade out of the slash in the fabric. Her pretty face was contorted in hatred as she jumped onto the low table, the knife held close inside the limits of her body, the stance of someone experienced in knife fighting.

Jason backed away, eliminating the height advantage the table gave her. "Damn, Natalia—or should I say Habiba? I've had women get pissed at how long I stayed in the john, but never *that* pissed!"

"Make your stupid joke, Peters. It will be your last."

Jason's right hand went to the small of his back, the touch of the Glock comforting. No. Easy enough to shoot this woman, not so easy to explain to the local authorities, who would, at the very least, be less than thrilled with the gun he was carrying in undoubted violation of national law. The killing knife on his leg was useless for the moment: She was too close for him to stoop and pull up his pants leg to draw his own knife from its scabbard.

She took a step forward, her eyes searching to try to find a clue as to his next move. In training for what the army described as "close combat," Jason had learned that watching your opponent's eyes could get you killed. Arms, hands, feet, and legs, as well as hips and elbows, cleared the way for the fatal opening to slide a blade into another body. Eyes were merely a distraction for the unwary.

Her shoulder tipped off her next move, a mere twitch but Jason saw it coming: a wide swipe of the blade, one meant not to kill but to disable. In the confines of the railroad car, the standard counter-move, ducking the opposite way and coming up under the arm wielding the knife, was not possible and she knew it.

"Not so easy," he said evenly. "Burning woman, children, and the elderly in their homes is one thing, maybe even easier than planting a bomb to kill Australian tourists. Facing someone not totally defenseless must be unnerving. You have become used to killing only the innocent."

Taunting to distract an opponent.

"Among the infidels there are no innocents!" she spat.

Behind her, the conductor entered the car from the one in front. She must have seen his reflection in a window.

"Lock the door," she ordered. "We need no one to enter this car until I have finished."

With a dull sense of surprise, Jason watched him comply. That explained why the lights had not come on. This was no longer a two-person show.

That was Natalia's first mistake, not coordinating exactly with the conductor so that Jason would be between the two.

If she saw it as error, she didn't show it. Instead, she advanced with the knife. Jason had little choice but retreat. His back came up against the door to the car behind. His hand found the handle and he opened it. Now he was on the platform between cars enclosed by two doors through which passengers would board or depart. He could ill afford to let himself be distracted by the view rushing by, a snowy precipice barely wider than the train itself. He thought he saw the silver ribbon of a river half a mile straight down. The other side was a wall of granite.

No time for sightseeing.

He stretched out as though participating in some form of calisthenics, his left foot jamming the latch that allowed the door to slide open. His right leg extended toward the following car as he used both hands to furiously roll up his pants leg. It was a position he could not long maintain. But he didn't have to.

The door flew open just as Jason snatched the killing knife from its scabbard, throwing him against the door to the next car. He rolled violently to his left as Natalia's knife thumped against the metal, a strike that would have gutted him like a fish had it found its mark.

It was then she saw what he held for the first time.

She backed up warily. "How unchivalrous, using a larger weapon. And against a woman, too."

They were circling each other, a move that would not have been possible with seats and tables on each side.

"I must admit, I don't recall killing a woman before. But then I've never had one attack me with anything sharper than fingernails, either. I doubt that's something you learned in school as a young girl."

She had counted on an instant of distraction. She flicked the blade upward, toward the hand holding the killing knife. Jason easily deflected it so it clanged harmlessly off the swordlike hilt.

He had the advantage at the moment and both knew it. He was larger, stronger, and had several more inches of reach. His weapon was longer and designed to stab or slash. She had counted on a single deadly stroke in the darkness of a tunnel, not prolonged combat. Her only hope was that her confederate, the conductor, would come to her aid. But to do so, he would have to come within the deadly arc of Jason's blade. Jason was certain she was as aware of all this, as was he.

"Tell you what," he said amiably, "you put down that pig sticker, and I'll let you off at the next stop, no hard feelings."

23

Croatia

"You will let *me* get off? Peters, you will be dead before then. You Westerners have no heart for what must be done, like killing a woman."

He didn't want to admit it to himself, certainly not to Natalia, but, yeah, he really did have qualms about killing a woman.

The thought vanished as she flicked her weapon at him, ripping the arm of his jacket with a tearing sound.

Fuck chivalry.

What she did next was as unorthodox as it was unexpected. With a move like a striking snake, she bent low, swiping his left calf with steel.

Jason's reaction was to try to reposition the tip of his knife for a stab into her exposed back. But she was too quick.

Either too fast or his reservations were clouding his mind.

It took maybe a full second before the sensation arrived, a searing hot pain that brought tears to his eyes, tears she saw.

"Tell you what," she said with a smile, "put down your weapon and I'll let you live. No hard feelings."

The thin carpet of the platform was getting slick with Jason's blood. He was careful where he placed his feet and how he shifted his weight. A slip, certainly a fall, would be fatal.

He feigned a jab from the right, his plan to slash from the left instead, a maneuver requiring a minimum of movement. Even so, the poor footing caused him to slip, the aggressive sortie of a boxer rather than the graceful lunge of a fencer. He twisted frantically to avoid Natalia's blade and his feet went out from under him, sending him crashing into the exit to outside hard enough to knock the breath out of him.

Worse, the killing knife clattered against the far door as it slipped from his hand.

He must have hit the button that slid the door open, leaving him on his back gasping for air, his head hanging outside the train with half a mile drop below.

Recognizing an easy kill, Natalia dropped to her knees, leaning over him. Her blade was raised for the coup de grâce. The knife was just before beginning its deadly down stroke when there was a woman's scream.

Without completely taking his eyes from his opponent, Jason saw a woman's horrified face through the glass of the following car. Natalia hesitated a fraction of a second.

Not much time, but all Jason had. Grabbing the vertical rails beside the open door, the very ones he had used to pull himself aboard, he brought his knees nearly to his chin at the instant Natalia put her weight down behind the killing stroke. For an instant, her body was balanced on Jason's knees, an instant in which her face was frozen in the horror of realization.

Like a circus acrobat, Jason flipped his knees over his head, a backward somersault, flinging Natalia through the open door and into space.

Jason saw, or thought he saw, a figure, stiff with arms outstretched like a paper doll cut from black paper, that got smaller and smaller until it disappeared against the landscape half a mile down.

As he scrambled to his feet, the woman who had been looking through the glass had both hands over her mouth as though to staunch the low moaning sound she made as her eyes went from the open door to Jason's bloody leg to the killing knife on the blood-soaked carpet. If ever Jason had seen sheer terror in someone's eyes, he was looking at it now.

"These domestic quarrels can be a bitch," he said before realizing how slim was the chance this woman understood a word of English.

No time to comfort strangers. The conductor was still around somewhere. He picked up his knife. Hugging the wall, Jason cautiously peered around the door and into the car in which he and Natalia had been sitting only minutes before.

Empty.

The burning agony of his leg was difficult to ignore, but the threat of the conductor made it imperative to do so. Jason did take the time to roll up his pant leg and note he had sustained a wound to the flesh only. Though deep, he could only hope there had been no, or minimal, damage to the muscle. Either way, he was already becoming light-headed from the loss of blood.

He used seat backs to help him walk to the quartet of seats where he and Natalia had sat. He picked up her purse, took out the wallet, and stuffed it in his jacket pocket. Doubtful a professional would be carrying anything of use, but he would look when he had time anyway.

Every second or two, he glanced up, making sure the complicit conductor didn't surprise him. Eyes flicking toward the forward car. He used the knife to sever the shoulder strap of the Hermès purse.

Next, he used the knife's razor edge to cut her jacket into strips. He could not help but note the four-pocket model had the distinctive interlocking Cs of Chanel on each pocket. Natalia and her fanatical Islamists might preach hatred for the West, but they had little reluctance to avail themselves of its luxuries.

He used the purse strap to bind the soft suede of the strips to the bleeding wound in his calf—possibly the world's most expensive bandage. But it should prevent him from bleeding to death before he could get the cut stitched shut.

Returning the knife to its sheath, he drew the Glock. The police were going to get involved now for certain; Jason just had to make sure the conductor was accounted for and depart the train before the local heat arrived.

24

Federal Bureau of Investigation
Re: Nikola Tesla
File No. 2121-70
TOP SECRET

February 3, 1943
To: William Donovan, Director, Office of Strategic
Services
From: J. Edgar Hoover

Bill:
   The Bureau has completed its search of the
effects of the above-styled, including a War
Powers Act secret order to drill and inspect
his bank box. We searched the two rooms he
occupied at the Hotel New Yorker within hours
of his death. We have found no evidence of contact of any sort with an Axis power. Of course,
it is unlikely the subject would have left evidence of treason lying around.
   We did find the names in his address book of
members of both the Swiss and Swedish Embassies
here in Washington. Unfortunately, neither man

is still here, both being sent to other postings in late 1942. Both embassies disclaim any knowledge or record any contact between their staff and the subject, and both are equally disinclined to allow the Bureau to pursue the matter. I don't think either of us expected a lot of help from pantywaist neutrals anyway.

The only thing of possible interest we turned up was a Railway Express Agency receipt for what appears to be a large package shipped from New York to the Savannah, Georgia, offices of Norddeutscher Lloyd. See below as to why the subject went to the trouble to send something to the shipping company in Georgia when the company had offices here in New York until the United States became involved in the war when, as an enemy alien corporation, it ceased operation on U.S. soil in early 1942.

We interviewed Kolman Cazo, one of the subject's assistants, who is presently in infantry training at Fort Ord, California. Although his memory is not as clear as we might wish, he said the subject frequently sent packages to relatives in Croatia. Subject believed the U.S. government had been intercepting and reading his mail and spying on him ever since the military declined to purchase subject's so-called "Death Ray." He went to great lengths to avoid observation. Cazo remembered subject originally demanded he (Cazo) carry a large package by train to Savannah but relented and allowed it to go by R.E.A. He has no idea what might have been in the package but he was quite sure its final destination was Croatia, not Germany. Subject told him it was canned goods and clothing for his family there.

I regret not to have more specific information, but I believe we have no evidence that the subject gave aid or comfort of any sort to the enemy, nor do we have reason to believe he shared any information of military value.

Don't hesitate to call if I or the Bureau can be of further assistance. Give my warmest regards to Ruth.

J. Edgar

25

Hotel Ante
Jasikovacka 9
Gospić, Lika, Croatia
Three Hours Later

Jason stiffly eased himself into one of the contemporary chairs that was every bit as uncomfortable as it looked. He propped his throbbing leg up on the chair's mate. The room was furnished in what some might call "Danish Modern." Others might call it IKEA. In any event, the room, one of only twenty-six, was clean and inexpensive, if totally bland. And cold. A cursory inspection had revealed no individual thermostat. Whoever controlled the central heat either planned on saving money on creature comforts or enjoyed arctic temperatures. Jason had never stayed in a hotel where he could see his own breath before. He should have guessed heat was not a significant amenity of the hotel when he had presented his George Simmons passport to a desk clerk in a fur-lined parka.

Jason turned to look out of the room's window, where swirling snowflakes were comets in the light from the hotel's windows. Cold or not, he should consider himself lucky. He had disembarked from the train at the next stop, one of those for which there seemed no reason other than a man and woman, cardboard suitcases or boxes in hands, waiting to board. The conductor had been conspicuous in his absence. Jason surmised Natalia had bribed the regular conductor to render whatever assistance she might need and he'd taken the money and then kept out of sight. Had he earned whatever he had been paid, it would be Jason, not Natalia, at the bottom of that ravine.

It was hard to find good help.

Jason guessed he must have made quite an appearance as he painfully climbed down from the railcar with his trouser leg slashed and bloody. His jacket covered the blood his shirt had absorbed from the drenched carpet. He did draw the attention of a walrus-mustached old man wearing some sort of military colored jacket in a very dated Zastava 750 automobile, a product of the same company who had unsuccessfully inflicted the Yugo on the United States a couple of decades ago.

Mustache watched with open curiosity as Jason limped across the single track, looking both ways for possible transportation. He had exited the train prematurely to avoid the police likely to be swarming all over it once the near hysterical woman who had witnessed Natalia's last moments could summon them. Now he needed medical help, but as far as he could see, he was in open country.

Clutching his suitcase, he limped toward the only vehicle in sight, the Zastava. The driver rolled down the window.

"Speak English?" Jason asked.

The answer was definitely not. Not a good sign.

Jason pointed to his bloody pants leg, making a sewing motion.

Mustache replied by rubbing a thumb against the fingers of one hand, the universal sign money was required.

Jason dug into a pocket and held out a handful of kuna.

Mustache considered the money, took it, counted it out, and returned some bills to Jason.

He motioned for Jason to go around and get in the passenger door. Grateful, Jason climbed in, the squeeze making him mindful the car had been designed under license from Fiat, a version of its diminutive 500.

Mustache's lack of English skills did nothing to discourage conversation, or at least, his side of one. He chatted away, the inflection of his voice indicating questions Jason could neither understand nor answer. He could only hope the man understood he needed to see a physician.

Five minutes later, the little car rounded a curve in the mountainous combination of asphalt and potholes. Half a dozen houses, each a single story with red-tile roofs, bracketed the road. By now, flakes of snow were drifting down from higher elevations. Beyond the village, if it was large enough to deserve the description, a valley was filled with fog like a lake of mist. Jason would not have been surprised to see the clouds sweep aside like a stage curtain to reveal Count Dracula's castle adorning one of the far peaks.

The car came to a stop in front of one of the houses. There was nothing to distinguish it from its neighbors other than the small red cross beside the door. Getting out of the tiny car, Jason almost fell. His head was spinning at a dizzying rate, and his legs felt like spaghetti. Mustache caught him, swinging an arm over his shoulder, and somehow managed to wrestle him inside. Bandage or not, Jason had lost more blood than he had thought.

The clinic was tidy, clean, and empty. Helping Jason onto the room's examination table, Mustache pressed a buzzer. Less than a minute later, a middle-aged woman strode into the room, steel gray hair in a no-nonsense bun and still struggling into a long white lab coat. Jason guessed that, like many European doctors, she had set up practice in her home.

Mustache and the doctor exchanged words, possible greetings, and a question or two. He sat in the room's only chair and lit a cigarette. Jason was so accustomed to the American Health Gestapo, he was surprised when there was no rebuke forthcoming from the doctor. Coat finally straight, she turned her attention to Jason. She produced a pair of surgical scissors and snipped away the bloody pant leg. Jason was thankful the killing knife was strapped to the other leg, sparing him questions best left unasked.

After applying a stinging antiseptic to the wound, she regarded him with a suspicion that needed no translation. "How?"

Stalling for an answer might result in a call to the police. Jason blurted out the first thing he could think of. "Slipped on the train, cut myself on the edge of the door."

He was not certain she understood, but it was clear she was skeptical at the least. Wordlessly, she finished sterilizing the cut and turned to a metal cabinet. She held up a needle and sutures.

"No anesthetic," she announced as she began to thread the needle.

She made no effort to explain whether she simply had none or chose not to use it. He decided not to ask for a bullet to bite.

Jason had endured worse. As an adviser to the mujahideen in Afghanistan, he had had a Russian bullet dug out of his back by a bayonet under flickering candlelight. A covert operation in Sub-Saharan Africa had ended with a two-day donkey ride with a broken leg using a rifle stock as a splint. The recollections did little to dim his present discomfort. Besides, the only mercy shown by pain was that it fades from memory almost as soon as it ends. We remember precisely the smell of a rose, the flavor of a favorite wine on the back of the tongue, but not the degree of agony. We recall there was pain but, once ceased, our brains have no measure of it.

Jason clinched his teeth. His eyes searched the room until they focused on a case clock in a far corner. The grain of the wood in which it was encased was without knots, indicating it had been taken from the heart of the tree. What tree? Jason concentrated on the swirls of the grain and the depth of color. Oak? No, more like walnut. He imagined the feel, the cool smoothness of the wood as it had been sanded, smelled the sawdust that had swirled around the skilled craftsman who had made that case.

Slowly, grudgingly, the pain of each stitch diminished ever so slightly with each new observation. During Jason's special Delta Force training, a psychiatrist or psychologist, some brand of head shrinker, had lectured on the subject of meditation as a tool for pain control. At the time, Jason had accepted the message as so much psychobabble. Subsequently, he found there was some truth to what he had been told. Meditation was not an opiate to pain, more like aspirin. But better than no relief at all.

There had been some respite from the pain certainly, for Jason was surprised when he noticed the doctor was no longer stitching but almost finished bandaging.

She motioned, and he gingerly climbed down from the table. He tested his left leg by putting weight on it. It hurt, but that was hardly news. He could flex the calf, though, an indication the muscle had not been severed.

The physician handed him a bottle of pills with one hand, a syringe in the other. "Pills three times a day," she ordered, holding up three fingers as though she doubted he was bright enough to understand and motioning for his arm.

He guessed the injection was a tetanus shot, the pills an antibiotic. Whatever, it had to be more beneficial than the one he had averted at Heathrow.

She put the empty syringe into a tin tray. "Two hundred."

This time, she was holding up two fingers with one hand, pointing to his hip pocket with the other. Jason counted out 200 kuna, marveling that medical services anywhere could be priced at the equivalent of, what, ten bucks?

Mustache stubbed out a third cigarette into a small ceramic bowl and offered his shoulder.

Jason took it and started out.

"Sir?" The doctor asked in clear English. "Next time you fall on train, try not to land on only door that has a knife edge."

She was chuckling to herself as he and Mustache left.

After a meal in the hotel's starkly modern restaurant—*odojak*, pork roasted over an open fire, washed down with *stoino vino*, table wine recommended by the chef himself—Jason felt pleasantly drowsy. His leg throbbed with a pain that was easily bearable. The doctor had given him no pain pills, nor would he have taken any. The slothfulness induced by painkillers was something he didn't want. If he needed to wake suddenly, act quickly, or make a decision in an instant, drugs were not for him.

He shoved one of the chairs under the doorknob of his room, stripped, and lingered under the shower for the four or five minutes it took for the hot water to run out. He was drying himself when there was a knock at his door. Wrapping the towel around his waist, he slipped the Glock from its holster lying on the dresser and went to the door.

"Yeah?"

"Mr. Simmons?"

English was not the speaker's first language.

"What is it?"

"A Mr. Džaja wants to know if you will need him tomorrow."

Jason knew no one named Džaja. Could be the police? Or whoever sent Natalia. Had they had identified him from the train and tracked him to this hotel? That would have required neither Sherlock Holmes nor bloodhounds. There were few hotels in the area.

"Just a minute," he called.

Crossing the room, he looked at the window. The old-fashioned kind that still opened, probably because air-conditioning in summer was used as sparingly as heat in winter. Jason had requested and gotten a room on the second, top, floor. Ground-floor rooms made for poor security. It was only twenty feet or less down to the snow-soaked lawn below, a relatively safe drop Jason could reduce considerably by hanging from the sill before letting go.

He opened the window.

"I'm coming!" he called in response to another knock as he slipped into a pair of jeans and his feet into shoes.

He was contemplating departing the room without further conversation when it occurred to him: "Need him tomorrow"?

Going back to the door, he asked. "Who is Džaja?"

"The man driving you here," the desk clerk's voice answered.

A quick glance confirmed what Jason already knew: There was no phone in the room. His driver could not simply have the clerk call up.

Jason chuckled, both at his own overreaction and the relief there was no danger. But paranoia trumped foolish risks. "Tell him I'll see him right after breakfast."

As footsteps receded, Jason risked cracking the door. Even from the back, he recognized the fur parka of the desk clerk and that old army jacket Mustache wore. He shut the door quietly, locked it, and shoved the chair back under the knob. Only then did he realize how much colder the room had become.

Small wonder. The window was still open, snow blowing in onto the threadbare carpet. Jason was glad he wasn't going to be going out.

For the first time in many years, Jason had difficulty in falling asleep, a problem he attributed to the throbbing pain in his leg, not allowing himself to consider the possibility the cause might lay elsewhere. The fact he had been forced to kill someone had never kept him awake before. But then, none of his victims had been a woman, albeit a deadly one.

When sleep finally came, it was thin and troubled. More than once, Jason awoke after his dreams replayed that figure falling, falling . . .

26

Budačka ulica 16
Gospić, Lika, Croatia
The Next Morning
Day 3

Džaja shared the front seat with Jason. The hotel's desk clerk, Aleksandar, now off-duty, had eagerly accepted Jason's offer to come along
and act as interpreter should one be needed. His enthusiasm at the
prospect of extra cash was undiminished by being stuffed into a space
that was a backseat in name only. He and Džaja chattered away with
only an occasional translation.

The house was on the edge of town, a single-story clapboard a
few kilometers past the rail station and the cobblestone square with
its circular fountain. As the houses became farther apart, the spaces
were frequently filled with crude roadside shrines, some still bearing the dried flowers of summer. Beyond the house lay the high,
flat, mountain-rimmed plateau above the Novčića River, land that
reminded Jason of the high plains of the United States.

Džaja pointed at the street number and swerved across the road
to park the little Zastava in the otherwise barren yard where patches
of winter-yellowed grass were islands in the sea of snow. The house's

occupant must have seen them coming, for she opened the door just as Jason was getting ready to knock.

At least seventy, the woman's face was road map of furrows. Wisps of gray hair had escaped the bun at the back of her head, and blue veins were the only color in the white hands that held the door. But there was nothing old or decrepit about the sky blue eyes that peered out from the drooping lids that gave the face a sleepy look.

"Herka Kerjck?" Jason asked.

She nodded as her eyes went to the two men behind him. *"Da."*

"I'm George Simmons. Someone told you I was coming I believe."

She started at him blankly until the hotel clerk translated. She stepped aside, opened the door wider. *"Dobro jutro. Uci."*

The three men entered a room that reminded Jason of his grandmother's house. Knitted doilies occupied every horizontal space above floor level. A sofa and two chairs were covered in a cabbage-rose pattern through which stuffing escaped along seams long parted. The halo of the crucified plaster Christ gleamed from the far wall just above the rabbit ears of a small-screen television. What was really reminiscent for Jason was the sterile cleanliness. Not a mote of dust dared to be seen. The glass of the room's two windows showed recent attention and even the faded patterned rug, though showing threads, was without stain. The room smelled vaguely of lye soap and stale tobacco.

She indicated a chair for Jason and sat opposite on the sofa. She crossed her arms and waited expectantly. Džaja found an ashtray and applied a wooden match to a cigarette before he sat. The thing smelled like silage. Apparently, Croatians did not ask permission before lighting up in someone's home.

Jason spoke to the desk clerk. "Ask her who she told I was coming."

After a brief exchange, the woman looked at Jason though speaking to Aleksandar.

"No one, she says. No one other than a few neighbors and her daughter who comes to visit every Sunday."

Hardly a secure network, but that explained Natalia. Well, Momma could hardly have expected an old woman, this old woman, to keep a tight lip without an explanation that would have put Jason in more jeopardy than he already was.

"Is she related to the scientist Nikola Tesla?"

At the mention of the name, the old woman sat up straight, full of pride. She didn't wait for the translation. *"Da!"*

She continued.

"He was her father's uncle," Aleksandar translated.

And so the interrogation went, question, translation, next question. She remembered that, when she was a very little girl, the Nazis came, men dressed in frightening black uniforms with lightning bolts on them and high boots, boots like no local people wore.

"I thought the German army wore a shade of gray," Aleksandar observed.

"They did," Jason replied, impatient to get back to the subject at hand. "But SS, Schutzstaffel, uniform is what she described."

Wait a minute, Jason thought. *Why would the elite of the German military bother with an out-of-the-way place such as this?*

"Ask her if these men in black were really Germans or just local men who had joined."

She was quite sure they were real Germans. What they wanted, she answered when asked, was the box that had come from America, the box that came a few days before her father returned home from Russia, miraculously excused from further military service on behalf of the Third Reich.

"The box, what happened to it?"

She shrugged as the question was translated.

"She doesn't know."

Jason was becoming increasingly impatient, both with the cumbersome process of translating back and forth and with what seemed to be a dead end. "Ask her to explain, tell us when she last saw the box."

The family, it seemed, lived on adjacent farms, of which the present house was one. The SS had arrived within hours of the mysterious box. They had moved the animals out of the barn, taken the box there, and put a guard on duty to make certain only those permitted entered. For the next several days, strange noises had come from the barn, and weird lights at night. There was much speculation among the locals as to what was being done there. One or two of the more superstitious recalled old legends about conjuring up the devil. One night, the Allies dropped a single bomb that destroyed the barn, but oddly did no damage to surrounding structures.

"A bomb?" Jason asked.

She nodded. At least that was the only thing the townsfolk could think of that could have caused the explosion, though no one had heard an aircraft overhead. The device must have fallen through the roof and exploded inside, for the walls were blown out, not in. But this was not an ordinary bomb, those who knew of such things said. The bodies of the dead Germans had shrunk, she understood, although, as a small child, she was not allowed to see such a thing for herself.

Jason glanced out of a window. "I don't see any barn."

An exchange between the old woman and the translator ensued before the latter said, "It was never rebuilt. As a matter of fact, some of the rubble is still there. Her father said it was a bad place, forbade the children to go near it. They did, of course. The box had been opened, and there was a machine that looked like it had been partially assembled. Or perhaps partially destroyed by the bomb."

"What kind of a machine?" Jason wanted to know.

The old woman shrugged again as she fished a cigarette from somewhere in the folds of her dress. She accepted a light from one of Džaja's wooden matches. If anything, the tobacco smelled worse than his.

"Other than her sewing machine, she knows little of machinery," the clerk translated. "Besides the fact this one was about the size of her sewing machine and its table, she remembers little about it."

Jason did a masterful job of concealing his growing frustration. "I thought she didn't know what happened to the box."

"She doesn't. She never saw it again after the Germans took it to the barn. She's guessing they threw it away after they took the machine out."

Was the woman dense or simply being intentionally difficult?

"OK, ask her about the machine. What happened to it?"

The clerk asked.

"The machine stayed where it was. Odd thing, it didn't rust in all those years of sitting in the weeds. Then came the Bosniaks . . ."

"The who?"

"Bosniaks, Moslems."

The clerk must have seen the puzzled look on Jason's face. "October of 1991, the so-called Gospić Massacre. Serb troops shot at least fifty people in the town, some Moslems. The Moslems took it as a renewal of the conflict between them and Christians, wanted revenge."

He said something to the old woman and she responded.

"A number of them came here, burned the next house down, the one where her relatives lived."

She became agitated, moving her hands in a parody of aircraft and making a *whoosh*-ing sound as the translation continued, "But two American jets came over the hills, scattered the Bosniaks."

"What does that have to do with the machine in the yard?" Jason wanted to know.

"After the Bosniaks left, it was gone. She is sure they took it."

27

Hotel Ante
Jasikovacka 9
Gospić, Lika, Croatia

Back at the hotel, Jason had the current desk clerk add up his bill while he went to his room to pack his single bag. Finished, he set the bag on the bed and took out his iPhone, a specially modified device with a few apps not available in the basic phone shop in malls across America.

He texted Momma a brief review of the morning's conversation, hit a button, and sent the entire message as a millisecond burst that, without the appropriate equipment, would register as no more than an electronic mini-surge. Minutes later, he was proffering the red-white-and-blue-on-silver Bank of America Visa card of Mr. George Simmons in payment of a bill that was modest by the standards of the day.

Outside, Džaja and his trusty, if diminutive, Zastava 750 waited to begin the mirror image of the trip Jason had taken yesterday. Unlike the unmanned stop at which Jason had disembarked in haste the day before, Gospić had a rail station. A small one-room building heated by a wood-burning stove, but a station nonetheless. Džaja insisted on carrying the bag inside, where Jason paid him and shook his hand.

"*Do viđenja*," the Croatian said as sorrowfully as though losing his best friend.

Perhaps he was. Or close to it. Jason guessed fares were few in this part of the world. He repeated the phrase, assuming it to be appropriate to parting.

In addition to the wood stove, the room featured a pair of back-to-back benches on which an elderly couple sat, surrounded by half a dozen cardboard suitcases. Their clothes, though worn, were clean and pressed. The grime under the man's fingernails and the obvious calluses on his large hands suggested farming as an occupation. Whatever their purpose in traveling, Jason had a hard time seeing them as a potential threat. There was no Natalia-type visible.

The man behind the ticket counter eyed him tentatively when Jason presented the credit card in payment. He held out both hands together like the opening and closing of a book. It took Jason a second to comprehend. The man wanted papers, identification. He seemed satisfied when Jason handed him the Simmons passport.

Required procedure, or had identity theft reached the Balkans?

Jason returned to sit on the bench just as his iPhone vibrated. He took it out of his pocket and read the message, a single line of an address in Paris in the 20th Arrondissement. He knew it well, well enough that he didn't have to memorize it before deleting it.

When he looked up, the elderly couple, unfamiliar with current technology, was staring at him as if he had sprouted horns. Perhaps he had; the woman was definitely making signs to counter the evil eye.

28

141 Boulevard Mortier
Paris, France
Six Hours Later

The train to Zagreb and the three-hour Air France flight into a foggy, rainy Orly merged into one miserable journey. First, Jason had been faced with the choice: abandon his weapons or check them. As much as standing around a baggage carousel flew in the face of his training and experience, being unarmed for whatever period was required to either ship the weapons or replace them was worse. He would be relatively safe in the air, at risk once on the ground. Paris, after all, had around 155,000 Moslems, almost 7½ percent of the city's population.

It would be a good bet some of them wanted Jason dead.

That was the reason he retreated to the nearest men's room after retrieving his bag. In a stall, he strapped the killing knife to his leg and the Glock in its holster at the small of his back.

He took a cab, which was soon cruising Paris's 20th Arrondissement through a section of single houses. The soggy day made the stone walls of Père Lachaise Cemetery weep as though mourning the passing of such diverse talents as Oscar Wilde, Chopin, Pissarro, and the Doors' Jim Morrison. Past the cemetery, they turned left and stopped.

Jason gritted his teeth as he climbed from the cab onto the drizzle-moistened sidewalk. After hours of enforced idleness, the wound in his calf resented the sudden action. He paid the driver with euros he had gotten at the airport's exchange booth, looked both ways, and crossed the street to an unremarkable wall. Behind the bricks adorned with razor wire, Jason could see the top story of the rather ordinary-looking two-story, freestanding house that was home to France's Direction Générale de la Sécurité Extérieure, the DGSE, France's CIA. Because of its proximity to the Piscine des Tourelles, its habitués referred to it as the swimming pool. As he stood before the massive wooden gate, he pulled his jacket collar flat to give a better view to the concealed cameras he knew were transmitting his image to the facial recognition technology.

He couldn't resist. Putting down his bag, he used both hands to pull his jaws back and stick out his tongue as he gave the invisible speakers the raspberry.

The mechanical voice that followed was not amused. It requested he identify himself and state his business here.

"Jason Peters. René de Terre is expecting me."

The gates swung open. Picking up his bag, Jason followed paving stones glistening with winter moisture oozing from lead skies, as typical of Paris's winters as the chestnut blossoms are of spring. He entered a marble foyer. In the center of the floor was a blue mosaic disk, criss-crossed by white lines with a red hexagon in the center, a symbol as enigmatic as the French words for "In every place where necessity makes law" that surrounded the disk.

Jason had long ago abandoned hope of understanding either women or the French.

The room was bare of furnishings or people. There was no need for a receptionist. No one got this far without identifying both self and purpose.

From an entrance Jason hadn't seen, a dark-skinned, white-haired man in a stylish pinstripe suit appeared. "Jason! Good to see you again, lad!"

Jason submitted to a one-armed embrace and air kissing in the vicinity of each cheek before shaking René's right hand. René had lost his left arm to a FLN bomb as the eight-year Algerian War wound down in the early sixties and the Fourth Republic was collapsing along with the last vestige of French imperialism. With the advent of de Gaulle and the Fifth Republic, France's reforming intelligence agencies recognized the Ouled Aissim tribesman's usefulness. He spoke Arabic, Farsi, and several Berber dialects in addition to impeccable French and Oxford-accented English. Not only had much of North Africa been in turmoil when René had joined the organization, but France had had a long policy of treating its colonials as full citizens of France, thereby causing a migration of poor Moslems whose culture would never be assimilated into that of France no matter how much French liberals had hoped. Instead, the culture and laws of Islam would threaten the nation's very existence as the pall of Islamic extremism spread across Europe in the following half century.

René's talents had been useful in the sixties and were even more so as time passed, so useful that France's mandatory retirement age of sixty-two had been waived, ignored, or simply swept under the rug of bureaucracy.

René shepherded Jason to a section of wall that silently slid open, revealing an elevator. It hummed upward, opening onto an anteroom with a steel door. René leaned toward the door and stood still for a second before it swung open.

He confirmed what Jason had guessed, "Iris recognition. Bloody ingenious!"

After a few steps down a hall lit to operating room standards, they stopped in front of what appeared to be a normal wooden door. Jason knew case-hardened steel was sandwiched between the oak panels. Inside was an office remarkable only for its economy. Two nondescript club chairs faced a desk that had seen long and hard service. On it, sat a computer monitor, a key pad, telephone, a file folder, and a hand-tooled leather desk blotter. A Kerman rug in pale pinks and blues and a well-done reproduction of Renoir's *Luncheon of the Boating Party* in a golden frame softened the austerity of the room. Men in straw hats, women in summer frocks. An unidentified but recognizable bottle of wine dark against a tablecloth.

Jason was examining the painting as René slid behind the desk. "I'm rather fond of that picture. The depiction of frivolity lessens the burden of the more serious matters that pass through this office."

René always talked like that, a professor standing behind a lectern.

This was no art-store print, but an actual painting. The artist had even mimicked the original by using a palette knife to apply a coat of white over the empty canvass before he had begun, giving a translucence to his subjects. Jason was noting the strokes that arranged color rather than applied it, sculpted rather than brushed.

"As delighted as I am to see you, Jason, I was informed you are here for specific information this organization is willing to share, not to admire my art."

Reluctantly, Jason turned from the painting and sank into one of the chairs, not conscious he was massaging the throbbing calf. "You have already been briefed on what I'm looking for?"

René opened the file folder and handed over several typed sheets. "Here is the official BEA report. Attached are some pages that are anything but official. I've taken the liberty of having both translated into English."

"Thanks, but I'll try the original French. Don't want risk the translator missing something."

"As you wish. Read all you like, but these papers don't leave this room."

Jason was already absorbing the information before him. He acquiesced with a nod of the head. René began work at the computer.

Twenty minutes later, Jason leaned forward and placed the papers on the desk. "The official report is amazing enough. The unofficial part is right out of some sci-fi story."

René's bushy eyebrows lifted, small furry animals arching their backs. "Sci-fi?"

"Science fiction. You know, like *Star Wars*."

"Regrettably, this didn't happen in some galaxy far, far away."

Jason was rubbing his leg again. "May as well have. Death ray, earthquake machines."

René was puzzled. "I don't understand."

Jason zipped open his bag and handed the man a sheaf of papers. "I'll wait while you read this."

After a few minutes, René looked up. "Are you telling me someone has resurrected this man's inventions, this man . . ."

"Tesla."

"Tesla. You Yanks think somehow the jihadists have gotten their hands on his inventions?"

Jason told René of his trip to Croatia, finishing with, "Apparently, the man made a deal with the Croatian Fascists to furnish them his machine—or the one he was working on—to get his nephew out of military service. The Germans couldn't perfect it, and the Moslems got hold of whatever remained and have finished what Tesla started."

René stared into space. "The bunch who participated in the massacre, the Bosniaks, they are Sunni, I believe."

"So?"

If you read the report I gave you carefully, you'll note whatever impacted that aircraft came at a certain angle."

Jason stopped rubbing his leg. "I'm not following you."

René peered over the edge of his desk. "You might want to get that sodding wound looked at."

Jason averted his eyes downward. A dark stain was spreading across his pants leg. The damn stiches!

René was muttering into the phone. "Help is on the way, old chappie. We have a physician on call, specializes in trauma. Every so often, one of our lads gets banged about, a trauma we had rather not be made public, you understand. He'll fix you right up."

"Thanks. But while we wait, you were saying something about the aircraft and an angle."

René stared at him blankly as though trying to remember, blinked, and stood. Turning, he reached up and pulled down a map of the world, a map that, like those used in schools, unrolled like a window shade.

Using a pen, he indicated a point in mid-South Atlantic. "This is the area where Flight 447 went down." He moved his makeshift pointer to the skull-like bulge of western Africa. "The angle of impact would place the origins of whatever hit the aircraft roughly here, in the nation of Mali."

"I understand some sort of triangulation was used to pinpoint the source." Ignoring the pain in his leg, Jason stood and leaned over the desk for a better view. "In the middle of the desert?"

"Our people used a number of methods to locate the source. They all agreed on this location. You'll note there's a city, a town, rather, in the general area. Interestingly enough, we—the Western intelligence communities—have noted a decided uptick in activity there by people we believe to be the Islamic Maghreb."

Jason inhaled audibly. "The North African arm of Al Qaeda."

"Not exactly, the Maghreb have allied themselves with Al Qaeda, but they are a separate entity. And they are Sunni just like your Bosniaks and just like Al Qaeda."

"Same difference."

"Perhaps. Sat-intel tells us the activity is centered around Timbuktu."

Jason squinted to make out the print on the map. "Timbuktu?"

"More or less."

Jason hobbled back to his chair. "If you guys know where the missile or whatever came from, why haven't you sent someone to investigate? After all, it was your plane that went down."

René let the map roll itself back up before taking a seat. "Same reasons I'm sure you've already heard. Why should we when your chaps are so accommodating?" Elbows on the desk, René made a steeple of his fingers. "Which raises a question of why this matter didn't refer itself to one of your intelligence organizations, CIA, NIA, et cetera."

Jason leaned back in the chair and tried to stretch his wounded leg out. The pain continued unabated. "Ordinarily, it would. Problem as I understand it, reason my employer was hired, was that the American intelligence folks want plausible deniability if things go in the crapper. It looks very much like this op is going to be wet and take place in a Moslem country. After the United States' engagement in Iraq and Afghanistan, after what amounted to an invasion of Pakistan to take out Osama bin Laden . . . Well, the powers that be in Washington don't want to take any action that could be construed as anti-Islamic."

René was now leaning forward, his arms crossed on the desk top. "And if, as you so picturesquely phrase it, 'things go in the crapper' . . . ?"

"It's my ass. The bad guys will know Washington's behind it, but they won't be able to prove it."

"You think you could resist, ah, what is the delightfully euphemistic phrase your CIA uses? . . . 'Enhanced interrogation,' that's it. You think you could withstand enhanced interrogation?"

Jason's hand grew still on his leg. "I don't think anyone expects me to resist. If I'm taken, no one expects me to be alive."

29

Gare de Marseille-Saint-Charles
Marseille, France
Three Hours, Twenty Minutes Later

Constructed in 1848, the Marseille train station is U-shaped, built around a rooftop canopy. It is perched on a plateau and reached by an outdoor grand staircase lined with African and Mideastern statuary reflecting the station's earlier significance as a waypoint to either destination. It is also the southern terminal of the TGV bullet train's line from Paris on which it is capable of exceeding 540 kilometers per hour.

At that speed, it is unnecessary to suffer the inconveniences of air travel.

With new sutures in his calf, Jason's leg felt stiff. He limped slowly down the stairs. At the bottom, he chose a cab at random, a Mercedes, and began the southern ride into the city.

The driver's skin was black, the color of an eight ball, toned, no doubt, by the French West African, Cameroonian, or Senegalese sun. Marseille had long been home to immigrants from former French colonies seeking jobs that did not exist under the new regimes of their homelands. Jason could see the man's eyes checking him out him in the rearview mirror.

"Where to, monsieur?"

"Perhaps you know of a man called Le Couteau?"

The eyes were studying him closely. "The knife? Marseille is large, monsieur. There are many people who may have such a . . . a *nom de guerre.*"

The voice was a pleasant baritone mix of deep African melody and French accent.

Jason reached into his pocket and produced a wad of euro. Leaning forward, he dropped them on the front passenger seat. "I would appreciate you searching for one of them."

The driver cut an eye from the road to appraise the amount. "Perhaps this 'Knife' does not wish to see you."

"Perhaps," Jason agreed amiably. "But if you tell people Jason Peters is looking for him, he might."

They were passing l'Hôtel du Département, the local government headquarters—Big Blue, as it was known locally—bright blue structures that reminded Jason of a child's garish toy on stilts. The French seemed to prefer a modern aesthetic in their architecture, no matter how ugly— a passion that apparently exceeded national pride; the building had been designed not by a Frenchman, but a Brit, Will Alsop.

They drove in silence until they turned off the crowded boulevard La Canebière. Passing several narrow stepped streets, the Mercedes started down a steep hill to the Old Harbor, presided over by the huge gilded virgin atop the 151-foot belfry of the neo-Byzantine basilica of Notre-Dame de la Garde. The church sat on its hill overlooking a collection of private motor yachts, fishing craft, and sailboats like a hen towering above her chicks.

Jason had a perfect view of the harbor, long known as a center of smuggling and corruption. It was the crossroads where raw paste of Afghan poppy sap would be refined into powder and cut with flour, baby laxative, or, frequently, insecticides or other toxins before moving over the hill to the Vieux-Port, the main commercial harbor, where it would be hidden aboard ships of all flags bound for North America and its insatiable craving for heroin.

Narcotics was only one illicit item moving through Marseille. It had long been the point of disembarkation for illegal immigrants from Africa just across the Mediterranean as well as from the Near and Far East. Even though the European Common Market had put an end to the traditional smuggling of tobacco and alcohol products by removing the tariffs, the proscribed and forbidden was still available.

The visible business of the harbor was fishing. Nets hung like moss from masts as small trawlers wallowed in a gentle tide. Men climbed over some of the vessels, scraping, painting, or adjusting lines. Other craft were deserted, their crews either finishing the day in any of a number of seamen's taverns lining the quay or busy at the open-air market hawking the morning's catch.

The Mercedes rumbled over cobblestones to the Quai de Rive Neuve, a line of four- and five-story buildings with plain stucco or cement facades and the red tile roofs common to the south of France. Each of the ground floors was occupied by shops—a bakery, a greengrocer, a butcher, a tobacconist. Even though the car windows were rolled up, Jason could smell a mixture of salt water, freshly baked bread, slightly spoiled vegetables, and tobacco smoke. Between each shop was at least one, and perhaps several, café, brasserie, or bar. Outside the latter, men sat at tables littered with overflowing ashtrays, wine and beer bottles, or small glasses holding some more potent drinks. They were hard-looking men wearing watch caps and pea jackets against the chill of the sea breeze, men of every color who stared unabashedly at the sleek Mercedes.

The car stopped in front of one of the more disreputable-looking bistros. Refuse from the tables had simply been mounded at the curb rather than removed. From open second-story windows, white curtains fluttered like welcoming arms. Through one, Jason could glimpse the top of a bedstead, through another a pine armoire. As is common in Europe, the proprietor no doubt lived above his business.

Closer scrutiny revealed paint was only a distant memory to the door and window frames. A wooden fish hung over the door with some of its gilt remaining, along with the weathered words LE POISSON D'OR, "the Golden Fish." Without a word, the driver got out of the Mercedes and went in. Several tables of men followed his progress with eyes barely showing above glasses of drink. Jason noted most of the clientele were not the stubble-bearded fishermen he had seen patronizing the other establishments. This one had a predominance of Africans, Asians, and various racial blends too subtle to identify. One thing they all had in common: the cold stares at Jason.

The driver returned. Behind him was a black man whose shaved scalp shone so brightly Jason suspected he polished it. A faded blue denim shirt stretched tightly across broad shoulders and chest. His nose was flat, more so on one side than the other, as though it had been smashed more than once. A pink scar stitched its way from right eyebrow to left cheek. His walk could be mistaken for a swagger instead of the limp Jason knew it was, a swaying like a ship under sail that seemed to emphasize his 250 plus pounds, weight that included little fat.

His face had the look of a scowl permanently frozen in place, a grimace that metamorphosed into a smile the second he recognized Jason in the back of the car.

He almost ripped the car's door from its hinges in his eagerness to open it. "I greet you, Jason Peters! Have you have finally come to visit your old friend?"

Jason felt himself snatched from his seat and dragged onto the curb where he feared his back would snap under the pressure of the hug he was given amid shouts of glee in English, French, and various African dialects.

Jason managed to wiggle free, laughing. "I greet you, too, Emphani! You're looking fine, ugly as ever."

"You have won a beauty contest since last I saw you? Come, let us sit at a table and share a bottle of spirits I have made myself and the very best fish soup in all of France."

Jason remembered too well the fiery, brain-numbing liquor Emphani distilled from fruit. His head ached every time he thought about it. "Make that a beer or wine, if you don't mind."

The fish soup was another matter. Thinner than the bouillabaisse, seafood stew popular here, the soup used the stock of the rouget, a small, red fish found only in the warm waters of the coast of southern France. Thickened with toasted bread and mayonnaise-like sauce, it was a meal in itself.

Jason literally felt his mouth water. It had been since . . . since last night that he had even been close to food. Was it really last night, not an evening a week ago? Jason paid the cab driver and retrieved his single bag before sitting at a table. Moments later, a fragrant bowl of reddish liquid appeared before him. Emphani sat across from him, a sweating bottle of white Burgundy in one hand, two glasses in the other. Wordlessly, he poured a little into one, stuck in his finger, and flipped away a droplet.

"The Prophet, peace be upon him, tells his people not to drink a drop of wine," he explained.

Jason grinned, remembering the ritual. "And that is the drop you will not drink."

Emphani was filling Jason's glass. "Just so. Now, tell me of yourself, what you are doing, how you have been. Have you taken another wife? Has Allah blessed you yet with sons?"

In the Moslem custom, the meal was accompanied by small talk, news exchanged by men who had not seen each other in a long time. Jason spoke and listened, recalling other meals, some neither as pleasant or leisurely.

Emphani had served in the French Foreign Legion, stationed at their headquarters in Calvi, Corsica, one of the few "foreign" places France still controlled since the independence of her African colonies. In an unusual display of international cooperation, the French government had allowed Jason's Delta Force team to train along the nearby, and largely uninhabited, cliffs of Cap Corse for two weeks. Emphani had captained a squad of legionaries who had been attacked at dinner one night by an overpowering force of Corsica's own brand of terrorists, the Italian-speaking separatists who had been waging their battle since Louis XV bought the island from Genoa in 1769. The ensuing fight had produced both Emphani's scar and his nickname after he killed a man using only his table knife.

Hearing the ruckus, the nearby encampment of Delta Force men had joined the beleaguered French just in time to turn what could have been a massacre into a victory.

Jason and Emphani had crossed paths only twice since then: Once when the latter had been included in a complement of legionaries sent to quash a coup in a former African colony where Delta Force was already, if unofficially, engaged, and once when Emphani and his wife had appeared in Washington on a tour of America. Laurin had taken an instant liking to both of them and they, in turn, had sent flowers to her memorial service after 9/11.

From irregular e-mails, Jason knew Emphani had bought the bistro with his retirement income. From the looks of the place, it was fairly clear the business did not provide a living even here, where life was substantially less expensive than in, say, Paris. If forced to guess, Jason would have hazarded that, like so many citizens of Marseille, his friend was engaged in other, if not quite so legal, enterprises. Arms smuggling came to mind, as did an occasional stint as a mercenary. It would be impolite, of course, to be the first to mention such activities.

Emphani watched Jason scrape his bowl clean. "The hunger of my friend Jason is that of one who has not eaten in a long time. The soup pot may have a few more drops in it, should you desire."

Jason drained the dregs of his glass. "Thanks, but the hospitality of my friend Emphani has been more than sufficient."

He watched Emphani produce a blue box of Gitanes and proffer it. "No thanks."

Emphani struck a wooden match on the sole of his shoe and lit his cigarette. "You still do not have the tobacco habit, I see."

Jason was looking at a NO SMOKING sign. The government required no smoking areas upon request of patrons. "I have enough of the others."

Emphani got up and turned the sign to the wall before returning to the table. "You have come to see me for more than my excellent fish soup, I think."

"You mean your *wife's* excellent fish soup and, yes, I have."

"Tell me."

Jason did.

When he had finished, Emphani lit another Gitanes. "You will contact each of the men you will need? It sounds as though you do not have the time."

"I don't," Jason admitted. "But I wanted to speak to you personally."

Emphani stared at the tip of his cigarette. "Because I am Moslem, you fear I will not fight these heaps of camel dung?"

"Mainly because you speak Arabic. But, yeah, the thought entered my mind."

Emphani spat. "Moustaph! May the womb of the bitch dog that bore him be cursed! He and his fellows disgrace the name of the Prophet, may it always be honored! Would you not fight fellow Christians such as the cowardly jackals that bombed the building in your Oklahoma City? Or the son of a dog that set a bomb at your Olympics?"

"Just asking."

"Moustaph, Bin Laden, Al Qaeda leadership! Like the cowards they are, or were, they hide while they bid others to die attempting to kill women and children. No true believer in the Prophet, may glory be upon him, would do such things. We leave mass slaughter to those of your religion such as Hitler."

Jason was unsure how much of a Christian the late German dictator had been, but he did not pursue the matter. "So, you'll be with me?"

Emphani shrugged. "If the pay is good enough and there is, er, action as you call it. I grow bored as well as old here." He smiled. "Besides, I will add diversion to your plan. You Americans love to mix many different races to your enterprises, your schools, and your government. Sometimes you do so even if it means the better-equipped man is not included. I am both black and Moslem. Diversion."

"Diversity?" Jason asked. "You may add diversity, but what I'm interested in is that you're the best man with a knife or garrote I know."

Before Emphani could answer, a young girl came out of the building. She was toffee-colored, a beautiful blend of Emphani's ebony skin and the whiteness of his wife. Her eyes were a deep brown, evenly set in a round face that was split by a smile. Like most young European women, she wore skin-tight jeans that displayed her figure to advantage. She said something in a tongue Jason did not understand.

Emphani rose to embrace her. "The flower of my garden, the sun of my sky, my daughter, Margot."

Jason stood and nodded. "A pleasure."

Recognizing the men were speaking English, Margot switched to that language. "Mother says if you want dinner for the customers tonight, you need to stop sitting around drinking and go to the market."

Emphani gave a theatric sigh. "As you can see, unlike my Moslem forebears, I am no longer the head of my house, nor the terror of my children."

Margot leaned on tip toe to kiss his cheek. "But you are the sweetest papa in all of Marseille, perhaps all of France."

Jason was fairly certain that had it been possible to detect a blush, he would have seen one.

"Tell that woman, your mother, that I am discussing business with an old friend, one she would also like to greet into our home."

Margot was scrutinizing Jason. "You are an American?"

"I am."

"Do you know anyone at Harvard near Boston, Massachusetts? That is where I wish to go to school when I finish the academy here."

Jason could not miss the sadness in Emphani's eyes, the look of a parent who knows his child's dream will never come true. "I'm afraid not, not a single one."

Clearly disappointed, she managed a smile. "No matter. I will find someone who can help me gain admission."

Jason stood, aware that traditional Moslem hospitality would require an invitation to a festive dinner, one that could take hours he did not have to spare. "I fear I must go, though it saddens me that I will not be able to see your beautiful wife again. I must be satisfied I have met such an attractive child."

Emphani held up a hand. "Wait but a minute longer. I will go with you."

"Not necessary. I have a few more things to do. I'll give you a destination and an airline ticket in a day or two. In the meantime, you can explain that you will be gone to your wife."

Emphani shrugged as he led Jason through the bistro. "They understand. My . . . er . . . other businesses frequently require sudden absence."

"You are blessed with an understanding family. But then, I suppose were you not, you could take another wife. Does not your religion allow this?"

Emphani grinned. "It does. If your culture permitted it, would you have taken a second wife?"

Jason smiled at the thought of Laurin's reaction to a polygamous relationship. "Are you kidding? Laurin would have made my life miserable."

"Just so. And why do you think wives of Moslems are different?"

"Mohammad took multiple wives."

"Possessing the wisdom and patience required to live under the same roof with more than a single woman is why he is the Prophet and ascended into paradise. I am but a man. Come, we will drive you to the airport."

From the rear door, they entered a car park that extended behind the adjacent buildings. Margot was already in the driver's seat of an ancient and diminutive Peugeot Junior, a box with a tiny wheel at each corner.

Emphani climbed in beside his daughter leaving Jason to squeeze in behind them. "The airport," he informed her.

Jason was trying to get comfortable in less square feet than his body occupied. "Yes. I'm headed to . . ."

Emphani somehow found the space to turn around, a finger across his lips. "One cannot unintentionally tell what one does not know. We must act as though the enemy has ears everywhere."

Good advice.

30

Plage de Gouverneur
Saint-Barthélemy, French West Indies
12:40 p.m. Local Time
The Next Day
Day 4

The beach at Gouverneur is a three-quarter mile crescent of golden sand embracing turquoise waters. At the moment, it was populated by winter visitors in various states of dress and undress at the eastern tip, to the more avant-garde at the western, where the sand ended in a sheer hundred-foot hill, and swimwear was notable only for its absence.

In swimsuit and T-shirt, and with a beach bag containing his weapons, Jason was not interested in the lithe, nude, and semi-nude bodies frolicking within a few feet of the beach blanket he had borrowed from his hotel in the hills above Saint-Jean. Instead, his eyes were fixed on a pair of burly men in black shirts and shorts who were busily planting beach umbrellas in a twenty-foot square.

These men were definitely staking out territory. As a practical matter, a slice of sand was being carved out for the owner of a large villa, a former Rockefeller property that fronted on the beach, the only habitation that did so. Information Jason had received during the Paris–

Saint Martin flight had revealed a certain Viktor Karavich, recently of Yekaterinburg, had joined the growing number of Russian industrial oligarchs acquiring property on the island, either by purchase or mere possession, such as what was transpiring in front of Jason.

A third man, also in black, trudged over the sand dunes that separated the villa owner's property from the beach. This one was carrying a stack of folding chairs. His shadow fell across Jason. Jason looked up. The man was larger than the other two, perhaps somewhere north of 250. His biceps filled the short sleeves of the shirt that didn't quite reach his waist. Jason shaded his eyes to get a better look. The man's face had the look of one that had been rearranged violently: a nose pushed to one side, scars in the brows that overhung ratlike eyes, ears that would delight a cauliflower farmer. And there was only one thing that left those pock-shaped scars right above his belt buckle: bullets. Beyond that, he had the slightly Oriental look of a Russian peasant.

The man set his burden of chairs down next to Jason. "Is necessary you move, please."

There was nothing polite in the tone.

Jason shook his head slowly. "Is public beach."

The guy was obviously not used to being refused. It seemed to take a second or two for the response to register. "You not move?"

A threat.

"I not move."

"Is Mr. Karavich's property. You must move."

Jason did move. To a squatting position, his legs bent as he looked up at the man. "Is the property of the public."

"Mr. Karavich not like."

"Mr. Karavich can get fucked."

The big man moved with a speed belying his bulk. Had Jason not anticipated it, a knee would have smashed into his skull hard enough to cause a concussion at the least. As it was, Jason ducked. Springing up from knees bent beneath him like springs, he was able to put every bit of his weight into the open-handed punch that smashed the heel of his right hand into the Russian's nose.

The snap of breaking cartilage was quite audible.

Though rarely fatal or even dispositive, there are few blows more painful than one to the nose. Pain, in and of itself, is disabling, distracting an opponent's attention from an effective counterattack. So it was here. The big man staggered backward, both hands unable to staunch the blood that was making Rorschach blots in the sand. The steep incline of the beach caused him to stumble, nearly losing his balance.

Only a fool gives his antagonist a chance to recover from the initial assault, and Jason was no fool. He chose that instant to charge the tottering Russian, lowering his shoulder to slam into the other man's midsection. Two things were simultaneous: a *whoosh* of expelled breath and a *splash* as the man fell backward into the water.

Jason thought he heard one or two screams from the beach bunnies as he pounced. Ignoring the painful sting of the salt water in his bandaged wound, he knelt in the surge. He locked his right and left forearms around the Russian's neck, tightening the grip by grasping his elbows. With pressure on one arm, Jason could crush the larynx. Sufficient pressure on the other separated the second and third cervical vertebra and, quite likely, the spinal cord.

Jason's opponent realized the futility of struggling. He went dead still, other than the arms he raised above his head. Surrender.

Jason maneuvered him around so they were both facing the beach. He was not surprised to see the man's two comrades racing toward him.

"Right there," Jason shouted above the crash of the surf. "Hold it right there, or your pal is so much shark bait!"

The two came to an abrupt stop, each looking at the other as though seeking a solution to the problem. The bleating of a police siren was getting louder. The curse of cell phones.

Someone shouted words Jason didn't understand. A man stood at the top of the line of dunes. The light breeze whipped a bathrobe around him, but what Jason found most noticeable was he had the immediate attention of the two men headed to aid their comrade. They stopped dead, tide swirling at their knees. Then they turned back toward Jason.

"Don't worry, American, they will only collect the mess you have made," the man in the dunes yelled.

Jason grinned and waved his acknowledgment before handing his choking, sputtering former adversary off to the two men from the beach.

He sloshed his way back ashore, picked up his bag, and scrambled up the dunes. A small crowd of the curious had gathered. Only on a French beach would a fight draw more attention than topless young women.

"Hello, Viktor."

The man in the bathrobe smiled, a metallic grimace of Soviet-era dentistry, and held out his hand. "Did you have to, er, destroy one of my men? He will be useless to me for days. Could you not come to my door instead?"

Jason shook the hand. "And how do I get to your door? I'm sure you have more deterrents than the NO TRESPASSING signs in English, French, and I'm guessing Russian. Knowing your background, I wouldn't be surprised if you had some really nasty surprises for those who come uninvited."

The conversation was interrupted by the arrival of two men in police uniform from the eastern end of the beach, the only access for the public. Viktor put a finger to his lips, motioning Jason to stay where he was. Sliding down the sand to the beach, the Russian greeted the two cops, apparently by name from what words the wind brought to Jason. The body language, including handshakes and shoulder patting, gave the definite impression Viktor was well acquainted with the local gendarmerie. Now Viktor was dismissing a young man who appeared to have a version of what had happened somewhat different from his. Within minutes, the police were gone and the beach returned to normal.

Viktor trudged up to resume his spot beside Jason. "Now, American, perhaps we may attend to whatever you have in mind. Come."

Jason followed him along a bougainvillea-lined path. The red and purple flower-bearing branches of the bushes made it impossible to walk side-by-side. Rounding a turn, Jason was looking at what at one time had been a village brought intact from the South Pacific: bungalow-style houses scattered around round, elongated, or irregular-shaped pools. Winding trails were dotted with native-style statuary. Jason would not have been surprised to see long-dead author Somerset Maugham step out from under the low thatch roof of the veranda. Between him and the house, a lawn cut to putting-green standards surrounded another pool, this one fed by a trickling stream from rocks high above on the hill.

Viktor was aware of the impression the place made, for he stopped, smiling. "Is nice, no? Far nicer than a simple *soldat* would deserve, no?"

Viktor had never been a simple soldier, a fact of which Jason started to remind him when they were suddenly surrounded by a laughing, chatting group of ten or more teenaged girls, all dressed for the beach.

Viktor took a girl by the hand, a pretty blonde who had not yet put on the weight that seemed to follow Russian puberty. Like her female companions, she wore a brief bikini. "My daughter, Vasillisa. Say hello the American, Vasillisa."

She dipped a shallow curtsy. "Hello, Mr. American."

Before Jason could reply, she tried to slip from her father's grasp. He spoke to her in Russian. Ignorant of the language, Jason still knew a reprimand when he heard one.

Vasillisa replied in English. "But, Papa, it is no more naked than my friends . . ."

A tirade of Russian followed, making Vasillisa blush. She did not reply. With the hint of a tear in her eye, she made a dash for the house.

Viktor snorted. "The young! Wants to parade about without decent clothing because her friends do."

"Didn't look to me like her swimsuit was any smaller than the others," Jason observed mildly.

"I have no control, really, what her friends do, but I will not have my daughter parading about like some . . . some French . . . French . . . What do you say, like a pastry?"

"Tart?"

"Tart, yes. Those French tarts on the beach. I bring Vasillisa and a few of her friends here each winter. Winter in Yekaterinburg miserable, snow, wind blow off Urals. No sun for weeks. Anyway, I bring to sun, warm, along with teacher so school, it not missed. Only thing they learn is to show tits."

Jason was trying to stifle a smile. This was serious to a Russian parent. "What does her mother have to say?"

Viktor looked at him as though he had not heard correctly. "Mother?"

Jason had forgotten that in the Russian peasant class from which

Viktor had come, the man's word was more than law: It was an edict from heaven. "Nevermind. Where can we talk?"

Silently, Jason followed Viktor into the dark coolness of the house, his mind racing backward.

It had been April 1989. Near Bagram, Afghanistan. Jason's first overseas assignment, the U.S. not-so-covert aid program to the mujahideen, those largely unorganized tribal guerrilla fighters who had opposed the Soviet puppet regime whose call for help had provided an excuse for Russian invasion ten years earlier.

The Russians had had it. Not only was their army tired, hungry, and ill equipped, the economy back in the mother country was rapidly collapsing. Intel reports were full of desertions, both by the Russians and the Afghan Communists. The Reds were beat and they knew it. So beat, they had become sloppy in their duties, including guard duty. That had caused a problem.

In the early morning darkness of that day, Jason's patrol of freedom fighters had slipped past a slumbering sentry, not even pausing to slit his throat. The urgency had come from word by the increasing number of Afghan defectors to the mujahideen that a specific Russian was encamped here, a Viktor Karavich. What made Karavich so special was his talent with explosives. Not only roadside bombs (improvised explosive devices had not yet found their way into the lexicon of war), but cleverly designed and hidden remote explosives. Karavich boasted he had once blown a man's head off with a bomb concealed in a pair of stereo earphones without getting a splatter of blood on the victim's shirt. Rumor had it Karavich occasionally wore the garment in question. He was a prestidigitator of plastique, conjurer of combustion, and necromancer of nitramine.

Rumor or truth, the sleepy Russian had been drugged and dragged out of his tent and smuggled past inattentive sentries in the darkness.

That caused the problem Jason faced. Aarash, the leader of Jason's group and the only member who spoke a smattering of English, wanted to turn the Russian over to Mullah Osman, the local leader of the Taliban, the fundamentalist religious militia that Jason suspected was going to cause problems long after both the Russians and the Americans were gone. The problem with Mullah Osman was his habit of slowly removing body parts from infidels, frequently making video recordings.

Atrocities had been common on both sides. Flaying skin from living bodies and burying alive were only a couple of the quaint local customs Jason had seen. But it was over. Karavich had made his last bomb, at least there. His agonizing death would accomplish no end Jason could see other than an evening's entertainment for Mullah Osman and his demented followers.

Jason left camp for a short scouting mission, or so he told Aarash. Instead, he had doubled back, entering the tent from ther rear, where the Russian bomber lay awaiting interrogation, hands and feet tied like a hog prepared for slaughter. Karavich's eyes doubled in size as he wordlessly watched Jason slide a long knife from his boot.

"No sweat, Viktor, old buddy," Jason whispered, using the blade to pry knots apart. Cutting them would be too obvious to Aarash and his men.

Moments later, Viktor Karavich stood, rubbing arms and legs. Jason listened carefully. There was no sound of anyone nearby. Lifting the canvas at the rear of the tent, he motioned to the Russian, who looked confused, to say the least.

"C'mon," Jason urged. "I'm not standing here, risking my ass all day."

The Russian understood the tone of urgency, if not the English. He stooped to slide under the canvas, paused, stood, and embraced Jason. Then he was gone.

It was sometime later Jason noticed his dog tags were missing from around his neck.

Cut to a miserable, blustery December night a year later. It was a Sunday night. Second Lieutenant Jason Peters was in the small efficiency he rented in the basement of a Georgetown townhouse. He was packing his gear for a joint training exercise with select Marines at Paris Island that would begin the next day when the doorbell of his apartment rang.

Certain someone had the wrong address, he trudged to the door and swung it open. He didn't recognize the big man with the fur coat and hat standing in the swirling snow until a hand came out of a pocket and dangled a military dog tag on a chain.

"Is yours. I come to return."

Jason examined the piece of tin in the dim light from the street, not believing what he was seeing. "From Afghanistan? You came all the way here to return ten cents' worth of U.S. Army dog tags?"

The figure in front of him stamped his feet, knocking muddy snow onto the mat. "*Da.* Is cold."

Jason stepped aside. "If you've come this far, may as well come inside."

Fifteen minutes and two drinks later (vodka for the Russian, single-malt scotch for the American), Jason learned his visitor had actually come from no farther than Wisconsin Avenue and the Russian embassy where he had been assigned to the military attaché. Although he declined to say how, he had traced Jason through his dog tags.

Jason tinkled the ice in his glass. "You've learned English since we last met."

The man nodded. "Required for posting to the United States. I do it good, no?"

"Hell of a lot better than my Russian."

"You speak Russian?"

"Not a word."

The two drank in companionable silence for a few minutes before Jason observed, "You didn't come here just to return the dog tags."

Viktor shook his head. "No. I come to have great capitalist enemy of peace-loving Soviet people show me Washington, DC."

"On a Sunday night?"

"Is small favor, nothing like what you do in Afghanistan."

Jason wasn't quite sure of the logic of that, how a great favor begat a smaller one. "Anything in particular you want to see, the Washington Monument, the Capitol Building?"

"Tonight, supermarket. Tomorrow or next week, Aerospace Museum."

Jason was unsure he had heard the man. "Supermarket, as in a grocery store?"

"Supermarket tonight. Aerospace Museum closed for night. American film show hectare after hectare of food to sell. Is propaganda, no?"

Jason took his coat from the sofa where he had thrown it earlier.

"Maybe not hectares. But big enough. You can't see one by yourself?"

"Is thinking is only propaganda."

Jason sighed, trying to remember the nearest. "Come on; we'll find one."

They had been in Jason's secondhand Jeep Cherokee only a few minutes when Jason noticed a car behind them.

"You wouldn't happen to know who is following us?"

The Russian nodded. "Embassy KGB."

"But why . . . ?"

Viktor turned in his seat to look directly at Jason. "They worry I detect."

"Defect?"

"*Da,* defect. Last military attaché in Washington disappear, leave wife in Russia. I have no wife."

Swell.

Here he was, driving along Rock Creek Parkway in his nation's capital, to prove that grocery stores really existed to a man he had met only once while being shadowed by one of the world's nastier intelligence agencies.

What next, encountering Dorothy and Toto at the store?

His attention was diverted by bright lights ahead.

He waited to make a turn. "Here we are, big as life: Food Lion."

The car behind, a dark four-door Ford, pulled to the far end of the lot. Apparently, they were there for observation purposes only.

Viktor got out of the car and stared at the cars scattered about. "One must have automobile to be allowed into this store?"

"One must have automobile to *get* to this store."

"Ha! Store is exclusive province of proletariat-oppressing bourgeois!"

Jason was beginning to detect what might, just might, be a touch of sarcasm in his new friend's use of Marxist-Communist dogma. At least, he hoped it was sarcasm.

He took the Russian by the arm. "C'mon. It's cold out here."

For a full twenty minutes, he and Viktor prowled each aisle of the store, scrutinizing labels and prices. The Russian was clearly shaken by what he saw.

"Like GUM?" Jason asked.

The Russian shook his head at the reference to the high-end, for-tourist-and-ranking-party-members-only Moscow store where only foreign currency was accepted. "GUM never have eight brands of canned beans, four types frozen. No toilet paper claim softness. In Russia, toilet paper, how you say, rare?"

"A luxury?" Jason supplied.

"Luxury. Many people choose between *Pravda* and *Isvestia* based on softness."

"We have a lot of newspapers best used that way, too."

The Russian shook his head sadly. "A nation that can provide its people with eight types of canned beans, ceiling-high stack of soft toilet paper . . ."

"It's called the capitalist system, free enterprise. Everyone is free to produce what he thinks will sell rather than what government tells him to."

Viktor sighed deeply. "Berlin Wall come down, Soviet army ready to leave Bulgaria, Yugoslavia. All because of canned beans and toilet paper."

It took Jason a moment to understand what he meant. "You mean the freedom to produce them."

"Is same thing."

Outside, the two headed for the Cherokee when three young black men blocked their path. Each wore the uniform of pants barely above buttocks and baseball caps either backward or askew. One of them held a small automatic pistol.

He extended the other hand. "Yo' wallet, give it up, mu'fucker."

"Is capitalist-type hooligan?" Viktor was more amused than frightened. "He not speak American?"

"My friend does not understand . . ." Jason was about to say "English" but realized that was not what the youth was speaking.

"Gimme yo' watches, too." The kid motioned with the gun as he glanced around nervously.

Jason had rather face an armed professional than a skittish kid with a Saturday-night special.

He and Viktor exchanged glances. The Russian's nod was almost imperceptible.

Jason was reaching for his hip pocket. "Your money and your watch, he wants your money and watch."

Viktor feigned comprehension, his hand going to his own pocket.

In anticipation of receiving what he had demanded, the kid with the gun stepped forward, hand outstretched.

The Russian moved almost too fast for the eye to follow. His hand came up not with money but a knife. His other hand grabbed the gun and swung the arm holding it upward as the blade sank into the would-be robber's throat.

Snatching the pistol as the kid collapsed, Viktor pivoted and fired a single shot. The parking lot's lights showed the neat, round hole in the forehead of one mugger.

The remaining thief had had enough. Feet slipping, he turned to run. Viktor took a standard two-handed target-range stance and let the kid take a couple of full steps before firing. There was a whine as the bullet ricocheted from a lamppost. From somewhere, a woman screamed.

Taking his time, the Russian fired another, and then another round. The last sent the young criminal sprawling.

As though only out for a stroll, Viktor walked over to the form facedown on the asphalt and extended the pistol.

"Drop it!"

The voice was mechanical, one transmitted through a bullhorn.

Spinning around, Jason saw two police cars, blue lights flashing. Behind one of them, two uniformed men had shotguns trained on the big Russian.

Viktor saw them at the same time. Dropping his weapon, he slowly raised his hands.

The final line: Viktor was released on diplomatic immunity grounds. Jason spent an uncomfortable night in the DC jail before being released. In Jason's mind, the big Russian owed him once again.

"All you had to do," Jason said with mild reprove, "was to show your ID as a foreign diplomat and you walked. I spent the night in the DC slammer on D Street before we got it sorted out."

Air-conditioning made the room cold enough to be uncomfortable. Why Viktor fled the Russian winter only to re-create it in the tropics was incomprehensible. The two men had been sitting in cane-back rockers looking through a picture window at verdant hills tumbling into an azure sea. The view made Jason's hands itch to get hold of paint palette and brush.

Two of the men from the beach bracketed the room's entrance like sentries until Viktor shooed them away and closed the door. Jason supposed he should be flattered that Viktor trusted him enough to dismiss his bodyguards.

Viktor went to a refrigerator built into the rear wall. Next to it was a sofa upholstered in a garish Hawaiian pattern of palm trees. The motif was repeated in tropical-themed artwork that had its place among images of Elvis on black satin, coconut shell lamps, and glass bowls filled with seashells. The place could have been furnished by Daytona Beach street vendors.

Viktor was pouring from a frosty bottle of vodka. He held up the bottle in invitation.

"No thanks," Jason declined. "But if you have a beer, I'd love it."

There was a sibilant hiss as the Russian popped the top of a can of Carib and sat back beside Jason. "You did not come here to drink a beer, I think. Nor are you here into remind me I left you in church in Washington shopping mall."

The beer stopped halfway to Jason's lips. "Church?"

"Is not what Americans say? You leave someone in trouble, you leave in church, no?"

Jason had to think that one over while he took his first sip from the icy can. "Lurch. You leave them in the lurch."

"Where is this 'lurch'?"

Jason thought that over, too. "You're right: I didn't come here just to bust your chops about ancient history. But before we talk about why I'm here, give me an update. Last time I saw you, you were with the Russian military attaché in the Washington embassy. Now you have an estate of some of the world's most expensive real estate here in Saint Barts—"

"Also in Aspen for skiing," Viktor interrupted, adding proudly, "Also on Ibiza and on Fifth Avenue in New York."

"You didn't come by that on a soldier's pay."

Viktor emptied his glass and got up to refill it. "Not on soldier's pay, no. Yekaterinburg big city, produce much steel like Pittsburgh. Or like Pittsburgh before Japanese make cheaper steel. Soviet Union collapse, no one run steel mills, workers not paid. My *drook* and I hire soldiers out of work also. We open steel mills, pay workers."

The Soviet government had not just fallen; it had shattered. Even so, this was a stretch. "You mean you and your friend, you just walked in and took over the government steel mills?" Jason snapped his fingers. "Just like that?"

Viktor took a sip from his glass, icy-cold vodka straight up, and nodded as though admitting to something as trivial as possession of an overdue library book. "*Da!* Soldiers in town not paid, either. They help."

"But what about the administrators, mid-level managers? Surely they didn't just walk away?"

Viktor tossed his glass back, gulping the rest of the vodka. "Some not walk, carried. Most no longer needed. Was exciting. Now not so much."

Jason was having a hard time getting his mind around the fact that this man had simply mustered a small army and taken over the city's steel mills. But, then, in those chaotic days following Christmas Day, 1991, anything could have happened and frequently had. Who would have opposed him? The government had ceased to exist as a functioning body, the unpaid army refusing orders. The events had proven to be the perfect breeding ground for the economic oligarchy that had budded and flowered with the death of Russian Communism. By the time some semblance of order had been restored, possession of a number of the peoples' assets were in private hands, hands in a much better position to keep them than to take them back.

Privatization had been swift and irreversible; capitalism on steroids.

The door cracked open and a woman in a swimsuit quite modest by Saint Barts' standards stood there, looking surprised when she saw Jason. She quickly covered her already adequate bathing suit with a beach towel. Somewhere in her mid-forties, she was plump, if not fat, plain, though not quite unattractive. Her eyes moved from Jason to Viktor as she said something in Russian. The tone of his reply in the same language sounded annoyed, if not rude.

The door shut soundlessly.

"The woman knows better than to interrupt business," Viktor growled.

"I doubt she knew I was here," Jason replied, feeling an inexplicable need to defend the person he guessed was Viktor's wife.

Filling his glass again, Viktor returned to the pair of rockers, this time bringing the frosted bottle. He held it out toward Jason.

"Is, how you say, breakfast of champions."

Jason shook his head. "More like a nightcap if I started drinking vodka shooters in the middle of the day."

"Shooters?"

This conversation wasn't going anywhere, at least not anywhere that would accomplish Jason's purpose in coming to Saint Barts. At this time of year, the small planes that could negotiate the island's diminutive runway to ferry passengers to and from the major international airport at Saint Martin were booked months, if not years, in advance. If he missed his late-afternoon flight, Jason could be stuck here for days while he tried to find a boat not already employed, a craft to take him across the twenty miles to the larger island. Or he would have to admit his mistake to Momma by requesting a chartered helicopter that would draw unwanted attention

No, Jason did not have time for an etymological discussion.

"You were right: As much as I'm enjoying renewing our acquaintance and the beer, neither were my reason for being here."

He had Viktor's attention.

"I'm here because I'm in need of your talent."

Viktor forgot his newly filled glass. "I do not think you wish me to operate a steel mill."

"Correct. I'm referring to your handiness with explosives."

The Russian grinned, again exposing a steel incisor. "You have someone you wish to be exploded?"

"Perhaps. Are you interested?"

Viktor emptied his glass in a single gulp in true Russian fashion and narrowed his eyes as he faced Jason. "You are talking money?"

Jason stood. "A lot, but probably not so much to a man like you. In fact, it was silly of me to think you might be persuaded. I mean, you have this beautiful villa on one of the world's most exclusive pieces of real estate. You must be making money faster than you can count it, let alone spend it, not to mention a daughter. Plus a wife who would be very unhappy with you if she knew you were traipsing off to some faraway place to risk your ass for less money than you make in a month."

He was turning toward the door. "Sorry to have bothered you, but thanks for the beer."

Jason could only hope he had accurately accessed Viktor's character. The two of them, American and Russian, were alike though they had served different masters. Jason had known only two types of warriors: those who turned their backs on the profession of arms as easily as they might change a shirt to follow peaceful pursuits—men who devoutly wished to avoid conflict, or at least battle—and those of intense competiveness, men who relished competition whether in business or in more deadly endeavors. These men could no more walk way from a fight than they could give up breathing. Bored by extended periods of peace and tranquillity, they became edgy, if not irritable. They could be called mercenaries, extreme thrill seekers, or simply victims of their own DNA.

Jason knew the latter well. Though he tried to deny it, he suspected the breed included himself.

The question was: Did it also include Viktor?

As his hand touched the door knob, Jason realized he had been wrong. Viktor had the means to obtain anything he might desire. The good life had extinguished the warrior spirit. Jason had wasted a precious day in a futile effort.

"Wait! Just what did you have in mind?"

Helping himself to a second Carib from the refrigerator, Jason returned to the still warm seat of the rocker to explain what was wanted. A few minutes later, he and Viktor were haggling over price. Jason had offered a fraction of what he intended to pay and was only halfheartedly letting himself be bargained upward. He was aware the argument was not really about money; Viktor had more than he could ever wish. It was a matter of pride, price reflecting the degree of respect for the Russian's talents.

At last, they agreed.

Viktor produced another bottle of vodka from the refrigerator and placed a glass in Jason's hand. "Is Russian custom to seal bargain."

Jason managed to beg off after a second shot, telling Viktor he would be in touch in a few days and securing the number of an account in the Cook Islands into which he was to wire half a million dollars as an advance.

Jason checked his watch as he climbed into the battered Suzuki Samurai he had rented at the airport. He was relieved to see he had plenty of time to catch his flight. Enough time, in fact, to pause at the top of the hill behind Gouverneur, get out of the car, and admire a view of golden sand, green hills, and blue waters, all framed by the blood red of trumpet-shaped hibiscus blooms along the corkscrew road. The sense of loss that he had no means to put the view on canvas was near tragedy, assuaged only by a promise to himself he would return, supplies in hand. A few minutes later, he was treated to a different, but equally spectacular, sight as the hill dropped down into Baie de Saint-Jean. He would not have been the first visitor to the island to run off the cliff that yawned beneath each hairpin turn, too enchanted with the scenery to pay attention to the snakelike road.

The road ran flat as it briefly paralleled the beach at Saint-Jean, a strand divided by the jutting prow of a rock formation upon which perched the Eden Rock hotel, where rooms ran thousands of dollars per night during high season. That, of course, included a complimentary bottle of reasonably good Champagne upon check-in and a daily breakfast buffet. The road, already narrow, was squeezed tighter by cars more abandoned than parked by beachgoers.

Jason took a right and began the ridiculously steep climb to a group of small cottages, the Village Saint-Jean. It had been the only place he could find without a reservation. Though the bedroom, bath, deck, and tiny two-burner-stove kitchen hardly warranted the price, the view of beach and sea were as magnificent as any on the island, with the airport thrown in. He parked under an arbor of bougainvillea and walked out onto the deck that would lead to his door.

He rounded a corner, key in hand, and stopped as though he had hit an invisible wall.

"Hello, Jason."

Languishing on one of the two chaise longues was Dr. Maria Bergenghetti.

The ample amount of taunt skin revealed by a bikini was light olive-colored, the hair knotted into a bun black as a crow's wing, so black as to be iridescent. Skin and hair betrayed her Campania linage. The blue eyes that were staring over the tops of the oversize Foster

Grants, though, spoke of ancient Norman or Viking intrusion into the bloodline.

She took off the sunglasses. "You don't look happy to see me."

"I . . . I . . . I'm surprised. Astonished, actually," Jason verbally back-pedaled. "I mean, how did you . . . ?"

Good question. Jason had both arrived on the island and registered at the hotel under the George Simmons identity.

"You don't seem overjoyed that I did, find you, that is. If I didn't know better, I'd suspect you were here with another woman, but yours are the only clothes in the room."

Better another woman than she find out why he really was here. An affair might be forgiven; planning violence would not.

She sat up straight, spreading her arms. "Aren't you going to at least give me a kiss? We haven't laid eyes on each other in, what, five or six weeks?"

That was one thing he could do. Stepping forward, he leaned over. Her arms encircled him. The next thing he knew, swimsuits were flying. He was kissing her nipple. "Shouldn't we go inside?"

Her hand searched for and found his crotch. "Why? No one can see us up here."

Jason wasn't sure he cared.

31

Sankore Mosque
Timbuktu, Mali
8:20 p.m., Local Time
The Same Day

Abu Bakr ibn Ahmad Bian was puzzled by the nozzle's inability to receive the proper pressure. Just this afternoon, the device had tested perfectly. Of course, under test conditions, water was used instead of the mercury particles that had destroyed Flight 447 and would soon bring down another planeload of infidels. Using the real ammunition for trial purposes was impractical for a number of reasons.

First, it had taken over a year to produce and accumulate enough mercury particles to destroy another airliner. Working with the volatile element was slow, tedious, and dangerous. Plus, there were few facilities in the Arab world possessing the equipment or know-how to make the production process work. Complicating that problem was the necessity for secrecy. Unlike those fools in Iran with their nuclear program, Abu Bakr had no intention of being in a position to have to claim his project's use was peaceful. No one who had basic knowledge of chemistry or physics would believe the civilian use of reducing mercury to its basic atoms and propelling those atoms high enough to substantially reduce gravity and then cutting the nozzle pressure to bring them down on the target was peaceful.

Abu Bakr liked that: The idea of striking from the sky. Like the fist of Allah smiting the enemies of His people. Hence, the code name of the project, the Fist of Allah.

Second, the operation was not without risk. A malfunction or miscalculation could bring the entire mass of atomic-size mercury particles down on this very mosque. Abu Bakr was a devout Moslem, but he was no fanatic willing to sacrifice his life for a cause. That cause needed scientists like him, not jihadists willing to die for an unverified promise of seventy-two virgins. No, he could advance the cause of the Second Caliphate, the expulsion of the infidel Zionists from this part of the world, or whatever, much more effectively with science than an explosives belt.

That risk had been the reason he supposed Moustaph had chosen this place, whose very name was synonymous with obscure places.

It had not always been so. The courtyard of this mosque had been laid out in the eighth or ninth century. The present building dated back to the fourteenth. On the southern periphery of the Sahara Desert, Timbuktu had been a center of commerce and trading then, crossroads for the treasure of Africa to begin its journey to Europe and Asia. The city had been a center for learning, also. This mosque was one of three that had become a madrassa, a Moslem school. The Sankore Mosque had gone on to become not just a place for study of the Koran, but of science and mathematics as well.

That also might have been a reason for Moustaph's choice.

Another might have been the unique minarets of the mosque. Instead of the needle with the bulging top common to most such places of worship, this one had thin pyramids towering above its walls, almost a custom fit for the giant nozzle.

Abu Bakr smiled. Even if the infidel should discover the existence of the weapon, the idiots would shrink from the prospect of damaging a UNESCO World Heritage site, as was the Sankore Mosque and all of Timbuktu. The infidel held places and things above Allah's law.

The sound of a door opening at the bottom of the stairs that led to this room made him forget his thoughts. It was past the time for the *Maghrib,* the prayer said after sunset, and not yet time for the *Isha,* the call to the final of the day's five prayers, *so* there could be only one person to whom the ascending footsteps belonged.

Abu Bakr hurried to undo the lock in response to the brisk knock on the door. Outside stood a man of indeterminate age, although his beard was more white than black. He wore the traditional Moslem clothing: a *taqiyah*, the small brimless hat; a *thobe*, the collarless long-sleeved robe, splattered with mud; and sandals caked with it. His only distinguishing features were a scar on his right cheek and eyes that seemed to burn with a light from within with such intensity that Abu Bakr found it uncomfortable to look the man in the eye when addressing him.

Mahomet Moustaph, now the most wanted terrorist in the world.

"Peace be upon you," the newcomer said, giving the traditional Islamic greeting as he crossed the threshold.

Abu Bakr shot a quick glance down the steps, verifying Moustaph had not come alone. At least two figures stood in the shadows.

He gave the traditional response. "And may Allah's blessing be upon you."

Moustaph wasted no more time on the niceties. Crossing the room, he stood before the nozzle, an object shaped like what one might find on the business end of a fire hose. This nozzle, though, was the size of a mini bus and rested on a steel gantry, which had been assembled from pieces small enough to be smuggled into the mosque under coats, robes, or other exterior clothing. The mosque's imam knew what was going on in the northwest minaret, but few, if any, of his congregation did.

Moustaph noted Abu Bakr's stare at the muddy footprints he was leaving. "*Mashā' Allāh*, it is God's will. The river floods; the streets' dirt has become mud."

He was referring to the annual late-fall flooding of the Niger River Delta reaching Mali in January. It was paradoxical that an area so close to the world's largest desert would flood.

Abu Bakr shrugged, a matter of no concern. "The reason I sent for you, *Sidi*, is that there is a difficulty."

If possible, Moustaph's eyes grew even brighter. "Explain."

Abu Bakr indicated a low table surrounded by cushions. A teapot and several glasses were arranged on its top.

Moustaph shook his head, rudely declining this basic Arab hospitality. He was known as a man with little patience for time-consuming customs. Rumor had it he had become even more brusque since his escape from the infidels. Many an elderly mullah took umbrage at what could be perceived as rudeness. Like a number of the younger jihadists, Abu Bakr believed custom and ritual got in the way of efficiency too often. The time for manners and the old ways would return when the devil himself—in the form of the United States and its imp, Israel—were wiped from the face of the earth.

So he answered the question on his feet instead of seated with a glass of tea in his hand. "It is the nozzle. For some reason, we are losing pressure."

"You have checked the equipment below, to which it is attached."

A statement, not a question.

"Of course, *Sidi*. All works as it should. The problem lies between the moving parts that create pressure and the hose itself."

"A fitting?"

"Checked thoroughly."

Moustaph caressed his beard in silence for a moment. "You have consulted an engineer?"

Abu Bakr tried with only modest success to keep the annoyance out of his voice. "I am an engineer, a graduate of MIT in Boston."

The other man could not have been less impressed. "Then find an engineer from a good Moslem university, one who knows his Koran as well as his calculus. Make no mistake about it: In six days, we will bring down an infidel aircraft, a very special infidel aircraft. *In shā' Allāh*, if Allah wills it."

32

Village Saint-Jean
Saint Barthélemy, French West Indies
1:40 p.m. Local Time

Jason had dozed off after making love. He awoke with a start. Had it been the sound of airplanes from the airport a mile or so away? Probably not. The uninterrupted drone of arriving and departing aircraft had become unnoticed white noise. More likely the departure of direct warmth of the sun as afternoon shadows engulfed the deck along with an increasing sea breeze. Or it could have been Maria leaving the chaise longue. The space she had occupied was still warm to the touch.

Her expedition to the volcanic eruption in Indonesia had been interrupted by a need for additional scientific instruments. Rather than awaiting their arrival in what she described as conditions not quite up to primitive, she had elected to surprise him with a visit to Sark, only to learn he wasn't there.

From inside, he could hear the sound of the open shower.

Now what? He could still catch his plane, but what was he going to tell Maria? Try as he might, he could think of only one rational reason for immediate departure: the truth. He stretched, got up, and went inside in time to see Maria wind an enormous orange beach towel with the hotel's logo around her body.

He reached past her to test the running shower. "You still haven't told me how you knew I was here."

She was winding a smaller towel, turban-like, around her wet hair. She grinned impishly. "Suppose I decide I don't want to?"

Jason pursed his lips, the expression of man making a serious choice. "This isn't some game." He stepped into the shower. "If you found me, some people I might not be quite as happy to see might find me, too."

She clearly hadn't thought of this possibility and gave it consideration as he lathered up. Although Jason had foresworn the violence and death of his past, Maria knew there were still enemies out there, people who had vowed to see Jason dead. She also knew that these enemies were the reason for frequent changes in residences. She could accept that. She could not and would not accept the reality that mayhem, murder, and assassination were sometimes necessary.

She slipped out of the bathroom to return to sit on the chaise longue. He followed, leaving wet tracks on the tile floor.

"Really very simple," she said. "The volcanic expedition is waiting for additional equipment, and I decided to spend the time with you rather than just sitting around with a bunch of boring scientists. You gave Mrs. Prince an itinerary and told her to ask for a man called Simmons in case there was some emergency with the house or the menagerie, the cat or dog. I remembered that horrid affair in Sicily. You went by the name of Simmons then, too."

And people thought elephants never forgot.

Complete professional craft would have required Jason to cut himself off from his normal world entirely, not leave possible clues as to his destinations. But he couldn't ignore the responsibility of the house, Pangloss, or even the truculent Robespierre. Not to mention a way to learn if Maria was in trouble and without her ever-present iPhone.

"But you had no way to know at what hotel I was," Jason protested, unwilling to admit he had taken more of a risk than he had thought.

She reached an arm behind his neck, pulling his head down close enough to kiss his nose. "You arrived via Windward Air at three twenty-four p.m., local time yesterday." She leaned over, exposing impressive cleavage. "It was not so difficult to convince the nice Frenchman at the customs office that I wanted to surprise my husband, Mr. Simmons. He let me go through yesterday's arrival manifests. I knew you were here somewhere."

"That wouldn't have given you the name of the hotel," Jason argued, "When I arrived, I didn't know where I was staying."

She got up, removed the towel from her head, and gave a shake, sending dark tresses flying. "But this morning, you rented a car. You have to put where you are staying on the rental agreement."

Nailed.

"And," she continued, "you didn't explain that bandage on your leg." She wrinkled her nose. "From the looks of it, you need to change it."

Jason glanced down. The morning's encounter with salt water and sand had soiled the gauze. "Er, yeah. I'll run by the pharmacy in Saint-Jean and get a clean bandage."

Maria was still looking at it. "A Band-Aid won't do the trick. You are going to need a roll of gauze and adhesive tape. Just how did you hurt yourself?"

"You wouldn't believe."

"Try me."

"OK. I was on this train, see? I got into a knife fight with a woman. She sliced my leg before I managed to throw her off the train."

Maria gave him a look very much like she might have shown a puppy difficult to housebreak. "I only asked because I care. You can spare me the sarcasm; I won't ask again."

And that was fine with Jason.

33

Realizing Maria's reaction to his imminent departure might be softened by an evening together, Jason had made arrangements to be picked up by a charter aircraft the following day and flown to San Juan, where his travel options would be far greater than those out of Saint Martin. He really wouldn't lose a day.

That's what he told himself. In a remarkable job of self-delusion, he convinced himself not having seen Maria for over a month, not even having lived with a woman's company (the grandmotherly Mrs. Price excepted) had no more to do with the decision than, say, the fact the afternoon's activities had whetted a sexual appetite he had all but forgotten.

Pulling the Suzuki's right two wheels up onto the curb, the locally accepted manner of parking, he managed to wedge the diminutive vehicle between one of the ubiquitous motor scooters and another rental car, identified as such by the quaint custom of leasing the car without the spare tire. He joined Maria at the open entrance through a brick wall. Next to the opening, so narrow as to admit one person at a time, was only a faded wooden sign, EDDY'S.

Eddy's is as much a Saint Barts' tradition as are one-piece bikinis. Entering tropical landscaping, Jason and Maria were under what appeared to be a thatched roof, although closer inspection revealed a more conventional ceiling above. The theme of wood was everywhere from tables of highly polished teak to massive posts supporting the faux roof to primitive carvings. A long bar ran along the right-hand side of the room with the kitchen area behind. In organized chaos, serving personnel scurried back in forth bearing trays of drink and food. No one was busier than Eddy himself. Salt-and-pepper beard and queue hung down the front and back of his white chef's coat as he stopped at each table, old customer or novice, to exchange a few pleasantries. As they were seated by a young woman, Jason and Maria declined menus.

"Do you always have to take the Wild Bill Hiccup seat?" she asked.

Though educated in America, her familiarity with folk heroes was not always right on.

"I believe the gentleman's name was Hickock."

"Whatever. You always take the seat with its back to the wall."

Basic security training.

But he said, "I understand it's good for the health."

"It wasn't for Hiccup or whatever his name was. He was shot in the back, wasn't he?"

"Point made. He wasn't facing the door at the time."

The waitress's arrival interrupted.

"Do you have the tuna, tuna, tuna?" Maria asked hopefully.

A combination of tuna—sashimi, sushi, and seared—served with rice and wasabi ice cream. It was the favorite of Eddy's habitués. Due to the vagaries of cooperation from the local fish population, it was not printed on the menu. It was with anticipation that the couple sampled a pre-dinner cocktail of Havana Club Añejo Blanco and tonic. Jason would have preferred scotch, but the house's choices of rum were far superior to its selection of whiskey. Oh well, when in Rome . . .

"You never told me you were leaving Sark," Maria observed with more than an ascertainable trace of bitterness. "I was going to surprise you by showing up. Can you imagine how embarrassing it was to admit to Mrs. Price I had no idea you had left?"

"Mrs. Price isn't paid to embarrass; she's paid to keep house. Besides, I left unexpectedly."

Her eyes narrowed slightly, a certain signal Jason was about to be subjected to an old-fashioned third degree. "An unexpected trip to Saint Barts? You can do better than that." She waved a hand indicating the whole room. "Just what business on Saint Barts was so urgent you didn't have time to text me?"

The question was never answered. Instead, Jason's attention was on two men who had just entered the dining area. They had not come in the main entrance, but from the side, where a door from the adjacent dress shop opened into a small space flanked by Eddy's toilets. These men did not look like they had been shopping for dresses.

They looked more like they were shopping for trouble. Big, dark men with hard faces, eyes that searched the room, light jackets despite the air's moist warmth. Jackets to conceal weapons. Each with the beard decreed by Mohammed to distinguish his people from the pagans.

Someone had tracked him here by following Maria, no doubt the same someone who had employed Natalia, the female assassin.

And the killing knife and Glock were safely hidden from Maria's view at the Village Saint-Jean, so certain he had been they would be not be needed for one evening on Saint Barts. He felt as though he had just entered a formal ball room only to discover he was naked.

"You haven't answered the question," Maria persisted.

Jason stood, pointing across the room and smiling like a man who has just recognized an acquaintance. "I'm going to walk away from the table," he said as quietly as the room's noise would permit. "Two men, maybe more, will follow. No, don't look around! As soon as they are no longer between you and the exit, get out of here."

He pushed the car keys across the table.

"But, I don't understand. Why are they . . . ?"

"Maria, we don't have time for explanations. Just do as I say."

"But, where will I go?"

Jason was already backing away. "The bar at the Carl Gustaf. If I don't show, just stay out of sight until tomorrow. A Tradewind

Aviation charter will be at the airport tomorrow around eleven a.m. Be on it!"

She protested something he couldn't hear as he crossed the room, selecting a table next to the bar. A man and a woman looked up from their dinner as Jason sat between them.

He put an arm around the astonished man, leaning over to kiss the cheek of the equally surprised woman. "Jack and Mary!" Jason was speaking loudly. "God, I haven't seen you since . . . When? Was it two years ago at Saint-Tropez?"

The man struggled free of Jason's grasp. "I think you make the mistake," he protested with heavy French accent.

The two men flanked the left side of the table. In the background, Jason saw Maria headed for the street.

"And you, Mary," Jason continued boisterously, "how do you do it? I mean, you look younger than ever!"

Jason could only get brief glances of the approaching men as he carried out his plan. By now, they were within a few steps of the table, each reaching inside his jacket. Nearby conversations went quiet, aware something unusual was going on.

In near choreographed unison, both men withdrew pistols, Russian Makarovs, the knock-off of the Walther PPK that had been the standard Soviet military sidearm until 1991. There were screams and sounds of chairs crashing to the floor as Eddy's customers forgot dinner and drinks and headed for the exit.

Jason waited for the men's arms to straighten, bringing the guns to bear. A split second before that happened, he lunged to his feet, fingers gripping the table.

Table, chairs, dishes, glasses crashed to the floor, sending the two gunmen stumbling backward. They regained balance and now stood behind the overturned table. Jason was jumping up on the bar. In a single motion, he stooped, scooping up a filet knife from where a gaping chef had been preparing a snapper. Spinning like a ballerina, he threw the blade, sending steel glittering in the dim light like a comet.

There was a thump, as steel bit into wooden tabletop. Not exactly the result Jason had hoped for, but enough to make the two would-be assassins keep their heads down long enough for him to reach a cluster of plates under a heat lamp awaiting delivery to tables now largely empty. The first one skimmed a head that had popped up from behind the table. The next left a reddish goo as it shattered against the teak tabletop.

One of Eddy's better Creoles.

A food fight out of *Animal House* wasn't going to keep two killers at bay very long, and Jason was running out of ammunition anyway. He was taking aim, though, making sure each plate hit the center of the tabletop so as not to alert his adversaries that he was moving toward the street entrance.

Outside, a group of the curious had gathered.

"What's going on?"

"Who are those guys with the guns?"

"Are you the one they're after?"

For the second time that day, Jason heard the pulsation of a police siren. Judging by the distance, plus the normal evening traffic jam on Gustavia's streets, they weren't going to get there in time to be of any help. He took a quick look around. Those guys inside were going to come spilling out there any second, ready to start shooting. Jason seriously doubted they would give a damn whom they shot as long as the tally included him. A quick calculation told him he probably did not have the time to get out of sight before the excitement got under way. Without success, he tried to shoo away the closest gawkers.

He returned to the street entrance of the restaurant and grabbed the worn wooden sign. The rotted wood tore from its securing nails with little effort. By the time the first assailant emerged from Eddy's, Jason had the sign firmly in both hands. Holding it like a bat, Jason delivered a home run cut that caught the man across the forehead. The man dropped to his knees as though shot.

The Makarov slid from his hand just as the second man squeezed through the wall's narrow aperture. Jason dove for the sidewalk as a shot sent the crowd scattering. Rolling to his left, he snatched the pistol the first man had dropped. He hoped it was ready to fire; there was no time to cock it.

34

Andrews Air Force Base
Maryland
At the Same Time

The man with the silver eagles on his shoulders watched the nav lights of the pair of Boeing KC-135 Stratotankers fade into the winter sky. The two aircraft would be in the air fourteen hours before delivering their loads of fuel to a facility previously secured, where Jet-A would be locked and sealed with a device that would betray any tampering.

None of that was really any affair of William "Wild Bill" Hasty, Colonel, USAF, but the colonel was a meticulous man who made sure everything having to do with his assigned mission went off without a problem. That fuel so carefully inspected and guarded would be for the return trip of the highly customized 747-200B he would be flying in less than a week. His interest wasn't the fact the aircraft was the peak of aviation luxury—its two galleys could serve 160 people simultaneously. It wasn't that the plane cost more than $181,000 per hour to operate, or even that there were only two such airplanes like this in existence. His attention to details, even details over which he had no command, was based on a single passenger who would be on board just six days from now.

Twenty-two years in the Air Force, seventeen in the Air Force Materiel Command, and he'd never lost a passenger or a cargo, a record he intended to keep unblemished until three years from now, when he and Kate pulled the plug and retired to that little fishing shack on the Saint Mary's River near Palatka, Florida, where their closest neighbors would be deer and alligators. And bigmouth bass, the largest bigmouth bass Wild Bill had ever seen.

Bass or not, the fuel carrying aircraft were off, the first part of the mission begun. He turned his attention to the single closed hangar, the one guarded day and night by armed sentries with no-nonsense orders to shoot to kill anyone who approached without displaying the proper credentials. Bill had those credentials, of course, but there was nothing for him to do there tonight. His work, the actual mission, would begin five days from now. For the present, he contented himself with making sure the space on the tarmac was clear, the space where the C-141 StarLifters would load up the two armor-plated limousines and the half dozen or so equally armored SUVs.

Satisfied he had done all he could for the moment, he dug his fists into the pockets of his sage green MA-1 flight jacket and headed for the gate in the razor wire–topped chain-link fence where he exchanged salutes with two men stamping their feet against the night's damp cold.

35

Saint Barthélemy, French West Indies

On his back, Jason had the Makarov in both hands. The man who had just exited Eddy's was silhouetted against the streetlights, as featureless as a figure cut from black paper. Only a glimmer of light reflecting on metal from where Jason guessed his hands were told Jason he was holding the pistol he had brandished inside. As if he needed confirmation, Jason had the distinctly unpleasant experience of seeing the muzzle spit fire as he rolled violently to his right while trying to bring his newfound weapon to bear.

Pointing rather than aiming, Jason squeezed the trigger, gratified to feel the gun buck in his grip. He was partially blinded by the muzzle flash, but he squeezed off two more shots as the gun came back to point in the general direction of his first.

His initial clue that he had hit his opponent was the lack of return fire.

He scrambled to his feet, smoking pistol still in hand. The same streetlight that had limned his adversary now showed what at first glimpse looked like a pile of discarded clothing. A second look showed a dark trickle that was now dripping from the curb to the street.

He resisted the impulse to search for something to identify the man, a wallet, a passport perhaps. No point, and, as the siren grew louder, no time. Unlikely a professional like the man lying at his feet would carry anything that might be of use, and the police had obviously navigated the crowded streets. He stepped to his left where he could see small boats rocking in the breeze-caressed harbor. He tossed the gun, waiting until he heard the splash. He doubted the local heat had ever faced a man with a gun. Nervous and inexperienced police have a tendency to shoot first and ask questions later where armed men are concerned.

A Range Rover with blue lights flashing howled to a stop in front of Eddy's. Jason calmly blended into the crowd, sought the shadows, and began his trek up a steep hill avoiding light as much as possible as he went.

The grade was such that his calves were aching by the time he reached the entrance to the Hotel Carl Gustaf. He passed the vacant registration desk into the lobby/bar/restaurant, a large space open on one side with a view of the harbor and town below. Other than the bored bartender, Maria had the room to herself. She sat, hands clasped around a tall glass, staring into space as she munched from a small bowl of nuts, olives, and chips. She didn't acknowledge Jason as he slid into the seat across from her.

"You don't look overjoyed to see me."

"I'm happy you are alive," she replied flatly

"Unfinished business."

For the first time since his arrival, she looked at him. "It is always 'unfinished business.' "

Jason knew better than to reply. Instead, he signaled the bartender, who grudgingly wandered over.

When in the tropics, Jason normally enjoyed rum and tonic, particularly Havana Club. Experience told him he was going to need something more potent.

"Gin martini, straight up, olive."

The barkeep shuffled off.

If Maria noted the change in beverage preference, she didn't comment on it. Instead, she said, "Jason, it will not end until you are dead. The constant moving from one place to another, always looking over your shoulder, I cannot live that way."

He could have pointed out that most of the time she didn't, that she was gone. He also might point out that it had been his lifestyle, his employment by Narcom, that had brought them together. He could, but he knew better. He never won arguments with Maria. The few times he thought he had, he subsequently learned the dispute simply wasn't over.

So he held his tongue as she continued, "Has it ever occurred to you that you might get me killed, too? I mean, those men at Eddy's didn't look like they cared who got shot along with you."

At least they were in agreement on that point.

"Jason, your past follows you around like a bad smell."

He doubted she would be any happier if he pointed out the men with guns in Eddy's were here because of a job he had so far concealed from her, not the past.

So he said the only thing he could think of that was true, relevant, and non-incriminating. "I can't change the past, Maria."

"No, you cannot. After, what, three or four years . . . ?"

She knew how long to the day. Further, she knew he knew she knew. "More like five."

"Five years together, I thought your past would, would . . ."

"Fade away?"

"Something like that. But it hasn't. We had to leave Ischia because your enemies found you there. Now I am curious why you left Sark."

Jason paused to accept, taste, and nod his approval of the martini. The Carl Gustaf was one of the few places in the French-speaking world that understood a martini required dry, rather than sweet, vermouth and that in minimal quantity. Jason was not in the mood for creative drinks.

"Who said I left?"

"Well, you are obviously not there."

"But Pangloss and Robespierre are, as are my easel, paints, brushes, and unfinished paintings."

"You are saying you will return to Sark?"

Jason took a long sip from the stem glass, giving him time to compose a truthful, if deceiving, answer. "I certainly don't intend to abandon what you refer to as 'the menagerie.'"

That seemed to mollify her. "You are returning when you finish whatever brought you to Saint Barts?"

"The sun and sand brought me here," he said. "I thought getting away from the Channel winter for a few days might do me some good. This is a resort area, you know."

Well, he *had* been on the beach this morning.

"And you are returning to Sark?" she persisted.

"Not just yet."

Her raised eyebrows asked the question.

"I've got business on the continent," he said.

She visibly relaxed. Several times a year, he visited one or more of the financial institutions where he had accounts, trips like the one to Liechtenstein. After accompanying him on one or two, she elected to stay home. After all, the most secure banks were not in the more exciting countries.

Her untouched drink in one hand, she was twirling a strand of hair with the other, an indication of thought process. "When I finish this expedition," she said at last, "we need to have a talk, a serious talk about our future . . . if we have one."

From Jason's viewpoint, one of the great things about their relationship was that each had so far been willing to live it a day at a time, neither seeking nor offering commitment. Now the subject seemed to be lurking nearby as unbidden as Banquo's ghost. Jason supposed he should have seen it coming.

Like Jason, Maria had been married once. Her husband had been a lying cheat she referred to as Casanova. The marriage had lasted little more than a year. In addition to repeated infidelities, the man had been a *mammone* one of those Italian men who suffer separation anxiety when away from the mother with whom they had lived their entire life before marriage. From their honeymoon, Casanova had called home twice a day. Upon their return, he took his laundry for his mother to do, returning with a week's worth of her cooking. Maria couldn't decide which of the women in Casanova's life were worse: the meddling mother-in-law whom she could never please and who was always present in spirit, if not in body, or the unknowns whose cheap perfume clung to the shirts the man had his mother launder.

Jason had thought from Maria's point of view, a second marriage seemed a triumph of optimism over reality.

But then, he wasn't Maria.

He trolled a change of subject by her. "When do you think you'll be finished in Indonesia?" Adding diplomatically, "We all miss you."

The bait was rejected. "In a week, two at the most, once our equipment arrives. But don't change the subject, Jason. When I get back, I want some answers."

The questions were all the more ominous by not being asked.

A group of three couples came to Jason's rescue. Babbling excitedly in French, they took the table nearest the bar before ordering a bottle of Perrier-Jouët. There was some discussion of vintages before the 2004 was reached as a compromise. Jason smiled. The Perrier-Jouët was expensive enough in France. Add shipping and the generous price boost given to anything consumed in Saint Barts' eating establishments and the Champagne would be costly indeed.

"The 2002 Piper-Heidsieck would be a better value," Maria offered. "Better Champagne, less expensive."

Jason was about to ask when she had become a Champagne connoisseur when the conversation at the other table, or that part of it his limited French allowed him to understand, caught his attention.

"Were you downtown when the shooting took place?" a woman asked.

"Yes," a man responded. "But we were in front of the post office, looking for a parking space. I understand it was some sort of turf war between some of the Russians."

"A man was shot right in front of our car," a second woman volunteered. "I'm almost certain the man who did it was one of the Russians at the next table at Le Wall House last night."

She turned to the man next to her for confirmation. He nodded. "I'm sure it was. I never forget a face, particularly of someone causing a disturbance over dinner."

The eighth deadly sin in France.

"There were four of them, two men, two women. The men were

shouting at each other," the second woman said. "I'm sure that argument was why someone got shot tonight."

Jason managed not to grin. A dozen untrained observers would, more often than not, produce twelve different versions of the same event. Policemen lamented the fact; defense lawyers counted on it.

Maria had been listening, too. "You had nothing to do with the men with guns?"

Jason smiled and shrugged. "If I had told you so, would you have believed me?"

By the time they ordered dinner, he still had no answer.

36

City of Pecos
Reeves County, West Texas
6:27 p.m. Local Time
The Next Day
Day 5

Jason slowed the rented Ford to exit I-20. He had picked the car up at Midland International Airport, an hour and twenty-five minutes northeast. He had arrived there by an unremarkable and indistinguishable series of airports from San Juan to Miami to Dallas. A dawn-to-dark day of surly airline staff, tasteless airline food, and schedules far more hopeful than accurate. Contemporary air travel might be efficient, but it was anything but enjoyable.

He noted he was on South Cedar Street. The downtown could have been any one of thousands across the United States: one- and two-story storefronts with the usual tenants. Connie's Cuts and Curls: If your hair doesn't become you, you should be coming to us. Chat and Chew: Texas breakfast $5.95 starting at 5:30. Pecos Feed & Seed.

There was also the usual empty windows induced by the Walmart he had passed on the way into town.

Following the signs, he made his way to a two-story brick building, a former hotel and now the site of the West of the Pecos Museum. At this hour, the parking lot was empty except for a gritty Dodge Ram truck under the security lights. It could have been black, blue, or dark green. Hard to tell under its coat of dust.

Jason stopped just before the parking lot's entrance and blinked his headlights once, counted to three and did it again. The truck came to life, its modified engine rumbling as headlights came on as though it were opening its eyes. Jason waited for it to pass him before pulling in behind.

Within a few minutes, the outskirts of Pecos were gone. Although darkness reigned outside the cones of their headlights, Jason got the impression there was no living soul within miles of the Ford and the truck, only the occasional ball of tumbleweed rolling across the road like an escaping child's toy. More to keep awake than for entertainment, he turned on the radio. His first sound was a high decibel plea to come to Jesus and, on the way, send a few dollars to the Cornerstone Church of San Antonio. A twist of the dial filled the car with the adenoidal twang of a man wronged by his woman. Jason switched the radio off.

What had he expected in West Texas, the London Symphony Orchestra?

Jason's inability to sleep on airplanes was catching up with him. The steady drone of tires on asphalt and the lack of anything of visual interest were tugging at his eyelids like lead weights.

This morning seemed like a week ago. He and Maria had met the charter, a single turbo-charged engine Piper Meridian with STOL capabilities to handle Saint Barts' less than generous runway. The four-person, pressurized, club-seating cabin had been quiet, too quiet. Maria had occupied herself with a women's magazine, a type Jason had never seen her read. After one or two efforts at conversation met with brief and frosty replies, Jason concluded that his participation in last night's fracas was suspected, if not proven. It was almost a relief when they parted in San Juan with a kiss that might have been shared by siblings rather than lovers. She took an American flight to New York to change planes and head back to Indonesia by routing that made Jason's head swim. An hour later, his Delta flight departed for Miami and the subsequent transfers that had brought him to Texas.

The truck up ahead was signaling for a right turn. Only seconds before Jason's Ford left the paved surface could he see the faint trace of twin tracks in the dirt. He had seen no sign or other indication of where to make the turn.

The truck was in the belly of a cloud of dust, its taillights only marginally visible. Dirt and pebbles scratched at Jason's windshield as though seeking admission. An occasional impact from below noted this path was better suited to a high-riding vehicle than a normal sedan.

After several minutes, the truck stopped. Jason could see its headlights reflecting from a gate in a fence that must have been fifteen feet high topped with razor wire. Although too far away to read, the lightning bolts and skull-and-crossbones on the adjacent sign made the POSTED and KEEP OUT notices redundant. In case a potential intruder still didn't get the message, surveillance cameras moved back and forth atop the gate posts. This was not some ranch fence erected as deterrent to straying cattle.

Somehow, the name over the gate seemed more ironic than informative: PEACE AND PLENTY RANCH. Jason knew this place represented neither.

Jason got his first view of the truck's occupant as he stood beside the open gate, motioning Jason through. Tall, with a broad-brimmed ten-gallon pulled low over his forehead. Leather vest and faded jeans stuffed into cowboy boots. All that was missing between this man and a B-grade western film was a six-shooter in a low-slung holster.

Jason waited for the man to climb back in the truck and lead the way. Minutes later, the two vehicles topped a slight rise. Below was a collection of single-story buildings that could have been bunkhouses from the same B-grade western. What no western, B-grade or otherwise, boasted was the mile-long runway Jason knew was on no aeronautical chart, or the collection of limousines that filled what would have been a real ranch's coral but here was a cement skid pad. In the widely scattered lights, the buildings, the cars, everything took on an ephemeral, almost ghostlike appearance.

But this was not a real ranch, nor, for that matter, did it pretend to be, despite the rustic appearance given to the casual observer, had one been allowed within a half mile of the place. It was a school of sorts, a place of learning things taught in no university. It was where the world's most skilled bodyguards came to perfect their craft. Its alumni included members of the security staff of the house of Saud, Bahrain, and a number of the other Emirates, as well as several countries where coups and assassinations played a significant role in the political process. From time to time, the U.S. Treasury Department contracted to send aspirants to the Secret Service's presidential detail there for training superior to their own. The CIA also sent an occasional honor graduate of The Farm, its own facility, there, although to what purpose was never made clear.

"He's in the laboratory," Jason's escort said from outside the car. "And he's expecting you."

Jason didn't reply that, had he not been expected, he would never have gotten there.

Instead, he got out of the Ford, noting the air had taken a decidedly chilly turn. He could see his breath as he asked, "Which building is that? They all look alike to me."

"The one with no number."

Jason squinted, unable in the dark to see numbers on any of the structures, and turned to ask the man to point it out for him, but he was gone, disappeared into the night. Only the sound of the truck's ignition proved he had been here at all.

Jason started down the slope, planting each foot with deliberation. This was not the time to suffer a debilitating fall. He yelped in surprise at an explosion of motion literally under his feet. Chagrinned at how easily he had been spooked, he listened to a buzz of wingbeats fading into the night. He had disturbed some prairie chicken's slumber. Oh well, be glad it wasn't a rattlesnake.

He was nearly startled into another exclamation when a voice came out of the dark. "Goddam, Artiste, you're the only person I know can wander around open country and make more noise than a punk rocker playing bagpipes! Louder than a pair of skeletons getting it on on a tin roof! You been in hostile territory, you'd be KIA."

A quick glance told Jason the speaker had somehow left the buildings and come up behind him without a sound. "Didn't know I was in hostile territory," Jason replied mildly. "How goes it, Chief?"

The shadow in front of him came closer. A tall man, long white hair in a braid. A hard, chiseled face that would have been at home on a buffalo nickel. And with good reason: James Whitefoot Andrews, Lieutenant Commander, USN (Ret.) was full-blooded Cheyenne. He traced his ancestry to Chief Black Kettle, who, unsuccessful in making peace with the white man through no fault of his own, was massacred by Custer at the Indians' camp along the Washita River, along with dozens of women, children, and the elderly.

Fortunately, Lieutenant Commander Andrews, or Chief, as he preferred to be called, held no grudges.

Andrews extended a hand which Jason took. "It goes well, Artiste." He started down the rest of the slope. "C'mon down to my laboratory, and I'll get you a decent cup of coffee. I doubt you had one on the plane."

Chief was either clairvoyant or had recently flown commercially.

37

Strait of Malacca
Indonesian Waters
1997

Then U.S. Navy Lieutenant Andrews had come up with a proposal involving minimum military or political risk to end piracy in the Malacca Strait, a problem that was a precursor to the troubles off the Somalian coast some years later. A rescued tramp freighter ready for the salvage yard, a month of ingenious retrofitting, and a squad ten Delta Force men under then First Lieutenant Jason Peters.

The nearly weeklong trip to the eastern entrance to the Strait of Malacca provided ample time to learn the singular attributes of the refitted ship. At the single refueling stop, a small corner of the massive port of Klang, Malaysia, the civilian-dressed crew enjoyed shore leave. The country, roughly half Moslem and half Christian, had reached a unique accommodation: Alcohol was forbidden to Moslems while freely available to Christians. If there were Islamic souls aboard the *Muriel*, they kept their religion to themselves as the crew en masse descended on those sleazy bars that line almost every large commercial harbor in the world. The local beer became a lubricant to tongues as the crew made acquaintance with the easy ladies who inhabit such places. The word changed from rumor to truth overnight: The ship was carrying a small but valuable cargo the exact nature of which was unknown to the crew, so valuable its composition was a deliberately kept secret between shipper and the ship's owners, who, in turn were unknown. An impartial observer might have wondered if an attack by pirates was being invited. Whether braggadocio or sheer stupidity were to blame, the value of the cargo was firmly established in the bars at well more than $500 million USD.

"You always carry a spare canvas and paint box?" Andrews asked, arms akimbo, as he looked over Jason's shoulder at the rendition of sky, water, and land. Andrews took a step closer. "Say, that isn't bad the way you do sunlight on water."

"You sound surprised."

"Guess I didn't expect talent like than in a ground pounder."

Jason grinned, "You have a discerning eye, Lieutenant."

Andrews took a deep drag and tossed a cigar butt overboard. "Let's hope so, Artiste. We may need it."

And they did in the later hours of that evening. It was two bells into the first watch by the Navy's arcane timekeeping system, or right at 11:00 by Jason's wristwatch. He was asleep in a bunk that seemed to never completely dry out, a fact he had accepted as part of naval life.

"Huh?"

In the dim glow of the night light, he could see Andrews's unmistakable profile. "It's time, Artiste."

"Time for what?'

"Time for you snake eaters to earn your keep. Radar has three craft approaching, all from different directions. Classic attack pattern."

Jason was instantly awake. Slipping his feet into a pair of deck shoes, he stuffed a denim shirt into the dungarees in which he had been sleeping. He had long ago learned the seconds required to fully dress could be the difference between just in time and too late.

Above and around him, members of his squad were silently rolling out of boxlike bunks that looked all too much like stacks of coffins. In the dim red of the combat lighting, the men reminded Jason of imps from hell. At the foot of the companionway leading up to the main deck, each man paused long enough to take a predetermined weapon from a rack: The new Colt M4 carbine with its collapsible stock and PAQ-4 infrared laser designator, some with the bulky new M-203 40-millimeter grenade launcher. The last man to leave the mess hall that also served as bunking area, Jason lifted down the chest containing his M24 Sniper Weapon System that represented the U.S. Army's return to bolt-action sniper rifles. Because of the weapon's inability to take the abuse to which most military rifles were subjected, it had been stored not in an open rack, but in a metal container.

He was carefully sliding the Leupold M3A scope into place along the track on the top of the barrel when Andrews appeared at his elbow. "Best get on it, Artiste. That long gun of yours won't be any help tomorrow morning."

Jason slowly hand tightened the securing screws. "Won't be any help tonight, I knock this scope off half a centimeter. At eight hundred yards, that would be a miss of over a foot. I . . ."

He realized he was talking to the space vacated by the lieutenant. Andrews was already halfway up the stairs.

Jason arrived on deck just in time to witness the last of organized confusion. Though the moonless night was too dark to see more than a few feet, the clink of metal on metal told him Delta Force men had taken pre-assigned positions along both the little ship's gunwales. Jason's post was atop the fo'c'sle just aft of the anchor wench.

He set the rifle on its two-legged stand underneath the barrel, uncapped the scope, and took a preliminary peek. Nothing but darkness. He opened the breach and jacked a shell into the chamber. There were four others in the clip, but only the first would really count. Either it struck home or the ambush was exposed. Although he had practiced his part in tonight's drama, he lacked the self-confidence for which the men of Delta Force were known. A shot over open sights or even the optically confined infrared scopes, yeah, sure. But a precisely placed bullet fired from a heaving ship with a wind that changed direction and velocity by the second? And, of course, there would be no time to correct the scope if the distance were far off that promised by Andrews.

He was spared further insecurity as events unfolded faster than he could follow.

First, a rocket screamed into the air from the bridge where Andrews had supposedly allowed the approaching craft to reach a point on the radar screen precisely 500 meters directly off the bow. Then night disappeared, stabbed by half a dozen high-intensity searchlights. Pinned to the black water like an insect in a viewing box, a steel motorized dhow churned toward the ship. At the bow stood a barefoot and shirtless man holding what Jason guessed was an old AK-74 with stubby under barrel GP-25 grenade launcher.

That would be consistent with what the Delta Force men had been told about the method of pirate attack: A warning shot fired to intimidate the victim vessel into heaving to, stopping, or risking a more damaging second shot.

Jason tried to ignore the yawing motion of his platform, to concentrate only on the man who filled his scope. Time went into slow motion, the fractions of seconds filling minutes as Jason made minute adjustments. Obviously surprised by the sudden light, the pirate at the bow hesitated a second too long.

In what seemed to take forever but actually occupied one or two seconds, Jason centered the crosshairs on the man's chest. A sure-kill head or heart shot would be pure luck from the swaying deck. Breathe in, breathe out, breathe in . . .

Through the scope it seemed the crack of the rifle itself knocked the man over backward, his AK-74 flying into space with a life of its own.

Not that it mattered. Behind him, Jason heard the groan of heavy metal. The much enlarged loading doors of the hold swung open. A Boeing AH-64 Apache helicopter rose from the depths, hovering over the deck for a second like a large, malevolent dragonfly. The spotlights seemed to slow its rotors as they spun in and out of darkness.

The chopper rose a few feet above the deck and rotated to face the dhow closest to the ship, the one from which the man with the grenade launcher had threatened. A couple of shots came up from the dhow before there was a *whoosh* as the Apache released the first of the four Hellfire missiles mounted between its main landing gear. The dhow simply vanished as though struck by a bolt from Olympus to be replaced by a light shower of parts, both mechanical and human, that dimpled the water where she had been.

As if by mutual agreement, the surviving pirates went overboard, several thrashing in the water as they remembered they could not swim. The remaining two pirate ships turned and fled. It took several repeated orders at the top of Andrews's voice before the ship's crew stopped shooting those helpless in the water.

"Goddammit," Andrews raged later. "The whole point was to have survivors, not shoot fish in a barrel."

Jason looked at him, a question on his face. "I thought the point of the exercise was to rid the strait of pirates."

"We can't kill 'em all, but we can sure scare the shit out of them. I want every boy along the strait to hear about the old rust bucket that turned around and bit them in the ass."

Jason was fascinated. "So, it was your idea to make a fighting vessel out of this old tub?"

"Yep. Not an easy sell to the brass, I admit. But I do have a reputation as a tinkerer. I was in charge of retrofitting this old tub."

The two were silent as Andrews produced a bottle of amber liquid, and two glasses. He filled each halfway. "Single-malt scotch?"

Jason reached for the one nearest. "I thought spirits were forbidden on U.S. naval vessels."

Andrews raised his glass in salute and nodded. "For medicinal purposes only. Fortunately, I am a very sick man."

38

Peace and Plenty Ranch
Reeves County, West Texas
9:26 p.m. Local Time

Andrews seated himself in a wooden rocker in a small cubicle whose only view through the single fly-specked window was a large warehouse-type floor. The space, perhaps 8,000 or so square feet, was broken up into sections, each containing mechanical-looking equipment Jason could not identify.

He followed his guest's gaze. "Not much to look at, I know, but it serves."

Jason took the mate to Andrews's rocker, extending a hand to accept a steaming mug bearing the logo of the U.S. Navy. Using the other to point toward the window, he said, "Surprised Deborah lets you keep it in a mess. Only time I met her, that time in Washington, she seemed to pretty well give the orders."

"*Gave*, past tense. She left out of here three, four years ago. Went to visit her sister in Omaha, never came back. Said she couldn't stand the loneliness, sound of the wind and coyotes drove her nuts. Guess she missed the society on naval bases."

"Ah . . ." Jason stumbled, a man committing an unintentional but very real faux pas, "I didn't know . . . I mean, I'm sorry."

"No need, Artiste. You couldn't have known."

Time for a quick change of subject.

"From the looks of that stuff out there, I see you are still . . . what did you call it? A tinkerer, I think you said. Like to fool around with gadgets."

Andrews nodded. "Yeah. Except now I don't have the brass looking over my shoulder, telling me what to do. Matter of fact . . ."

He stood, motioning Jason to follow.

Unable to find a convenient place for the coffee mug, Jason carried it out onto the floor. He followed Andrews past what resembled auto engine blocks. Another section contained robot-like devices. Jason was about to ask a question when Andrews stopped.

"Know what that is?"

Two tanks the size a scuba diver might wear, a hose leading to a nozzle device with trigger.

"Looks like a flamethrower."

"Bravo!"

"But what's with a flamethrower? I mean, there must be hundreds of them lying around in military warehouses."

Andrews stooped over to pick up the rig. "Actually, there aren't. Never have been like this one, anyway. The things were used in Vietnam and weren't made to last. I looked everywhere, the Internet, military surplus stores, the lot. The commander in chief decided flamethrowers, particularly napalm flamethrowers, were 'inhumane.' " He made quotation marks with his fingers. "Imagine that, worrying about inhumanity to some asshole who's trying to kill you. Jesus Christ on roller skates! Hell, the things were the number-one effective infantry weapon in the Pacific in World War II. Pretty effective in 'Nam, too. Nothing like a little napalm to get someone out of their spider hole in a hurry." He sighed. "But then, our great leader, the peanut farmer, decided newsreel pictures of flaming VCs or whoever we fought next were bad for our image, never mind how many American lives might be saved."

One thing about Andrews: His politics were never wishy-washy.

Jason sipped his rapidly cooling coffee. Definitely better than the airlines' brew, even if it was bitter enough to make him pucker his lips. "Wouldn't it be illegal to own a flamethrower?"

"Nope, at least not nationally. Not that the Alcohol, Tobacco, Firearms, and Explosives guys wouldn't be sniffing around here, they knew what I was doing."

"They check the ones I see in the war movies?"

Andrews snorted derisively. "What you see on the screen are giant cigarette lighters, propane for safety. A real flamethrower uses a mixture of benzene and gasoline with maybe a thickening agent like polystyrene to make sure the fire sticks to whatever it hits, like skin. Too dangerous to let anywhere near the likes of, say, Tom Hanks."

"Why a flamethrower? I mean, what's so special about this one?"

"Trouble with World War II types was they weren't specific enough. You point it and everything within fifty yards or so gets incinerated. Well enough if you're torching Japs in a cave or Vietcong in a tunnel. Not so good if there are friendlies in the area. Want me to show you?"

Jason took a step backward "No, no. I'll take your word for it. What made you decide to build flamethrowers? They aren't my idea of security measures."

Andrews shrugged. "Disguised freighters weren't the Navy's idea of fighting piracy, either."

"I get the connection, but flamethrowers . . . ?"

"What greater atavistic terror does man have than being cremated alive? Suppose some sand cretin terrorist wannabe knows that he might be dispatched to paradise as a cinder? But you didn't come all the way to Peace and Plenty to see an old man's play toys.

"You're right. Let me tell you a story."

Twenty minutes later, Andrews pushed back as far as the rocker would allow and stared at the ceiling, his coffee cup forgotten. "Wow! Right out of science fiction."

"So I've been told."

"How sure are you about this gizmo, this death ray?"

Jason shrugged. "I only know what I've been told. The French security folks believe in it, I can tell you that."

Andrews got up and went to the table on which the coffeepot sat. He lifted it above his cup. "Damn thing's empty. You gonna want more?"

Jason shook his head, his stomach already sour from the bitterness. "No thanks."

Andrews pursed his lips, a man making a decision. He nodded, decision made, and put the coffeemaker in a nearby sink. "How sure are you of the location of the source?"

"Once again, I'm relying on the French."

The Cheyenne was rinsing the pot out. "You didn't come all this way just to tell me about a plane crash."

A statement, not a question. Jason said nothing.

Andrews scowled as he concentrated on wiping the coffeemaker's innards clean. "OK, Artiste, exactly what role do you want me to play in this?"

"So far, there are three of us. You'll make four if you want to join the party. The mission profile calls for us to reconnoiter, confirm this machine is where we think it is, take it out by whatever means, and confirm that."

Andrews returned to his rocker. "Sounds like a job for one of the Air Force's drones."

"Except that a drone can only see what is outside of buildings, can't go inside. Plus we may well be dealing with not only a mosque, but one that's a World Heritage site. If you get a week of rioting and forty-plus deaths for accidentally burning a few Korans, you can imagine the reaction if we bombed the wrong one."

"That was Afghanistan, stirred up by the Taliban."

"You think the Maghreb would be more reasonable?"

Andrews nodded. "Point taken."

There was a brief silence before he said, "You have a plan for both insertion and extraction?"

"Depends."

"On what?"

"On whether you're with us or not."

Andrews gave a dry chuckle. "I 'spect you knew that before you came. Old war horse like me, put out to pasture . . ."

Jason couldn't suppress a smile. "Before you get teary-eyed feeling sorry for yourself, let me remind you: You have the best known security school in the United States of America, probably the world. You also have the most expensive. You're making, what, ten times what the Navy paid you?"

"Yeah, but there's no real excitement, nothing to get the adrenaline rushing. When I wake up in the morning, I know exactly what's going to happen that day. Biggest surprises in my life are when it rains."

"I take it that you'll be with us."

"When do you want me where?"

At Andrews's insistence, Jason spent the night. Breakfast, served before full light, was in one of the bunkhouse-like structures. Six men sitting around a long table reminded him of a scene out of a western. Except these cowboys wore suits tailored on Bond Street instead of flannel shirts and chaps, shoulder holsters instead of low-slung gun belts, cap toes and wingtips by Bruno Magli instead of boots.

The bodyguard business must pay well.

The sun was just beginning to swallow the night's shadows when Jason tossed his bag into the Ford's backseat and reached across his chest to extend his right hand out of the window. "I'll be in touch, next day or two, Chief."

Andrews leaned over, elbows on the sill of the car's open window to take Jason's hand. "Can't tell me more than that? Like where we're meeting, exactly when?"

"Don't know much of that yet. Think of standing by for orders."

In the rearview mirror, Andrews faded into the dust of Jason's departure.

39

Bamako-Sénou International Airport
Bamako, Mali
Two Days Later
Day 7

Smoke puffed from the tires of the Air France Airbus A330 as its wheels smacked onto Runway 06. The flight from Paris had been a little over five hours, not counting the time spent on the ground at Casablanca, the sole intermediate stop. Passengers stretched. Several lifted the window shades, squinting in the brilliance of the West African sun.

Despite the warning coming over the electronic speakers in French, English, and Bambara, most of the 300 passengers stood in the narrow aisles before the aircraft came to a stop beside the modern glass-and-steel terminal. They waited with the impatience of weary travelers for a pair of tractors to push twin air stairways against the forward and aft doors of the aircraft.

The four men of varying races remained where they sat with the assurance of experienced flyers that their business-class seats provided far more comfort than would the standing mob. As the lines in the double aisles began to shuffle toward the exit, each of the four stood and removed a single bag from the overhead bin.

The terminal was a single unairconditioned room, filled with shoulder-to-shoulder lines, a babble of a dozen languages and dialects, and the smell of sweat. The quartet joined the line at the far end of the building to exchange currency for West African CFA francs and paid the arrival fee to an official in camouflage army uniform and reflective sunglasses before presenting entry forms, passports with visas, and proof of yellow fever inoculation to his twin.

The latter spoke in French to one of the group of four who smiled and shook his head slowly. *"Je ne parle pas français."*

The official scowled with the ill-concealed hostility third-world officialdom display toward the more affluent. He turned his gaze to the next of the four, the only black man in the group. He noted the scar that divided the face from right to left, the muscles that strained the short sleeves of the khaki shirt, the shaved head. Then he spoke in French, a question. The black arrival replied and was answered with another string of French.

"What did he say?" Jason wanted to know.

Emphani flashed a bright smile. "Other than wishing upon us the peace of Allah, it seems he is having a hard time understanding exactly what of geographic interest we might find at Timbuktu."

"You told him we are researching the city's Askia Period on behalf of the National Geographic Society?"

"Of course. That explains why we each have passports from different countries." He lowered his voice "Even if the names are . . . er . . . um . . . *faux.*"

Another question and answer in French.

"He wants to know if we will need to be in the country longer than the three days the visa permits."

For reasons known only to the Maliese, the only visa available outside the country was for three days. Any extension had to be granted while in country. Jason suspected the practice generated additional income and more jobs for bureaucrats.

"Tell him I doubt very much we will need additional days this trip. If we find something of interest, we'll be back."

Emphani rattled a line of French and received another question in response.

"If we are from *National Geographic*, where are our cameras?" Emphani translated. "He says *National Geographic* always has pictures, color pictures."

"The cameras are with the rest of our equipment," Jason improvised. "It should have arrived this morning."

After another exchange in French, Emphani said, "He will come to the freight depot with us. He would like to have his picture taken." Then, in a lower tone, "Hope you have a camera. It would give much, er, er . . . How do you say *prestige* in English?"

"Prestige."

"It would give him much prestige to have his picture in *National Geographic*."

"Tell him if he will expedite our equipment through customs, I will see what I can do to put his picture on the cover."

Viktor and Andrews were watching the three-way exchange with growing impatience.

"Artiste,'" the latter said. If you can't—"

Jason silenced him with a wave of the hand while Emphani translated the offer into French. A broad smile spread across the official's face, and all traces of animosity disappeared as the man gave Jason a brotherly hug.

"He says he will give us a ride to the freight depot." Emphani said. "There will be no customs fees or . . ." Emphani rubbed the fingers of one hand together, the international sign a bribe was expected.

In this part of the world, a waiver of any fee plus the accompanying *pot-de-vin* was rare.

Twenty minutes later, one of the green minibuses that serve as taxis in Bamako was into the fifteen-kilometer trip into town. There had been so many crates, boxes, and bags addressed to the *National Geographic* expedition, there was no room for anyone other than the driver and his four passengers.

Andrews, seated next to Viktor in the second row of seats, leaned forward. "Artiste, was that a Canon AT-1 you used to take that man's picture?"

In the front seat between the driver and Viktor, Jason nodded. "Uh-huh."

185

"Not digital," Andrews persisted, "Film, right?"

Again, a nod.

"Didn't know anyone even made film anymore."

"They don't."

"But how. . . ?"

"Let's just say when the May issue of *National Geo* comes out, we would be wise to avoid the Bamako airport."

Viktor snorted a laugh. "You carry an old camera with no film?"

"Let's just say I've dealt with officials in this part of Africa before."

All four were silent as the minibus wove through increasing traffic—automotive, human, and animal. Loose cattle wandered at will among trucks, scooters, bicycles, and cars. The road sloped gently downward as mud-brick buildings became more numerous. A woman riding a donkey was dressed in a brilliantly colored pagne with matching turban. Another on foot, a basket of fruit balanced on her head. Although largely Islamic, Mali had not adopted the hijab or other Islamic dress. Men largely wore a *boubous*, full-length tunics made from rough cloth and dyed with patterns of varying colors of mud.

By Lumumba Square, the town's skyline was dominated by the minarets of the Grand Mosque towering above three or four stories of mud brick. The main feature of the city, and the reason Jason had chosen to enter the country there, was the seasonally flood-swollen Niger River. Dividing Bamako, its muddy waters swarmed with watercraft ranging from the multi-decked ferry to dugout canoes. At near seasonal flood stage, it was about a mile across here. Along its banks, fishermen haggled loudly with women over their catches while others mended their nets. Men stripped to the waist, ebony skin gleaming with sweat, loaded cargo into a *pinasse*, a twenty-five- to thirty-foot, high-prowed, canoe-like craft powered by outboard motors with a tentlike structure serving as a cabin at the stern. Nine or ten months of the year, Jason and his comrades would have had to travel slightly further to Mopti, where the river was always deep enough for commerce.

It was upstream of the traffic-clogged King Fahd Bridge and alongside one of these craft that Jason ordered the driver to stop. The four passengers quickly transferred the contents of the minibus into the slender craft, declining help from any of the native longshoremen. When they finished, they climbed aboard and the ship backed into the eddies of the current and headed north.

40

King Fahd Bridge
Bamako, Mali
The Same Time

Moussa was probably the richest twelve-year-old in Sikoro-Sourakabougou. This morning, he had left the single-room mud hut he shared with his mother, grandmother, and three siblings to beg, take odd jobs, steal, or do whatever he could for a few West African CFA francs. Like all the others in the slum, the house had no running water, sanitary facilities, electricity, or garbage removal. In fact, there was no reliable source of water within a mile or so, only a well that gave out during the dry season and carried evil vapors during the wet, vapors that caused over half the children to never reach half Moussa's age.

Had there been a school, he certainly would have attended. But there was none, so Moussa spent his days on the streets of Bamako.

That was where he had met the Arab.

Arabs were relatively rare here, and even more rare were Arabs that spoke Bambara, Mali's largest dialect. Those that did venture this far south usually prowled the streets for young boys. Moussa had had an experience with such an Arab, a very painful one, even if it had actually put the equivalent of five euros in his pocket. But the shame was worse than the pain, a shame only slightly mollified by his mother's joy at such a princely sum of cash.

She did not ask where he got it.

But this Arab was not looking for young boys, at least not in the sense Moussa feared. Instead he was offering untold riches in exchange for a simple task: Stand on the King Fahd Bridge and watch the river for four men. One black, two white, and one dark-skinned. They would be together and would load objects into some sort of rivercraft, most likely a *pinasse*. Moussa was to watch them and then call a number on the cell phone the Arab gave him.

Then he could keep the phone plus the hundred West African CFA francs the Arab shoved into his hand.

That was all. No pain, no humiliation.

Allah was indeed great.

41

Restaurant Amanar
23 Rue de la Paix
Timbuktu, Mali
Earlier the Same Day

The two men sat at a low table in a small garden enclosed by a high wall. One entrance was from the restaurant itself, the other through a wrought iron gate through which the Flamme de la Paix could be seen. It was early afternoon and the heat of the day was waning as shadows of two towering date palms lengthened. Both men were Arabs, not uncommon in Timbuktu, but not part of the majority, either, although the city's ancient past as a center of learning and commerce was largely attributable to Arab culture. Both were dressed in the traditional Bedouin garb: Loose-fitting robe or *thobe* reaching the ankles with large, triangular sleeves that could, and frequently did, conceal weapons. Over these were a striped sort of vest. Each wore a *kaffiyeh* on his head held by an *agal*, a strip of hair or fur. Each man had small cup of coffee in front of him.

"The nozzle is fixed." asked the younger of the two, Abu Bakr ibn Ahmad Bian.

"*Alhamdulillah.*"

"*Alhamdulillah,*" echoed the older, larger man.

"All is in readiness, then?"

"Almost all."

Abu Bakr's coffee cup stopped somewhere between the tabletop and his lips. "Almost?"

"Our friends in Paris tell us the infidel and three companions departed there last night for Bamako. A survey of rivercraft tells us it is most likely one of the *pinasses* has been chartered for a trip here by four men from the National Geographic Society."

"Which you believe to be the infidel Peters."

A single nod.

"But it takes four days to reach here from Bamako by river. By that time, we will have finished our mission, *In shā' Allāh.*"

The older man smiled, though there was little warmth in it. "That is why he is not planning on making the trip by water. That is why I have asked our Tuareg brothers for help, to operate a little south of their usual territory."

Abu Bakr asked, "They will intercept the infidel?"

"*In shā' Allāh.*"

42

Niger River

Mali is shaped roughly like an hourglass, tipped forty-five degrees to the right. The bottom half is largely the Niger Valley, fertile and by far the more populous of the two halves. Where the borders narrow, the river becomes shallow, navigable only a few months of the year. By the time one reaches the upper half, the land is largely barren, bordering on the desert. There the mighty Niger is but a trickle except in the winter months.

Approximately 900 kilometers lie between Bamako and Timbuktu, at least half of which traverse arid, inhospitable terrain, which is why most travelers take the four-day river route.

But Jason and his crew did not have four days for a leisurely cruise. Two hours after departing Bamako, the *pinasse* moved to the right bank of the river, making a detour around a herd of frolicking hippos. Any adult of the ill-tempered animals was more than large enough to do serious damage should it take offense at the ship's presence. The shallow draft boat slipped into a mangrove swamp. The captain, the sole crew member, jumped overboard into knee-deep water to take a bowline Jason tossed to him.

"Didn't I see crocodiles sunning on the bank a few miles back?" asked Andrews.

Jason was too busy playing out line to take his eyes off the man in the water. "Yep."

"Then that guy is either crazy or has the biggest balls I've seen lately."

"Or knows the current is too swift here for crocs."

The conversation ended with the squeak of the ship's keel on river-bottom sand. Jason and the other three went overboard, splashing in the shallow water. Although it was less than ten meters away on relatively dry land, the Toyota Series 70 Land Cruiser would have been invisible had the sun not reflected from its windshield. Jason ran a hand under the right front fender until he found the magnetized box with the key in it. Climbing into the cab, he sighed his relief as the engine turned over in response to the ignition. The gauge showed the tank was full. From the window behind his head, he could see three fifty-liter jerry cans strapped to the truck's bed. A fourth was marked in chalk "H2O." Two spare tires completed the trucks initial load.

Viktor's head appeared beside the driver's window. "If nothing else, American, you have organization," he commented admiringly. "Perhaps whoever delivered this splendid vehicle left a bottle of vodka, yes?"

Jason was climbing down from the cab. "Whoever delivered this splendid vehicle left a bottle of vodka, no. Now, give us a hand unloading the boat."

The Russian looked back at the ship, only its bow visible in the thicket of green leaves. "It is a pity to have to load and unload again, no?"

Jason was back in the water, sloshing toward the *pinasse*. "All the more pity if we don't. Must have been a thousand or more people saw us leave Bamako. You think any one of them would have qualms about selling that information?"

"Sell?"

"To bandits, to anyone who might be suspicious as to who we really are, curious enough to wait upriver for a better look."

Viktor was splashing right behind him. "In Russia we say, 'If you are afraid of wolves, stay out of the forest.' "

"Yeah, well in the United States we say, 'Better safe than sorry.' I'd just as soon avoid the wolves altogether."

Once the slender craft was unloaded, Jason peeled off bills from a roll of dollars and handed them to the smiling captain. He would sail the rest of the trip to Kabara, the port closest to Timbuktu, in case curious eyes were monitoring the vessel's progress. By that time, Jason would have either completed his mission or failed.

Either way, he would be long gone.

Or dead.

Before shifting the *pinasse*'s cargo to the truck's bed, each man rummaged through several packages, removing personal arms. Three men waited patiently for the few minutes it took Emphani to complete his afternoon prayers, roll his prayer rug, and join in the task. Pistols and knives went under sweat-soaked shirts. Unidentifiable packages and cases were placed in the truck's bed before Jason climbed into the driver's seat with Emphani beside him. Andrews and Viktor chose to ride in the open truck bed, a decision dictated by the vehicle's lack of front-seat space and air-conditioning. Having two men in the open was not a bad defensive measure, either, should it become necessary.

The Toyota slogged its way through mud that reached the middle of the wheels before reaching what Jason assumed was the road. Parallel tire tracks faded into a surface resembling a washboard more than a highway. As the truck jounced along, conversation was possible only through clinched teeth. Sixty kilometers per hour seemed to be the maximum speed at which the Toyota could proceed without vibrating apart or leaving the undercarriage in the road.

In the truck's bed, Andrews and Viktor were forced to hold on to the sides or risk being bounced onto the ground below. Using one hand, Andrews dumped a bag, from which came a hose-like apparatus that ended in what, to the Russian, looked like a gas pump's nozzle complete with trigger.

Viktor raised his voice above the rattle as the truck tried to shake itself apart. "We will not need that. We will pour petrol directly from the cans."

"We may not need it," Andrews replied, "but if we do, I want make sure it works. It's not your average gas pump hose."

By now, the sun was little more than a golden memory in the west.

To the north, Sirius, the sky's brightest star and central to the mythology of the Dogon people of Mali, was clearly visible. Waves of shadows had become a tide of darkness, obliterating the road. There was barely enough light to limn the trees against a deepening purple backdrop: the fullness of a baobab, the slender kapok, the massive mahogany. The Toyota's headlights were two converging scars across the breast of the fading twilight. From all directions and no direction at all came the howls, barks, and grunts of the local fauna, enough to make each man silently thankful for the steel between him and the African night.

The truck came to such an abrupt stop Viktor and Andrews nearly flipped over the cab. Andrews got to his knees to peer over the cab's roof. Squarely across the road were a pair of battered small Mitsubishi trucks. Behind them a half dozen men stared into the truck's headlights. Though black, they were dressed not in the colorful native garb, but like Bedouins. And though the dress had not changed for centuries, there was nothing traditional about the AK-47s each man held.

43

The window seemed to filter all life from the pale winter afternoon sunlight that was barely strong enough to cast shadows on the carpet of the Oval Office. Behind the Resolute desk, the president of the United States leaned back in his padded wooden-and-leather swivel chair, his fingers interlocked across his chest. Only a few inches of cigar butt were left, visible in the right corner of his mouth.

No matter what the decision on the trip, Chief of Staff Henry Hodges was thankful his boss wasn't babysitting today. The twins, Ches and Wes, were one of a number of reasons Hodges was thankful he had successfully eluded marriage.

Henry guessed the president's mind was made up, down, and locked. Henry could only sit on one of two wheat-colored sofas perpendicular to the desk, leftovers from the previous occupant. The chief of staff was convinced the former president had them placed so that no one could look at the desk without turning his head, a subtle means of discouraging arguments.

And arguments there had been aplenty as the past chief executive had not so subtly tried to overcome the constitutional restraints that had seriously hampered his plans for the country, plans the recent election had demonstrated were less than popular.

None of that, though, was why Henry was here today. His duty, as he saw it, was to do the near impossible: Change the president's mind. As the president's campaign manager, he had had to develop certain persuasive skills varying from diplomacy to the political equivalent of breaking legs.

The president, whose boyish good looks and a penetrating gaze that screamed sincerity had earned him comparisons to a young John F. Kennedy, shook his head. "Forget about it, Henry, I'm going."

"I'm not suggesting you cancel, Mr. President. I'm urging you, though, to reschedule." Hodges twisted on the sofa to put his body as close to face-to-face as the furniture arrangement permitted, a less than comfortable contortion and finally stood. "Give us a chance to verify this thing's location and destroy it."

The president unlocked his fingers and leaned forward, elbows on the desk. "I'm not going to postpone my meeting with the first democratically elected president of Egypt. I can't risk offending him or the rest of the Moslem world. Extending the hand of friendship to Egypt and all of Islam is the only solution to the conflict between the Middle East and the West."

More like extending the hand of friendship to an angry rattlesnake, Henry thought. But he said, "You won't achieve a hell of a lot if you're dead."

"Life is not without risk, Henry. *Audaces fortuna iuvat.*"

The president was fond of Latin aphorisms, a habit his class-warfaremongering opponents characterized as elitist. To their surprise, the electorate decided to restore a modicum of culture and learning to the White House.

"That may be so, Mr. President, but we have credible evidence Al Qaeda or their allies intend to shoot down Air Force One just like they did the Air France flight." Hodges stood and took a stroll around the sofa. "If nothing else, think of Suzanne. She's far too young to be a widow, and the twins need their father."

The president shook his head. "I can't be seen as cowering away from some sort of Star Wars weapon that we don't really even know exists. Can you imagine what the *Post* and *Times* et al would do with that? Hell, I can even see a *Saturday Night Live* skit."

Hodges was well aware the president was not the darling of the majority of the media. His promise to balance the budget in his first term had resulted in austerity programs that had already reduced the deficit while enraging those no longer subsidized by the government.

"I don't understand how this thing is supposed to work . . . if it works at all."

"We're not sure, Mr. President, other than it seems to be some sort of particle beam. Going back and looking at what remains of the notes of this man Tesla, it seems most likely it was powered by a huge electrostatic generator to accelerate tiny articles of mercury in a vacuum and spew them out through some sort of specialized nozzle at great distance."

"I'm no physicist," the president admitted, "but if you need a vacuum to accelerate particles, what happens when they're spewed out of the vacuum? Seems like they'd lose velocity. Sounds like nothing more than a crackpot idea."

Hodges returned to the sofa, this time giving himself more room to turn and face the president. "Don't be too sure. We know that, in 1908, Robert Peary was making his second attempt to reach the North Pole. Tesla sent him a pre-departure telegram, telling Peary he, Tesla, would try and contact the expedition and to please report anything unusual occurring on the tundra."

"North Pole? Robert Peary? C'mon, Henry, you're wasting my time!"

The chief of staff held up a protective hand. "Indulge me, Mr. President, please."

The man behind the desk didn't look pleased, but he wasn't shooing anyone out of the office either.

"Anyway, on the evening of June 29, Tesla and his associate George Scherff climbed up a tower Tesla had built in Shoreham, New York, and aimed the so-called 'Death Ray' across the Atlantic toward the Arctic at a spot Tesla had calculated would be west of where Peary's expedition should be.

"According to Scherff, Tesla turned the machine on. At first, there was nothing but a dull hum. They thought the device might have malfunctioned. Then an owl flew in front of them and seemed to disappear. Later, they found it dead and reduced to about the size of a sparrow."

"An owl? So the thing shoots down birds. Air Force One is a little larger than an owl."

"The damned owl isn't really important. What is, is that two days later the newspapers carried a story of a huge explosion devastating Tunguska, a remote area in the Siberian wilderness, about the same time Tesla and Scherff were on the tower. Five hundred thousand acres of timberland destroyed, an explosion greater than any nuclear device ever detonated since the bomb was invented, audible from more than six hundred miles away.

"The first explanation was an asteroid or comet but no exact point of impact was ever found nor was any trace of the asteroid or comet. Tesla had a different explanation: His death ray had overshot its intended target and leveled a good part of Siberia."

The president gave Hodges the famous look. "You believe that?"

"Tesla did. He dismantled the thing, put it away till the First World War when he tried to peddle it to Woodrow Wilson, offered to rebuild it."

"And?"

"All he got was a polite letter from Wilson's secretary."

The president leaned back in his chair. "And that was the end of it?"

"Not quite. When the Second World War came along, J. Edgar Hoover and William Donovan corresponded about it. There seemed to be some reason. To think the Germans might have gotten hold of Tesla's ray."

"Did they?"

"Inconclusive, but we know we won."

The president stood, a signal the conversation was at an end. "Which would seem to indicate this so-called death ray either doesn't exist or, more likely, never did."

Henry Hodges stood again. "I hope you'll reschedule, Mr. President."

"I'll give it some thought, Henry."

Which almost always meant the subject would not come up again.

44

Bamako-Timbuktu Highway
Mali

"Who . . . ?"

"Shh!" Andrews tugged Viktor's shirt, bringing the Russian's head below the top of the truck's cab.

"But who. . . ?" Viktor insisted, this time at a whisper.

"Tuareg rebels, National Movement for the Liberation of Azawad."

"Aza what?"

Andrews was pushing Viktor toward the truck's tailgate. "We can talk politics later. Right now, let's deploy into the brush before they figure out Jason and Emphani aren't alone."

Inside the truck's cab, Jason was staring into the barrel of an AK-47. From the passenger seat, Emphani was doing the same.

Jason rolled down his window, admitting a horde of mosquitos along with the warm night air. "You speak English?"

For an answer the door was snatched open, the hand not holding the automatic rifle grabbed the front of Jason's shirt, jerking him out of the truck. Jason struggled to maintain his balance, stumbled, and fell to the ground. His hand automatically reached for his right calf where, concealed by his pants leg, his killing knife was strapped.

It took only a fraction of a second to realize he would be dead before the blade cleared its scabbard. The muzzle of the AK-47 was never more than a foot from his head as he got to his feet.

"But we weren't speeding, Officer."

If any of the men in blue *thiyaab* understood him, it wasn't obvious.

Emphani, his hands over his head, came around the truck in front of another rifle. "They're NMLA."

"I thought the Tuareg rebellion ended in '09."

"So did I."

Jason searched his memory. The Tuaregs were a nomadic group who claimed to be seeking freedom of their homeland, Azawad, from portions of Mali, Niger, Algeria, and Nigeria. Since the areas included in the nonexistent Azawad were almost entirely in the sparsely populated Sahara Desert, the countries involved put up little resistance. The near dormant movement was revitalized when the fall of Qaddafi put Tuareg mercenaries out of work and the Libyan arsenal was pretty much open on a first-come-first-served basis. Those who had served the Libyan strong man now existed with the banner of a cause as an excuse for banditry. Many in Africa linked the rebels to Al Qaeda's African arm, an accusation the AQIM, or Al Qaeda in Islamic Maghreb, stoutly denied. Either possibility gave little comfort. Certainly the murdered unarmed civilians couldn't care less as couldn't the inhabitants of burned villages and raped women.

He could not be sure in the dark, but Jason identified six different men. Four of them had climbed into the truck's bed.

Wincing at the sound of equipment being dumped onto the ground, Jason whispered, "Any idea what they want?"

"Anything of value small enough for them to steal," Emphani replied. "And if they decide we might bring a ransom, they might let us live."

At the moment, Jason wished they really were with the venerable magazine they claimed to represent. *National Geo* would pay a ransom. Momma would make a decision based on economics. A captured operative who had failed his assignment would have scant worth.

Momma!

Germane to nothing in his present situation, the revelation came to Jason like a vision to an Old Testament prophet.

He had been had.

Really had.

The men in the Mercedes in Liechtenstein. The shot into his bedroom in Sark. The men in the Mercedes had made no overt effort to harm him, only to let him know they were there. Little chance a random shot into a windowpane would have hit him.

But Momma knew about both. She could have had spies in Liechtenstein, but Jason was quite sure he had not told her about the shooting incident. Yet she knew, knew he would immediately jump to the conclusion his presence on Sark was known to his enemies. An assignment was a way to get off the island, to go somewhere until he could decide on another base. Somewhere that served Narcom's purpose.

He didn't notice the sound of teeth grinding in chagrin.

Momma's duplicity wasn't the problem of the moment, however. The Tuaregs were shouting, motioning for him and Emphani to put hands behind their backs, no doubt to be tied up with the rope Jason could see one of them holding in the headlights. Once trussed up like a Sunday dinner chicken, there would be no chance of escape.

Where the hell were Chief and Viktor?

No matter, he realized. Two men, even armed, would stand little chance against six. There would be nothing the two could do. With resignation, Jason watched one of the Tuaregs approach with the coil of rope.

He was only a dozen or so feet away when there was a hiss like air escaping a punctured tire and the Tuareg burst into flame. It was right out of a Stephen King novel. One moment the man was there, the next instant he was a human torch, his flowing *thobe* a sheet of fire as he screamed and fell to the ground, writhing in his hellish death throws.

With the swiftness of a bat flying out of darkness, Emphani snatched the man's rifle, swung it around to bring the muzzle to bear. It would have been a futile effort; there were too many Tuaregs for the man to get them all before one got off a fatal shot.

Emphani didn't have to.

The two men closest to him simply ignited as though someone had put a torch to gasoline soaked cloth. Both jerked in a macabre dance of death as sizzling flames consumed them. The odor of burning meat filled still night air already pregnant with agonized screams.

In seconds, there were three charred forms, only remotely human, smoldering on the ground as starving flames licked away the last remnants of flesh.

It was enough for the remaining Tuaregs. Blinded by the sudden blazes, Jason could only hear terrified yells as bodies crashed through the impenetrable darkness of night in the African brush.

Like a genie out of the bottle, Andrews appeared, smoking flamethrower in hand. "Welcome to the barbecue, Artiste." He cocked his head, studying what he could see of Jason's face. "You don't look all that happy to see me. More like you're pissed off."

Jason couldn't get Momma out of his head. "Good guess. I am."

"Jesus Christ on a motorcycle, Artiste! I just saved your ass and you're pissed?"

Jason realized the absurdity. "Not at you."

"Well, what a relief that is. If there were one around, I'd guess a woman."

"How astute."

"There isn't one within miles."

"That's what pisses me off: I'm risking my ass in Mali because she tricked . . . Ah shit, guess all's fair in love and war, and she sure as hell isn't in love with those assholes with the Tesla device." Jason looked around. "Where's Viktor?"

"Is here," came the Russian's voice. "Looking through the trucks those *perhot' podzalupnaya* were driving."

Russian for "peehole dandruff," a picturesque epithet and one of the few Russian phrases Jason recognized. The others were largely swear words and the scatological or sexual sobriquets to be heard on any military base no matter the language.

"Anything useful?"

Viktor appeared in the truck's headlights. They were beginning to dim. "Is nothing but their extra clothes and food spoiled. Smells like someone *guano*, er, shit. No weapons, nothing." He bowed his head in mock sorrow. "And no, er, alcohol."

Jason was walking toward the vehicles with which the Tuaregs had blocked the road. "Let us be thankful for small favors. In the mean-time, cut off our lights before the battery runs down and give me a hand here." He lifted the hood of the first of the two Mitsubishis. "I'm pulling the distributor cap off both. The engines will never crank. If those bastards want to chase us, they'll have to do it on foot and in the dark."

45

The Toyota was coughing as though suffering terminal tuberculosis instead of terminal sand ingestion. The twin ruts that passed as the north-south highway had demonstrated why extra tires had been part of the equipment included with the little truck. Twice, jagged shale had forced the four to stop and change them by flashlight. Hours later, the sharp rock that seemed to line every foot of the road was replaced by sand—bottomless, shifting sand. Sand that made eyes sore with grit, clogged noses, and abraded throats as it bogged the truck down to the axles requiring nearly an hour to dig it out. Sand that sucked at the Toyota's wheels like water. Sand that quickly found its way into the carburetor, necessitating stopping to remove and clean the overwhelmed air filter.

Despite the ache the weight put on his wounded leg, Jason insisted on doing his share of the digging.

"I can see why most people take the boat," Andrews had grumbled after his third effort at wielding a shovel. "I'd take hippos and crocs over this any day."

Next to him, Emphani paused long enough to wipe sandy sweat from his forehead with the back of his hand. "The *pinasse* was, how do you say, never a *bateau mouche* anyway."

"Say what?"

"C'mon, guys," Jason had intervened. "We can stay here all night gabbing like a woman's bridge club, or we can get this job done and go home."

Daylight made visible the change in terrain the four could only guess at in the dark. The lush foliage of the Niger River valley now looked more like Death Valley. Scrubby trees, bushes really, sustained an existence distant from one another. This might have been south of the Sahara, but it certainly looked like the great desert. Instead of the animals of the day before, lizards scurried for protection both from the merciless sun and the intruders in the Toyota. The only other living creatures were occasional herds of sheep or goats, their shepherds eyeing the men in the truck with undisguised suspicion.

Viktor watched a small group of these animals from the open bed as the truck stood still, waiting for them to amble across the road.

"Sheep or goat. Sound the same, look the same, smell the same. How do you know . . . the . . . er . . . different?"

Andrews was carefully measuring out a drink from one of the five-liter jugs of water. "In this climate, sheep have no wool. They look like goats." He pointed to the animals as they moved away. "But at this angle, you can see the critters have their tails up. Goats. Sheep have tails down."

Viktor nodded slowly, absorbing this bit of bucolic wisdom. "Tail up, goat. Tail down, sheep."

So it had gone, monotonous hour after monotonous hour. As shadows awakened and began to stretch, traffic on the road increased: Camels, donkeys, and Japanese trucks, their paint scabrous from sand blasting. The air was not noticeably cooler; but the road, still no more than a trace, firmer. Cresting a slight rise, the yellow mud-brick walls of the city of Timbuktu had come into view, shimmering in the near-desert heat as though viewed through water.

It would have made an impressive painting. Though even if Jason had brought his supplies, there would be scant time or opportunity for artistic endeavors. Even so, Jason was thinking of how to render the chiaroscuro of afternoon shadows on mud brick.

Jason let go of the steering wheel long enough to stretch as the truck stuttered through low city gates. "This city has been here since the 1300s," he announced.

Then he noted Emphani, his only company in the truck's cab, was snoring gently.

So much for historical background.

The streets were narrow, lined by one- and two-story mud-brick houses, each with a window over the centered front door from which owl-eyed children stared in wonder. As he began to climb a slight rise, Jason could see roofs consisted of dirt poured over palm matting. He supposed the arrangement was not entirely waterproof; but, here adjacent to the desert, it didn't need to be.

He had been driving along the edge of a fairly steep ridge. Its conical shape suggested it might have been an ancient volcano. Something he would have to ask Maria about.

Maria.

Only a couple of brief texts since Saint Barts and no mention of her work.

Some relationship! But a normal family-type life as he had shared with Laurin was hardly possible, not until Moustaph was counting his virgins, a pursuit in which Jason intended to render every possible assistance. What would it be like, he wondered dreamily, having a real home again, a place where there was no need for motion detectors, weight sensors, and a personal arsenal? No apprehension he might have to leave on a moment's notice. A place where a knock on the door was more likely to be a neighbor dropping by unexpectedly than an assassin.

Sure, the irrepressible voice from inside said. *With a white picket fence and climbing roses around the door. Maybe even a couple of rug rats crawling around if Maria stood still long enough.*

So, what's wrong with that? Jason demanded.

Life-size vision of you holding a projectile-vomiting, screaming heir in one arm while you try to replace shitty diapers with the other. Enough domestic tranquility to have you in alcohol rehab in no time.

I had a life like that with Laurin, Jason rebutted, regretting he couldn't sound huffy in mental communications.

That was then, this is now, the voice replied with infuriating logic. *That was pre-Momma. No, old buddy, you are warrior class now, samurai, as it were. Adventure and excitement are as much a part of you as the Italian Baroque composers and acrylic land and seascapes. It's in your DNA, man. You couldn't quit if you really wanted to and you don't.*

Don't tell me what I want. Once Moustaph is dead, I . . .

Face it: There will be another Moustaph and another after that.

The potential truth of the observation had haunted the corners of Jason's mind from time to time: becoming an assassin's version of Hendrik van der Decken, captain of the ship *Flying Dutchman,* of legend and Wagnerian fame, doomed not to sail the Cape of Good Hope for eternity, but to pursue Islamic terrorists in perpetuity, never to have a life of domesticity.

No! Once Moustaph is done . . .

"Jason, who are you talking to?" Emphani had waked up.

Jason hadn't realized he had become so agitated he was speaking out loud. He thought he heard a distant snicker.

The Hotel la Colombe was an unremarkable two-story building surrounded by a low hedge that was fighting a losing battle with the sand and heat. The facade presented the traditional Islamic architecture of curved windows on the second floor. The air-conditioning was a pleasant surprise as the four men's steps echoed from the stone floor. The desk clerk in Western jacket and tie treated them to a dazzling smile.

"You are the gentlemen from the magazine?" he asked in Oxfordian English. "Perhaps you need assistance with your luggage?"

"We can handle most of it," Jason replied, holding up a camera on a tripod.

"Very well." The clerk studied the register in front of him. "I note you have four rooms on the southern, or outside, wall of the hotel. Whoever made your reservations did not understand the more desirable accommodations are on the other side, those that overlook the pool and patio. That side also receives much less sunlight and is therefore cooler and quieter than those on the street."

"Thanks," Jason said, "but we'll endure the heat and noise. We want the view of the town. That's what *National Geographic* sent us here for."

What Jason did not say was that southern exposure gave them an unobstructed view downward across the two courtyards of the Sankore Mosque and the pyramidal minaret on the structure's southern edge.

"Very well, sir. I will ask the dining room to remain open."

The prospect of a meal of something other MREs, the military's bags of self-heating cuisine, brought smiles to four sand-encrusted, unshaven faces.

Thirty minutes later, Jason, Andrews, and Emphani, bathed, in clean clothes, and smelling of herbal soap, were making their way down the stairs.

"The Russian," Emphani asked, "where is he?"

"If the hotel has a bar, that would be the first place I'd look," Andrews offered.

"*If* is the operative word," Jason observed. "Mali being a Moslem country, booze might not be available."

Viktor appeared at the foot of the stairs, swaying slightly and holding aloft an earthenware cup. "*Zdorovie!*"

"I'll not ruin my health drinking to yours," Andrews said good-naturedly.

"Perhaps there is wine wherever you got what may be in that cup?" Emphani asked hopefully. "Man was not made to drink only water."

"You guzzled your share," Jason reminded him.

"Man drinks water for thirst, wine for pleasure."

Viktor gave him a pat on the back and pointed to a small room where three or four tables were grouped in front of bottles on mostly empty shelves. "Is bar! If wine is as bad as vodka, is shit. Shit vodka better than no vodka."

"Old Russian proverb, no doubt," Jason noted dryly.

"First toast always to health," Viktor said with a grin. "Second to family. In army, third to fallen comrades. Fourth is to hope never to be in third toast."

Jason joined in the levity. "As you Russians say, 'Only a problem drinker drinks without a toast.'"

"Is true!" Viktor beamed before draping an arm around Emphani's shoulder. "Come, drink many toasts!"

After several vodkas for Viktor, one glass of wine for Emphani, who swore it had no relationship to the French vineyard on the bottle's label, and two room-temperature Budweisers for Andrews and Jason, which miraculously tasted like the Anheuser-Busch product, Jason put his empty bottle on the table.

"Gentlemen, dinner is waiting."

"Roast goat or sheep, take your choice," Andrews mumbled.

The sole entrée was *alabadjia,* according to the desk clerk, now maître d'. Goat, cooked separate from its juices, pounded tender, seasoned with ghee, the local butter, and then marinated with the juices served over rice. Both tasty and filling.

Jason declined the small cup of viscous after-dinner coffee that followed a meal in this part of the world, standing. "Not for me. Long day tomorrow, guys, deciding whether the town is worth a full shoot. I'm headed to bed."

A murmur of agreement went around the table until it reached Viktor who held up a hand, thumb, and forefinger inches apart. "A small, what you say . . . hat on the night?"

Jason stood. "Nightcap."

Viktor was the only person he knew who could literally drink himself sober. But then, he knew few, if any, other Russians. Viktor would be fine in the in the morning while any normal person would suffer the mother of all hangovers.

Upstairs, Jason paused outside his door to check the telltale, the hair he had pasted with saliva between door and jam. It was gone. Someone had opened the door.

Jason checked the hallway. Empty other than the shadows of low-wattage bulbs. Ear to the door, he heard nothing as he drew the killing knife. One breath, two.

He slammed the door open with a crash loud enough to at least momentarily distract the intruder.

Had there been one.

The room was quite empty, as was the small bath. In the simply furnished room, there was nowhere else to hide.

Jason turned slowly, befuddled, until he noted the sheets of the bunk-type bed had been neatly folded over. He had not expected maid service.

He sighed as he pulled his shirt over his head. Reaching into a pants pocket, he retrieved his iPhone and entered Maria's number. What time was it in Indonesia?

" 'Lo?" a sleepy voice answered. "Jason? Do you know it's five a.m. here? Where are you?"

"Timbuktu."

The voice came fully awake. "Timbuk . . . Oh, ha, ha, very funny. You wake me up in the middle of the night and don't want to tell me where you are." Pause. The tone became tender. "But it's good to hear from you."

"Mine isn't the only iPhone that makes outgoing calls, y'know."

"Don't be cross." Maria was saying. "I text you when I can. Remember, Indonesia doesn't exactly have complete satellite coverage."

Jason was grimacing at his reflection in the small mirror over the sink. The small vanity probably saved his life.

The mirror showed something behind Jason move. At least, he thought so. He listened to Maria's voice but his attention was on . . . what?

Nothing.

His imagination?

Unlikely. Delta Force trainees didn't imagine things.

"Jason, are you listening to me? Jason?"

There it was, something moved under the bed covers. Not much but just enough to be perceptible. Jason held his breath, listening, watching.

"Jason, you called me, remember? Now say something or I'm hanging up!"

"Good night, Maria. Love you, but I gotta go."

There it was again: the slightest of movement. Did he really hear the rustle of starched sheets?

46

Hangar 19
Andrews Air Force Base
Prince George's County, Maryland
At the Same Time

The huge hangar that was home to the two very special 747s was a scene of orderly activity, activity Colonel Bill Hasty watched closely. When one of those babies was going to fly in two days, there were a lot of necessary preparations; and, as pilot in command, it was his job to see they were made correctly. He observed the self-contained retractable stairway and baggage loader work over and over. Their function was part of the plane's extensive equipment that assured the aircraft was never dependent on airport facilities.

Inside the huge aircraft, he began his normal inspection of the entire 4,000 square feet on three levels, starting with the cockpit. The plane had all the electronics one would expect to see in a modern commercial airliner and a quite a few that might not be so normal: an antimissile defense activator switch, which would release clouds of super-heated metallic chaff to decoy heat-seeking weapons and defeat any guidance radar; surge protectors to ensure even the electromagnetic pulse of a nuclear weapon would not interrupt communications; an in-flight refueling system to give the aircraft unlimited range; and radar-jamming electronics were only a few. Then there were the 240 miles of internal wiring that assured all forty-eight telephones on board had full air-to-ground capability as well as the ability to speak to one another.

It took nearly a half hour to work through the extensive check list, flipping toggles, pushing test buttons, and cross-verifying instruments. Satisfied, he left the cockpit, entering the president's suite: an office with a full-size conference table, fax, shredder, computers, printers, and twin television screens. One of the latter was on, a twenty-four-hour commercial news station turned to low volume. Sitting at the table watching was a black woman wearing the stripes of an Airman First Class on the sleeves of her uniform. She jumped to her feet as Hasty entered.

He motioned her back into her seat "Stay put, Rosie. All the bells and whistles working?"

"Yes, sir! Any what aren't will be, time I leave this aircraft."

He touched the bill of his cap, not quite a salute but not not one, either, as he passed through to the presidential bedroom and bath. "Carry on, then."

Not a doubt in his mind. He had inherited Rosie Carpenter along with most of the Air Force One crew. If it was electric, she could fix it, from a toaster in one of the ship's two galleys to the most sophisticated computer. He had originally been suspicious of why she had stayed with the U.S. Air Force when her talents would bring a much higher salary on the civilian market. The answer had made him ashamed of his doubts: Her husband, confined to a wheelchair by incurable multiple sclerosis, would have had a difficult time affording treatment outside the military.

Two men were in the president's bedroom suite. One, earphones looped over his head, was vacuuming the lush carpet. The other could be seen through an open door polishing the bathroom fixtures. Neither man saw Hasty and he passed through unnoticed.

Ten minutes later, he was standing amid the gleaming stainless steel of the forward galley. A steady procession of uniforms was carrying provisions to the mammoth refrigerator, the huge freezer, or the cavernous pantry. All told, the plane could carry 2,000 meals. Hasty knew the non-coms doing the work had unloaded dozens of vehicles, mostly unmarked SUVs driven by men and women in civvies who had made the purchases at random grocery stores around the DC area. That, plus the rigid security surrounding the airplane until it was in the air, would make tampering with the food supply very difficult.

"Hungry, Colonel?"

Hasty turned to a man in turtleneck and jeans. "I'd known you were going to ask, I'd skipped McDonald's on the way here."

A bright smile split the swarthy face. Placide LeBrun, the president's famous Cajun cook. The president, from Louisiana, had brought the chef of his favorite Baton Rouge restaurant with him to Washington to ensure his fare did not suffer in quality. Admittedly, the practice of noisily sucking the juice from crawfish heads, adding hot sauce to everything except dessert, and serving fried alligator tail at state dinners had caused a stir in the ever-scandal-hungry city. But when the emir of Dubai pronounced LeBrun's sassafras-laced filet gumbo (minus the andouille pork sausage) "truly fit for the mouth of the Prophet," a Cajun craze raged through the nation's capital. Formal dinners were less likely to conclude with classical string quartets or piano concertos than appearances by Zachary Richard (pronounced "Ree-chard") or Gerald Thibedeaux's Cajun bands.

"Looks like you have everything under control here," Hasty observed.

"Colonel, if you manage this airplane with the care I manage its galleys, all will be well."

Hasty gave him a pat on the shoulder. "Sounds like we're in great shape, then."

Next, the colonel passed through the aircraft's medical facility, an office that could quickly be converted into a surgery should the need arise. Sam Silverstein, the full-time Air Force One doc, was inventorying the pharmacy. Long past retirement age, Sam had somehow evaded severing ties with the service. Popular rumor was that he had been around long enough to have a bit of dirt on those now in high places in the Air Force, and had every intention of using it should that be necessary to continue to enjoy the prestige and travel associated with his job.

"Got enough pills?" Hasty asked. "Eye of newt, toe of frog?"

Silverstein turned around, adjusting frameless glasses. "Oh, hi, Colonel. Nothing quite that exotic, I fear. Just making sure we have enough motion sickness medication. One little bit of turbulence and half the press corps are flipping their lunch, which, in turn, makes the others ill."

"See what you can do, Doc."

Finally, Hasty was in the cargo hold. A separate C-17 Globemaster III had already departed with the heavy stuff—two armored GMC TopKick trucks with Cadillac-like bodies, the Suburban that followed the presidential limo with various defensive mechanisms and the rest of the presidential cavalcade. Air Force One's cargo would largely contain scrupulously inspected baggage of the crew, the attending press, and the president. Two Airmen Third Class were already stacking suitcases.

"You men be careful with the president's golf clubs," Hasty admonished.

Both men snapped to attention.

"Sir!" One of the men's eyes were centered on a spot an inch or so above the colonel's head. "The president's golf clubs, along with the rest of his gear, will be loaded last, probably not until just hours before departure."

Again the fingers touched cap brim. "Very well, then."

Hasty stood akimbo on the cement floor of the hangar, looking up at the plane he had just vacated. He had done all he could at this stage to make sure the president was delivered safely to Egypt.

The rest was in the hands of what Hasty's experience had taught him was a very capricious God.

47

Hotel la Colombe
Rue Askia Mohammed
Timbuktu, Mali

Jason watched for what seemed an eternity, but the bedclothes remained as placid as a pond with no wind. He flicked his eyes around the room, searching for the phone.

There wasn't one.

As far away from the bed as he could get, perhaps three or four feet, he stooped, reached up his pants leg, and came up with his killing knife. One step and the tip of the blade was lifting the top sheet.

What happened next took place as a blur in his memory. The sheet lifted and something struck, something long and brown and angry.

The thing had made a leap, or strike, that was long enough to have reached Jason, had it not hit at the knife's point instead. Now it was on the floor, twin needles of fangs facing Jason. Anvil-headed, dappled brown, with Satanic horns above each catlike eye, and a flicking tongue that seemed to be savoring a victim already. From long ago desert training, Jason recognized the deadly horned desert viper.

A native of the nearby Sahara, this one was unusually large at just over a couple of feet. Its venom was a witch's brew of toxins that affected everything from kidneys to heart to bowels.

And it was definitely not in a good mood.

The snake had no intent of giving ground; and if the strike from the bed was any example, Jason was within easy range even adding the length of the blade. Attempting to use the knife was going to get him too close to those fangs. Keeping his eyes on those of the serpent as though they might telegraph intent, Jason poked the sheet with the knife again as he slowly backed up to put the bed between him and the snake. The creature advanced quickly across the tiled floor, a sideways movement like the sidewinder rattlesnake of the American Southwest, a movement adapted to the loose, shifting sands of the desert.

In less than a minute, Jason was going to be out of room.

Impaling the sheet on the tip of his knife, Jason waved it in front of the viper, drawing another strike, this time at the fabric.

A second attempt achieved what Jason had hoped for: The snake's fangs were caught in the cotton threads of the sheet.

Swallowing the almost atavistic fear of snakes, Jason quickly stepped on its head, pinning it to the floor. A single stroke of the knife and the headless body wriggled furiously, leaving a thin trace of blood and slime across the tiles before it went still.

Jason carefully lifted his foot, unsure if he might still be in danger from some death spasm that could send those fangs into his foot or leg. If he ever could have used a shot or two of Viktor's vodka, it was the time.

He started for the door, to get someone up there to remove that thing before he stepped on it in the dark.

No, wait.

The viper didn't get in here on its own, and there is no point in alerting the would-be assassin it failed. Let him wonder. Mental advantage Jason.

Jason speared the head on the tip of his knife, carried it into the bathroom, and flushed it down the toilet followed by sections of the snake's body he fed into the spinning waters one at a time.

Jason placed his knife and a recently unpacked .40-caliber Glock on the bedside table before turning out the light. Armed or not, sleep was not going to come easily.

48

Hotel la Colombe
Rue Askia Mohammed
Timbuktu, Mali
6:42 a.m. Local Time
Day 9

Breakfast consisted of rice porridge floating in sorghum and *injera*, a bread made from flour, honey, and rosemary. And, of course, coffee, thick, aromatic African-bean coffee. Overhead, a fan spun lazily, doing little but rearranging the already hot, dry air in a room empty except for the four men at the same table. The one next to theirs could have been a display case at a photography store: cameras with varying attachments, tripods, strobe lights and klieg lights on stands.

The four were dressed almost identically: khaki safari jackets over V-neck T-shirts and cargo pants stuffed into military-style combat boots. Only in headwear was there a difference: One Indiana Jones–style broad-brimmed hat, a tightly woven straw Stetson, and two long-billed caps.

Jason was finishing relating the events of last night. ". . . And I'll be damned if I can figure out why they didn't try something more certain. A gunshot, perhaps. Why would they put a two-foot horned viper in my bed?"

Emphani smiled. "Perhaps because they could not find a five-foot cobra."

"You complaining, Artiste?" Andrews chimed in. "Advantage of your dying of snakebite is that the police could treat it as something other than murder. I'm sure the one in your bed wasn't the first varmint to creep in from the desert."

Jason put down the piece of bread at which he had been nibbling. "Why do I have the feeling the sudden demise of a foreign infidel would not cause a great deal of concern among the local gendarmerie?"

Viktor, astonishingly chipper in view of the volume of vodka he had consumed the previous evening, spoke for the first time. "Important thing is someone knows is not crew from magazine."

"Thanks a lot, asshole," Jason said good-naturedly.

Viktor grinned, holding up both hands. "Mistake. Is important next to you being alive."

Andrews pushed back from the table, the legs of his chair protesting against the floor's tiles. "OK, now that someone knows our business isn't glossy pictures in a magazine, what do we do?"

Do? What the hell could they do, Jason thought. Damn Momma and her duplicity that put him and his men in a place synonymous for remoteness with their cover likely blown and no way to identify their enemies.

"Don't see we have much choice," he answered. "We continue the masquerade."

"Continue?" Viktor protested. "How is possible? Our enemies know we are here."

"What would you suggest?" Jason asked patiently, all too aware Emphani and Andrews were listening with more than passing interest. "We can pack up and run, leaving the good folks who tried to kill me in our rear, free to contact their Tuareg buddies to set up an ambush if they don't get to us first. It's not like we can just go to the airport and skedaddle."

"And why not, Artiste?" Andrews wanted to know. "You sure as shit aren't planning to return the same way we came."

Jason turned to face the former Navy man. "Our extraction plans do, in fact, call for us to depart by air, although hardly by commercial service. They also call for pretty precise timing, which we can discuss tonight along with our attack plan for tomorrow. The Timbuktu airport has only two flights a week direct Paris. All the others go to Mopi or Bamako. If we succeed, I doubt anyone will be eager to wait at either place for a flight out of country. No, I believe the safest thing is to stick with the plan we have. We'll just have to be extra careful."

There was grudging agreement around the table.

"OK, Artiste, you win. So, what are our plans for today?"

Jason glanced around assuring himself he would not be overheard. "Emphani, it's too late for *Fajr*, the prayer said before sunrise . . ."

"Tell me about it," Andrews grumbled. "Surely, I wasn't the only one that screeching from the mosques woke up."

"I was already awake," Emphani replied coolly. "Saying my *Fajr*."

"Sorry. I didn't mean . . ."

A smile twitched across Emphani's lips. "Recording the muezzin's call to prayer instead of having a live person call from the minarets hasn't done a lot for the tone."

Jason looked from one to the other. "If I may, gentlemen."

When he was certain he had their attention, he began. "Emphani, you are the only one who speaks both Arabic and French . . ."

"But not Koyra Chiini." The dialect spoken along the Niger Valley and by far the most popular dialect in Timbuktu, one of over fifty in Mali.

Jason continued. "Do the best you can. French is the country's official language and you're sure to hear some Arabic if the people we think are here are here. You go to *Dhur* prayers shortly after noon at the Sankore Mosque, snoop around. Oh yeah, no point in playing with a disguise. If anyone asks, you're with the magazine's mission here because of your linguistic skill but, more important, because you are a Moslem. The mosques here are not open to us infidels. And, of course, you want to look around, maybe take some pictures if the local imam doesn't mind. Naturally, you'd be interested in the older parts of the place like the southernmost of the two minarets.

"Chief, you take in Djinguereber, the Great Mosque, on the western side of the old town. Viktor, the Sidi Yahya Mosque. Don't slink around. You are legitimate journalists, OK? Just remember, non-believers are not welcome inside, and we don't want to cause a ruckus."

The rule regarding non-believers in mosques varied according to two seemingly conflicting verses of the Koran. In Turkey, for instance, tourists are welcome during non-prayer hours as long as dressed appropriately. In most African mosques, not so.

"No one ever accused Moslems of being open-minded," Andrews grumbled.

"That is one person's view," Emphani replied tartly. "Had it not been for such mathematical devices as the invention of zero as a number, you will still be counting on fingers and toes."

A glare from Jason silenced them both.

Andrews and Viktor exchanged glances before the former asked, "Anything in particular we should be looking for? I mean, if we can't go inside . . ."

"Well, from the wreckage of the Air France plane, the angle of damage to certain parts of the aircraft, the French triangulated back to this area of Africa, give or take a hundred kilometers or so. Assuming this ray, or whatever it is, can't jump sand dunes, trees, and the like, it would have to have been launched from a relatively high point . . ."

"Only one of which in maybe fifty kilometers of here would be tower, er, minaret of one of the mosques," Viktor interrupted.

"Precisely," Jason continued. "So, what we are looking for is anything suspicious around a mosque."

Emphani cleared his throat. "But you think it is the one we can see from our windows. Why?"

"Making another assumption, that the beam or missile or whatever moves in a more or less straight line, it would have had to depart in a westerly direction. According to the guidebook I read on the plane, the southern minaret of the Sankore Mosque is the only one with an opening facing away from Mecca, westerly."

"And you, Artiste, what is going to occupy you this morning?"

Jason drained the dregs of his coffee. "I'm going to take advantage of the height on which this place is built. I can see damn near the whole town."

49

Sankore Mosque
Timbuktu, Mali
Thirty Minutes Later

Emphani stood outside a heavy wooden door set into a wall from which regular rows of timbers extended, serving as a foundation for the mud brick beneath the adobe facade. He was reminded of a porcupine. To his left, men splashed water from a trough on face, hand, and feet, a ritual ablution preparatory to entering preparatory to *Dhur*, still several hours away.

Festooned with three cameras with varying sizes of lenses, he walked the sandy street along the outside wall to an arched opening. Inside was a courtyard surrounded by arcaded galleries. It was here, he thought, the great madrassah, Islamic university, had flourished in the fourteenth century. The city had been a crossroads of trade then: salt from the Arabic north, slaves and gold from the black African south. All that remained of the epicenter of culture and learning were a pair of anemic date palms with dusty fronds and the ever-shifting sands from the desert.

From the corner of his eye, that part of the human eye that best detects movement, Emphani saw something move in the shadows of the arcade to his left. Slowly, as though simply scratching, his fingers reached to touch the Glock in the small of his back.

Two figures emerged into the near blinding sunlight, both of whom wore Bedouin clothes.

"*As-salām 'alaykum*," one said, hand over his heart. A typical Sunni greeting.

Emphani had spent enough time in North Africa for his ears to pick up a mispronunciation like an orchestra conductor a false note.

But he replied, "*Wa 'alayakum as salām*," the appropriate response.

Emphani kept a little more than two arms lengths' distance, avoiding the handshake that would customarily follow. There was no profit in having his gun hand otherwise employed should he need it. Particularly as he could see neither man had the angular facial features or the dark desert-tanned skin of a Bedouin.

"You are a Moslem brother," the one who had spoken before said.

It was not a question but Emphani answered anyway. "Yes," he said also in Arabic.

For the first time, the other man spoke. "You are a visitor in Timbuktu."

Another statement.

"Yes. I am with a crew from the American magazine *National Geographic*. Perhaps you know of it?"

The reply, more grunt than words, had equal chances of being negative or affirmative.

"You live in the United States?" the first man wanted to know.

"No. I live in France among other Moslems."

The two exchanged glances before the first one said, "I hear of great oppression of our brothers and sisters there. The women are humiliated by being prohibited the wearing of the veil."

Emphani had to bite his tongue not to smile at the thought of his daughter, Margot, being told she had to wear a veil. Either open-mouthed disbelief or, more likely, unrestrained guffaws.

"The infidel oppresses the believers," he said simply.

"But you are employed by the infidel," the second man observed.

Emphani shook his head, holding up one of the cameras slung around his neck. "I am a photographer who takes work where he can find it. I am not in a position to refuse pay from a wealthy American magazine."

The answer seemed to satisfy whatever doubts the men had. The first one nodded in appreciation of financial realities. "You are a stranger here. Perhaps you might honor us by letting us guide you through both this holy mosque and the city so that you will have identified and photographed the important places. *In shā' Allāh*."

To refuse would only arouse suspicion if these men did not already know his real mission. "*Bāraka Allāhu*," may God bless you, the traditional response to a gift or gratuitous kindness.

Like so many mosques, parts of the Sankore had been used for secular purposes. Some, like this one, included schools. Others had and did encompass hospitals, tombs, libraries, gymnasiums, and civic centers. But when entering the *masjid*, the part that, once so designated, would remain holy ground until the last day, certain rituals had to be observed by all. Emphani sat on the sand-strewn floor, removing his boots. He placed them on one of several shelves beside the sandals of his companions and perhaps a dozen more of worshipers already inside.

Emphani stepped back, his camera raised. "Perhaps you would do me and the magazine the honor of letting readers see how the faithful remove their shoes?"

Smiling, the two reenacted the sandal removal before the three proceeded through Moorish-style archways to the *musallā*, or prayer room. By far the largest chamber in the mosque, it was two stories high, apparently the maximum height for mud-brick structures without supporting wood beams. Around the walls about ten feet above the floor, Islamic calligraphy spelled out verses of the Koran in faded gilt. The religion strictly forbade portrayal of any of Allah's creations, so there was no other art. To Emphani's right, the *qibla* wall ran perpendicular to a line directly to Mecca so that those before it would be facing the holy city. Several worshipers, on knees with foreheads touching prayer rugs—or, in this impoverished section of the world, reed mats—were already attending to their immortal souls well ahead of *Dhur*.

Emphani raised a camera only to feel a hand on his arm. The second man was scowling, shaking his head. No pictures during prayer. Emphani nodded his acknowledgment.

Passing out of the *musallā*, the three came to the base of one of the mosque's two minarets. An open entrance showed steps leading upward, but only a few before an iron gate blocked access.

"I would very much like to take pictures from the top," Emphani said, noting another pair of "Bedouins" had suddenly appeared.

"I fear that is not possible," the first of his escorts said. "The minaret is old and in poor repair, unsafe. With the *adhān*, call to prayer, prerecorded, there is no need for anyone to risk going up there."

Perhaps, but Emphani noticed that the lock securing the gate was new, shiny brass. And there were footprints in the sand that coated the steps, prints the dry breeze would have obliterated in less than an hour.

50

Djinguereber, the Great Mosque
Timbuktu, Mali
Thirty Minutes Later

Lieutenant Commander James Whitefoot Andrews, USN (Ret.), noted Timbuktu ran not on horsepower but donkey power. Donkeys pulled two-wheeled carts loaded high with bags of grain, charcoal, or vegetables. Donkeys carried bulging sacks across their backs. Men rode donkeys, their sandals nearly touching the sandy streets as they urged their diminutive mounts on with thin whips cut from branches.

An occasional mud-splattered truck roared by, trailing clouds of blue smoke, its muffler little more than a memory. Noise and air pollution maybe, but the trucks did not leave something for the unwary to step in.

Young boys in what Andrews guessed were school uniforms chattered like monkeys as they dashed by for the first class of the day, each laden with a knapsack.

In the square to his right, brightly striped fabric provided shade to women in garish-colored hijabs who squatted beside clay pots of what looked like fish or hunks of meat. There was no effort at refrigeration. Was Andrews only imagining he could hear the buzz of the clouds of flies attracted to the display? Other pots contained rice and vegetables not all of which he could identify. Babies, naked and semi-naked, dozed in mothers' arms while those slightly older chased one another noisily through stalls of weavers, fruit grocers, knife sharpeners, and bakers' ovens. The sound was a babel of voices, each trying to be heard above the others as merchants haggled with customers. The smell of charcoal, fresh dung, rotting vegetation, and human sweat hung in the air like an early morning fog.

He paused a moment, unslinging a camera from his shoulder. He framed a picture. Then from a slightly different angle. His subjects were colorful and exotic, so much so he might even like to keep the images being recorded on the camera's card. If it even had a card.

He was focusing on a woman taking something out of a mud-brick oven when two figures in white blurred in the lens. Irritated, he lowered the camera. Two men in what he would describe as Bedouin dress were carefully sorting through a collection of cheap beads on strings in front of a wrinkled woman who gestured wildly extolling the virtues of her wares.

Andrews knew next to nothing about Bedouins, but he'd bet a bottle of reasonably good scotch they didn't wear beads. Pretending to ignore them, he moved about the bazar, snapping pictures in what he hoped looked like a professional manner. Wherever he moved, the two positioned themselves so he was between them, classic surveillance technique.

Seeming only interested in what he could catch in his lens, Andrews carefully noted the available alleys and doorways. He could probably give these guys the slip, but to what end? Suddenly disappearing was not something a man on a legitimate mission would do. Better to continue the charade.

Leaving the bazar, Andrews walked purposefully toward Djinguereber, the Great Mosque, whose twin minarets were already visible. Like Sankore, this structure was largely built of earth although the northern facade and one minaret had been repaired in the 1960s with limestone blocks rendered with mud, according to the Google site he had called up earlier. Also like the Sankore Mosque, Djinguereber had been built in the fourteenth century. The two, along with the Sidi Yahya Mosque, had formed the University of Sankore.

The narrow street, lined with mud and mud-brick buildings, made a perfect frame for a photograph of the building as its earthen walls were turning a rich chocolate brown in the morning's sun. His two escorts, one on either side of the street, were making no efforts to conceal their interest in him. Ineptness or threat?

Andrews reached the wall of the mosque just as the last worshipers completed their ablutions, entered one of the three courtyards, and disappeared into the building. His two uninvited companions made a show of washing face, hands, and feet, but demonstrated no immediate intent to enter the prayer service. He resigned himself to their company.

51

Colonel Wild Bill Hasty had a corner office, perhaps the only one in the building occupied by anyone below the rank of brigadier general. His was a suite of three second-story offices facing the threshold of Runway 01R, the right of two parallel runways with a compass heading of ten degrees, almost due north, where a pair of DC Air National Guard F-16s were shooting touch and goes.

The colonel was too busy collecting the data necessary for tomorrow's flight to notice. He had already made certain his Jeppesen approach plates to both Cairo International and the military field, Cairo West, and his high altitude charts were current, both those in the loose-leaf binder and their electronic duplicates fed into the aircraft's GPS electronic display system. The ones published by NOAA, the AJV-3s, were furnished free by the Air Force; but, like so many products, those by the privately published Jeppesen Sanderson Company were superior to those offered by the government. They were both more likely to be current, and certainly more detailed.

He had already called up the Global Operators Flight Information Resource website. This privately owned company was the one place all applicable SIGMETs, METARs, and NOTAMs could be found. Turbulence above 35,000 feet over the Philippines, runway repair on 07R at Moscow's Sheremetyevo International Airport, all in one place. There were none applicable to tomorrow's flight.

Now he was calculating fuel burn based on the winds aloft. He frowned. The Air Force Weather Agency's prediction varied by a good six knots from NOAA's. The Boeing 747 had a potential range of 9,600 miles with all tanks topped off, but the destination was only 5,818 miles distant.

Rarely did the aircraft take off with full tanks. The weight of the unneeded Jet-A would only slow down the plane, burning yet more fuel. But a discrepancy of merely a few knots in wind speed could necessitate extra fuel. Conversely, the old pilot's adage noted few things were more useless than fuel left in the pumps back at the base.

Hasty got up, crossing his office to where a small blackboard hung, his pre-flight to-do list. There were already two numbered items. He added: "3. Check current winds aloft."

There were some parts of pre-flight planning that were best left to the last hour before takeoff, when he would file his international flight plan. His eyes went to a small frame on his desk where two lines of poetry reminded him,

The best laid schemes o' Mice an' Men
Gang aft agley.

The eighteenth-century Scottish poet Robert Burns thought like a pilot.

52

Hotel la Colombe
Rue Askia Mohammed
Timbuktu, Mali
7:23 p.m. Local Time

Jason believed the closer the equator, the briefer the dusk and sunrise. This evening had done nothing to disabuse him of that tenet. The bloodred African sun had seemed to visibly slide down that point at which sky met earth. Darkness followed sunset by minutes, heralded by pinpoints of bright stars in the pale blue between horizon and total nightfall.

The four men sat in Jason's room, two on the bed, one on the floor, and Jason in the sole chair. Emphani was speaking.

". . . Many, perhaps a dozen, men around the mosque in Bedouin dress though not Bedouins. The minaret with the western opening is closed off because it is said to be unsafe. But I saw tracks in the sand. Someone had been there within an hour."

"Guess those were the same Bedouins who kept me company," Andrews drawled from the bed. "Persistent as bedbugs. Didn't make a hostile move but didn't let me out of sight, either."

"Same," Viktor said. "Men in robes watch but do nothing."

"Sounds like we were right, it is the Sankore Mosque," Jason said.

"Now what?" Andrews asked.

"We do a little nighttime recon, maybe right after *Isha*, the last prayer of the day. That would be when, Emphani?"

"The last prayer before bed. Last night, the call to prayer was around nine p.m."

"OK, guys," Jason said. "Here's the plan."

53

Sankore Mosque
Timbuktu, Mali
At the Same Time

The low light of a single low-wattage bulb made Abu Bakr ibn Ahmad Bian squint through thick spectacles at a Jeppesen high altitude chart of the North Atlantic, the same chart Colonel Hasty had been studying earlier in the day. Next to it, a conventional map of much the same area. A red line stretched northwest from Timbuktu to a point about 300 miles off the Moroccan coast. In the background, the mosque's generator chugged softly.

Almost engulfed in a sea of shadows, Mahomet Moustaph watched as Abu Bakr used a compass to measure the distance for the third time. "They will die over water?"

The younger man nodded.

"*In shā' Allāh*. It is better that the infidel devils never find their president to bury just as they did with the martyred Bin Laden, peace be upon his soul."

Moustaph stepped closer to inspect the machine that occupied most of the small room as if he had never seen it before. "I am curious. How are you certain you will strike the infidel's aircraft from such a distance?"

"That was a problem when we obtained the first device. If we missed the target, the particles continued until they either ran out of energy and fell to the ground or the curvature of the earth brought them smashing into some part of the earth's surface, such as happened to a forest in Siberia when the machine's inventor overshot the North Pole."

"And now?"

Abu Bakr pointed to a laptop computer on the floor, wires disappearing into the larger machine. "GPS. I simply set the coordinates; and, Allah willing, the particles strike the target."

Moustaph was still not convinced. "That requires some precision, to make particles and target meet."

The other man nodded his agreement, holding up the high altitude chart. "It is made easier by the American devils themselves. The aircraft will be out of radio contact for several hours. Its first communication will be when it reaches this point." He placed a finger on the map.

Moustaph glowered at the Roman letters. "What does the English say?"

" 'Hamid.' It is what is called an intersection like the meeting of two streets, except here two vectors meet."

"Vectors?"

"Predetermined routes like a highway. With GPS, the concept of set vectors is all but obsolete, but intersections are useful in ascertaining an aircraft's position to a ground controller. For instance, the president's plane will become visible to civil ground radar just before Hamid, and it will so identify itself and give its altitude to Gibraltar Center on frequency 122.45, a broadcast we will monitor. One of our brothers has hacked the center's radar so we, too, have all the information we need as to speed, altitude, and heading. We will put that data into the computer, which will feed them to the machine, which will fire a burst of particles every fifteen seconds for a minute. May it please Allah, one or more of the bursts will rain down on the infidel aircraft just as it did the Air France plane with the same result."

Moustaph toyed uneasily with his beard, a man who was naturally suspicious of anyone with such scientific knowledge. "If these particles of yours may be directed with such accuracy over such distances, why not rain them down on Washington or New York?"

Abu Bakr shrugged. "It is not my decision, but I would speculate once the particles reach the altitudes necessary for such targets, they and their source would be apparent on military radar. In fact, once the American president's plane is struck, it may be possible to trace the direction of the particles back to here."

The thought of the death and destruction that could be wreaked on America gave almost sexual pleasure to Moustaph. The threat of retaliation against an obscure city such as Timbuktu was hardly a deterrent. He would not be here when the American drones came on silent wings to unleash their deadly missiles without warning. His experience and importance to the movement necessitated postponing blessed martyrdom. Only the young, inexperienced, and otherwise useless would voluntarily taste an early paradise.

His thoughts were interrupted by the sudden awareness Abu Bakr had asked a question.

"The infidel Peters and his band of devils are here in Timbuktu. You have taken precautions to make certain . . . ?"

Moustaph smiled though there was no humor in it. "May Allah will it, he will foolishly attack tonight or tomorrow morning. We are prepared for him."

54

Outside the Sankore Mosque
Timbuktu, Mali
At the Same Time

Men and women exited different doors shortly after *Isha* ended, the small crowd disbursing into streets illuminated only by such light as leaked around edges of closed doors and shuttered windows. In the dark, the four men in loose-fitting *thiyaab* could have easily been mistaken for Bedouins. The departure of worshipers lasted long enough for each to slip one by one into the mosque's main courtyard.

Wordlessly, Jason motioned toward two figures, also in Bedouin attire, standing beside the entrance to the minaret. Even in the near total absence of light, it was clear each held something that gave an occasional reflection. Jason had no doubt they were armed.

Stepping back into the deepest shadows given by the wall, Jason removed a pair of night-vision goggles from the billowing sleeve of his *thobe*. A detailed scan revealed only a pair of gray-bearded old men in the arm waving, head wagging, body language punctuating conversation common in this part of the world. Other than them, his crew and the two guards at the door, the courtyard was deserted.

He gave a low whistle he hoped would blend with the ceaseless breeze's whisper. No such luck. The two at the door turned, searching as they raised what were now unmistakably rifles, most likely the ubiquitous AK-47. At the same time, Emphani and Viktor glided silently across the sand toward them. The guards turned back just in time to detect movement. One had his weapon raised just as a blur of silver streaked the night like a comet. There was the sound of steel meeting flesh, a grunt and one of the two was on the ground. The second almost got off a shot before there was a single coughing sound, and he joined his companion.

At a run, Jason crossed the distance to the entrance where Emphani and Viktor were dragging two limp bodies out of sight. Even in his hurry, Jason noticed the neat round spot in the second guard's forehead. Viktor's skill with a pistol had not diminished since that frigid night in a Washington, DC, strip mall.

He was aware of Andrews next to him as the former Navy man applied a pair of man-size bolt cutters to the chain securing the iron gate on the stairs. Behind them, the other two men were furiously stripping the dead of items that might perfect their own disguises.

The chain made a dull thump as it hit the sandy floor. Andrews whispered, "This place was patrolled regularly today?"

"I watched from the hotel," Jason responded. "Timed it as every five to six minutes a couple of guys in Bedouin dress walked by this minaret. Far too regular to be coincidence, and I doubt there are that many Bedouins in town anyway. I guess at night they figured no one would notice if they posted guards."

"You watched all day?" Andrews wanted to know.

"From the time you guys left the hotel. I did take a piss break or two. Listened to Albinoni on my iPod and watched this mosque."

"Albinoni who?" Viktor asked.

"The sixteenth-century Italian Baroque composer who wrote the Adagio in G Minor."

"*Merci* for that *friandise*, tidbit," Emphani said. "My life will be complete now."

Humor and friendly sarcasm had relieved many tense moments in Jason's career. Warriors were frequently their most witty when facing death. Jason knew it was a healthy relief to the tension that naturally built before the shooting starts.

"Five to six minutes, huh?" Andrews returned to the task at hand. "They might not continue roving patrols since they have men posted. Still, no time to waste."

Andrews was already quickly and silently making his way up the stairs.

Jason's last view of the outside was of Emphani and Viktor taking up the position of the fallen men. Ahead, inside the minaret, was a tower of stygian darkness. Glock in one hand, Jason used the other to feel his way along the wall up a spiral. Relevant to nothing, he noted the turns were clockwise going up. Coincidence or was the minaret designed like midlevel fortresses so that a climbing attacker's right, the side carrying a weapon, would be hindered?

"Jesus Christ on a camel!" Andrews whispered angrily. "There's a fucking door here. No light coming under it, though."

Jason produced a penlight from his sleeve, its laser-like beam painting a steel door and its deadbolt lock. "Obviously not part of the original structure," he observed.

"Brilliant, Artiste! Don't suppose you brought along an acetylene torch?"

Jason shouldered his way next to Andrews. The stairs' builders had not planned on two adult men standing side by side. "Got something better, a lot quicker."

Again Jason went to his thobe's sleeves, groping until he found a small metal cylinder, a Brockhage battery-powered electric lock pick, available to anyone with 150 bucks plus postage, no questions asked.

Andrews watched for the few minutes before the spinning needle tumbled enough pins and the lock clicked open. He pointed. "You wouldn't have a decent bottle of scotch in there, would you?

"Huh?"

"Your sleeves. You seem to have everything else we need there."

Jason ignored the observation. "Cover me."

Glock in hand, he pushed open the door, hit the floor in a body roll and slammed his leg into something hard enough to blur his vision with blotches of color.

"Shit!" he cursed through teeth clinched as pain shot the length of the still-healing scar. He soon forgot it.

He had lunged into a device that left very little space in a room he estimated as no more than ten by fifteen feet. The machine was encased in roughly elliptical metal housing from which a long protuberance ended in what looked like a giant fire hose nozzle. A sweep of the narrow beam of his penlight revealed a battery of dials above a row of switches and a pair of hand clasps similar to those on a heavy machine gun except there was no visible trigger mechanism. Taking hold, Jason was surprised at how easily the bulky machine could be maneuvered by the grips alone. There must be a swivel beneath the floor.

Andrews was rubbernecking. "I'd say we found what we were looking for."

"Either that or the world's largest smoothie machine."

"Let's get the job done and get out of—"

Jason's iPod vibrated.

He held up a hand for silence as he put it to his ear. "Go!"

He listened for an instant, then said, "Get your asses out of there now! No, don't wait for me and the Chief. Wait at the hotel for thirty minutes, then get the hell out of Dodge if we haven't shown by then."

Jason shoved the device back into his sleeve. "At least eight bad guys headed this way."

Andrews shook his head. "Considering there's only one way in or out of here, that sucks. My momma always told me to avoid fast women, slow horses, and places with only one way out."

Jason was looking for an escape route. He saw none. "You might have mentioned that a little sooner."

55

Andrews Air Force Base
Prince George's County, Maryland
At the Same Time

Colonel William Hasty always spent the night before a presidential flight at the bachelor officers' quarters on base. The Boss liked to get an early start, like, say, five a.m., which meant, leaving from home, Hasty would wake his wife, Eugenia, in the wee hours. He would also disturb Tiny Tim, the 200-pound Newfoundland who howled most piteously whenever Hasty left the house with a suitcase, which would, in turn, wake little Jeannie, his granddaughter, staying with them during the last three months of her daddy's deployment in Afghanistan so Mommy could finish her MBA course at the University of Maryland.

Besides, he could sleep a little longer on base without the drive.

Of course, it wasn't technically night yet, and he hadn't had time to check into the BOQ, but there was still enough to keep him busy and still allow a few hours' sack time before takeoff for the approximately ten-and-a-half-hour flight.

He got up from the desk in his office, went out into the hall and into the adjacent office. A black man with the brass oak leaves of a major on the epaulets of his uniform was hunched over a desk running numbers on a calculator.

Jim Patterson.

Major was a relatively junior rank for the copilot of Air Force One, particularly the service's youngest major. Patterson had been promoted with unusual speed. But then, he was an unusually talented pilot.

Eighteen months ago, he had been a captain, transporting combat support material from Ramstein Air Base. It had been a cold March night, the rural Rheinland-Pfalz district in Germany shimmering white with snow and more forecast. The Lockheed Martin C-130J Super Hercules had a load of ninety-four paratroopers prepared for a night training exercise.

Clumsy on the runway, the aircraft climbed into the ragged sky with grace, its four turbo prop engines at full throttle as it was swallowed by low clouds. The problems started when the pilot, Patterson, eased back the throttles to climb power.

As is often the case in aviation, things happened all at once: The stall warning horn beeped frantically, the plane yawed violently to the left, and a red light was blinking from somewhere in the cluster of engine instruments.

"Sir, we've lost the number-two engine," the flight engineer's panicked voice would later be heard on the cockpit voice recorder.

Patterson lowered the nose of the climbing aircraft to regain airspeed, postponing, if not ending, the possibility of a stall. He quickly feathered the prop on the dead engine to present minimum resistance to the air. What happened next was best described by replaying the tape:

(Loud blast of stall warning)

Copilot: Captain, now the number one has quit!

Patterson (with the calmness of a man discussing his entrée with a waiter in a restaurant): I can see that from the panel. Wonder what the odds of that happening are?

Flight engineer: I don't know, but with the two left engines out, this plane isn't going to climb and we're below MOCA (minimum obstacle clearance altitude).

Patterson (to copilot): Lieutenant, put the emergency code on the transponder and tell Ramstein departure we'll be making a forced landing. Flight engineer, give me a GPS position.

Flight engineer (voice wavering): Sir, shouldn't we try to return to base?

Patterson: We have a line of hills to our right, if I recall, and I'm sure not going to put us in a graveyard spiral by turning into two dead engines.

Flight engineer: Captain, we're two and a half kilometers from the fence, flat farmland, but by the time you get down, we'll be less than a thousand from some woods. We'll hit the trees.

Patterson: This was built as a STOL aircraft. I'll get her stopped before then.

Flight engineer: Sir, the book says you'll need at least 3,000 feet to stop.

Patterson (annoyed): Lieutenant, I am flying this airplane, not some fucking book. Clear?

(Unintelligible voice, presumably copilot talking to Ramstein departure)

Copilot: Sir, departure orders you to attempt to return to base.

Patterson: Tell them to fly their fucking radar scopes. I'll fly this airplane. Now, give me ten degrees of flaps and tell those grunts in the cargo bay to tighten up their seat belts.

Captain Patterson made a gear-down landing, coming to a stop not fifty feet from a grove of very large oak trees. The only damage was large trenches in the wet ground of a potato field. The only injuries were the badly lacerated face and the broken ankle of two paratroopers who didn't buckle up quickly enough. The other ninety-two received only a bad scare. Patterson's skill and judgment had saved their lives, as well as those of his crew.

The ensuing inquiry found that one of the switches used to change fuel tanks after takeoff had jammed between tanks, starving both left engines. Although the problem could have been discovered in flight, the plane's low altitude and certain collision with ground obstacles did not leave time to do a thorough checklist of possible culprits. The ultimate result of the hearing was the red bar of the Legion of Merit Patterson wore among other decorative ribbons above his left breast pocket.

Patterson was definitely the man Hasty wanted in the right seat of any plane he flew.

Patterson looked up from his calculator, started to rise. Hasty waved him back into his seat.

"Colonel?"

"Weight and balance calculations?" Hasty asked.

Patterson nodded. "Almost everything except passengers and the president's personal baggage is aboard—food, fuel, oil, press's luggage, et cetera."

The aircraft must be loaded not just according to weight, but where that weight is placed so that the plane is balanced. A pound at the rear of the plane is given more significance than, say, the same pound at the center of gravity, usually right over the main wing spar. An improperly loaded ship will not handle properly and could become dangerous in turbulence.

"Be sure the president's golf clubs come off first."

Last year, the clubs had been misplaced. America's chief executive had played Scotland's St Andrews with borrowed equipment.

"I wasn't aware golf was on the agenda for this trip."

"It isn't but if the opportunity arises . . ."

Becoming serious, Hasty held up some papers in his hand. "When you get it all inside the envelope, take a look at this. I got a discrepancy in the fuel burn depending on whose winds-aloft forecast I use."

"Different winds, different air, and ground speed."

Hasty dropped the papers on Patterson's desk. "I'd take it as a favor if you'd take a crack at it."

Major Patterson suppressed a smile. He knew the colonel redid every calculation every crew member did. The man was a perfectionist. His job demanded it.

56

Sankore Mosque
Timbuktu, Mali

There was the sound of feet on the staircase. Jason turned the door's dead bolt.

"Swell," Andrews observed dryly. "They can't get in but we can't get out. Stalemate."

Jason went to the window and peered out.

"Thirty or forty feet down," Andrews said. "If you're lucky, a broken leg is all you'll get. At least until those assholes outside that door find you."

"You always this optimistic, or just having a bad day?"

His answer was the click of the knob turning, followed by beating on the door.

"How long you suppose until they get whoever has the key?" Andrews asked. "Any chance you can turn that machine around and blast them?"

Jason shook his head. "I don't think the power source is in this room. Besides, if this thing can bring down an airliner, I don't want to be that close to its beam or whatever when it strikes something."

Voices from the other side of the door were audible. Jason caught a few words his limited Arabic vocabulary allowed him to understand.

"At least they're not trying to break the door down," Andrews noted.

"No. They've probably sent for the man with the key."

"Now who's the optimist?"

Jason holstered his Glock and went to the window again. He stuck his head out. "I don't see anyone down there. They must all be in the stairwell."

"So? It's still too far to jump."

"Who said anything about jumping? The reason this minaret could be built higher than a couple of stories is the wooden beams sticking out of the side. C'mon."

The beams, though massive, were virtually invisible at night. Spaced in rows about ten vertical feet apart, they jutted about half that distance from the sides of the minaret. Jason recalled the rows being regularly spaced so that one telephone pole–size piece of wood was exactly above the one below except for the ones on the end of each row, which diminished in number as the pyramid-shape grew increasingly narrow as it rose.

Dangling by his arms from the sill of the open window, Jason's feet hung in space as they searched for traction. This wasn't going to be quite as simple as he had hoped. Reluctantly, he loosened his grip, holding on only with his fingers. The extra inch or so helped. The tips of his toes touched a solid surface but he couldn't stand on it flat-footed. He was going to have to chance it. He took a deep breath and let go.

He found footing on the wood but he was losing his balance. He tried to steady himself using his arms like a tightrope walker but to no avail. He fell and for one terrifying moment was certain he would plunge to the ground below. Instead, one hand grabbed the beam. In seconds, he was chinning himself up and was sitting astride it.

Now what? He certainly wasn't going to try free falling again in hopes he might be lucky enough to grab another of the wooden poles. Careful of his balance, he took off his belt. He looped it around the beam, holding both ends.

"Artiste!" A hoarse whisper from above. "How the hell do you get from one of these beams to the next without falling?"

"Good question. Hope to have an answer for you in a moment," Jason replied and swung into the void.

For an instant that seemed an eternity, he swung through the darkness before his right leg smashed into the beam below with an impact so painful he feared he might have broken a bone. Belt in one hand, he used the other arm to hold on to the wood until he could place the belt in his teeth and then use both arms to pull himself onto the protruding beam.

Andrews had obviously heard him. "What happened?"

"Use your belt to swing down to each beam."

Minutes later, both men were on the ground, concealed in the shadows.

"Think it's safe to head for the hotel?" Andrews asked.

"If we're going to move at all, I'd suggest doing it before they find we aren't still in the minaret."

The two men set out, resisting the temptation to run, thereby attracting the attention of whoever might be in the deserted streets.

Andrews gave a look over his shoulder although someone could have been an arm's length away and not be seen in the darkness. "They must know where we're staying. You suppose they plan to attack us there?"

"If they were going to do that, they already would have. I think they may be afraid of attracting attention to the fact Al Qaeda, or its North African affiliate, the Islamic Maghreb, is operating in Mali. They don't want a fuss until they are finished—or nearly finished—with their business here."

"Emphani spoke with some of them while he was at the mosque this morning. From the accent, he's pretty sure they aren't from anywhere in North Africa. His guess is Afghanistan."

"Al Qaeda on the half shell."

"Hell, Artiste," Andrews said, "we knew that coming in."

Viktor and Emphani met them at the door of the hotel.

Jason took in the small lobby. "Where are your bags? I thought I gave a direct order to hit the trail if the Chief and I weren't back in half an hour."

Emphani smiled holding up his wrist so Jason could see his watch. "Five, no, six minutes remain."

From the looks the African and Russian exchanged, it was obvious they had had no intent of deserting their comrades, orders or not. As a former officer, Jason appreciated loyalty, but not at the expense of disobeying orders. An overabundance of allegiance to one's fellows contrary to orders had gotten more than one man killed. On the other hand, he gained nothing from chewing out Viktor and Emphani.

"OK, I've got things to do for tomorrow and so do you, starting with checking your equipment. Plus, there's a change in our strategy."

Although the four deemed a direct attack in the hotel was unlikely, they moved their equipment and weapons into Jason's room, the one with the best view of the town, in general, and of the mosque, in particular. Like the veterans they all were, three were disassembling and cleaning a variety of firearms for the fourth or fifth time since arriving in Mali.

Jason was assembling the .50-caliber Barret M82A1 sniper rifle. It was not an attractive gun. Matte gray, its muzzle rested on a bipod while its unique recoil absorption system and side vent gave it a bulk uncommon to rifles. Instead of a stock, its rear end was no more than a loop of metal behind the pistol grip and trigger.

"What is kill range?" Viktor wanted to know as he walked around the weapon.

Jason was carefully attaching the Leupold Mark 4, a stubby but efficient scope, one of only two that could absorb the abuse delivered by such a large bore rifle. "It's been used effectively at three thousand meters, one-point-one miles."

"Originally used as an anti-matériel weapon, if I recall," Andrews chimed in. "In fact, there's a selection of ammo."

Jason placed two of the bulky ten-shot magazines beside the gun. "That's why I brought extra clips."

Emphani stuffed a fist into his yawning mouth as he stretched out on the floor beside the bed. "A long day. I sleep now."

Jason shook his head. "Not until we go over the new plan for tomorrow."

57

The 747 had become Air Force One five hours earlier, once the president stepped aboard. A breakfast of eggs Sardou, sausage bread, and grits had been served to all, the latter drawing the usual disparaging comments from the would-be elite press corps from the northern and West Coast media and retorts from those based in the Southeast. The chicory-laced coffee had been shipped to the White House directly from Baton Rouge, and was a favorite among those who liked their morning beverage to have the viscosity of used motor oil.

Many of the newsies had dozed off; the president's staff didn't dare. All too frequently, one or more might be summoned from their aft quarters to the office just behind the presidential suite. Woe betide the person who appeared with red-rimmed eyes and face puffy from sleep rather than crammed with every bit of information relative to his or her duties during the trip at hand.

In the cockpit, Colonel Wild Bill Hasty undid his seat harness, stood, and stretched. He put his hand on the copilot's shoulder. "Major, I'm going aft for a few minutes. Take a leak, shake hands with the passengers."

The latter practice reflected that of a time when air travel was both pleasant and gracious, passengers treated much like honored guests, a time as far distant as twenty-five-cents-a-gallon gasoline and civility in politics.

Major Patterson looked up. "OK, Colonel. I've got the ship."

Hasty stopped at the cockpit door, looking at the screen in front of a blonde woman whose otherwise curly hair was tethered in a tight bun, the flight engineer with twin bars on each shoulder. "Captain, how far out are we from radio contact with Gibraltar Center?"

She didn't look up. "That would be Hamid intersection, sir. I'd estimate forty-six minutes."

58

Sankore Mosque
Timbuktu, Mali
At the Same Time

Only a sharp eye could have detected any lightening of the dark in the east. The brightness of Venus, the morning star, alone announced the approach of dawn. Already, a few worshipers, mostly elderly, had gathered in the mosque's courtyard, robes and shawls drawn tight against the early-morning chill. They filed into the courtyard and lined up at the fountain-fed trough of water for *wudu*, the ritual ablutions required before prayer.

It would be almost an hour before the first of the five daily prayers, *Fajr*, the predawn worship service, began. Only a flickering gas lamp illuminated the protocol of the righteous. First, plunging the hands into the trough three times, being certain water ran between the fingers. Next, water applied three times to the mouth, sniffed into the nose, and then rubbed on face, arms, and feet as the worshiper recited the Arabic for "I witness that none should be worshipped except Allah and that Mohammed is his slave and messenger."

Once so cleansed, men and women used separate entrances, the

latter clad so that only face and hands showed from garments intentionally bulky enough to make the shape of the body indistinguishable.
Among the last to enter the courtyard were two men with the *cheche*,
the indigo blue veil worn by Tuareg men. Had anyone noticed, they
would have found it strange neither did more than mimic the rites of
purification even though they stood beside the trough. Stranger yet,
they made no effort to enter the mosque, edging toward the doorway
to one of the minarets where half a dozen men in Bedouin dress also
showed no inclination to join the worshipers inside. It would have
been obvious to the keen observer that something unusual was taking
place, something that had little to do with the religious service inside.

Six football fields away and up a steep slope, the 50-caliber Barrett's
bipod rested on a table, its muzzle only inches from the hotel room's
open window. But for the moment, the rifle was ignored. Jason was holding a Speedtech SM-28, a calculating device about the size and shape of
a photographer's light meter, but serving a far different purpose.

A 9-millimeter pistol shot at fifteen to twenty feet, a .30-30-round
from a hunter's rifle at a deer fifty yards away, if properly aimed, were
likely to find the mark. A shot from nearly half a mile's distance with
a projectile varying from 440 to 700 grains was another matter. Wind
velocity, for example, could push a bullet right or left of the target.
A hundredth of an inch deviation every hundred feet would make
the difference between a hit or miss at the yardage from which Jason
would be shooting. Friction with the air would slow down a bullet sig-
nificantly over long distances, heavy or humid air more so than lighter,
dry air. Distance, weight, temperature, relative humidity all needed
to be ascertained and figured into the equation. Add the fact that no
sound suppressor system yet invented would dampen the crack of a
high-powered rifle bullet shattering the sound barrier and the conclusion would be that the first shot was most probably the most effective.
No sane target would stand still awaiting the second.

The next ten shots in the clip would likely be for matériel, not personnel.

His calculations complete, Jason used a pair of night-vision binoc-
ulars to scan the mosque's courtyard. He could easily see Emphani and
the Chief and was relieved no one seemed to be paying them particu-

lar attention, not even the six Bedouin-dressed men none-too-subtly guarding the entrance to the minaret. They seemed more interested in cupping hands around a lighted match to ignite the single cigarette they shared like an Indian peace pipe.

And why not? Earlier that morning, they had departed the hotel, uniformed similar to the other home-bound members of the establishment's night crew. An observer would have seen nothing abnormal. At least, that was the plan—an apparently successful one if the inattention of the men at the minaret's door was any indication.

Reaching into a pocket of his cargo pants, he pressed the button on a miniature transmitter. "Chief, you got the guys in Bedouin costume?"

A voice made metallic by the tiny electronics but still recognizable as Andrews replied through the set wrapped in his turban-like headgear, "Got 'em, Artiste. Any word from the Roosian?"

"Not yet. But he's not supposed to move for another"—Jason consulted his watch—"twelve and a half minutes."

"Let's hope he gets his job done. We're royally fucked if he doesn't."

"Any reason to think he won't?"

"Depends on whether he found another bottle of that South African vodka."

"Black Horse?"

"Yeah," Andrews agreed, "the shit tastes like it came out of a horse, all right."

Jason's experience had been the no amount of vodka seemed to diminish Viktor's capability, but it didn't hurt to be sure. "Kremlin, you online?" Jason asked, using Viktor's code name.

No answer.

"Kremlin . . ."

There was nothing but a whisper of static.

59

Aboard Air Force One
Forty-Two Minutes Later

"Colonel," the blonde flight engineer said, "time to switch tanks."

At cruise, the 747 burned a gallon of fuel every second. With six separate tanks in the wings, one in the body of the aircraft and an auxiliary in the tail's horizontal stabilizer, allowing a disparity in the amount of jet fuel in any one tank would cause an imbalance of weight, hence the necessity of periodically alternating between the corresponding numbered tanks in left and right wings. The fuselage tank was used mainly for takeoffs and landings, the one in the tail should an additional 350 miles need to be added to the trip to reach an alternate.

Colonel Hasty touched the TRANSMIT button on the intra-cockpit communication system. "OK, Captain, switch to both number twos. Major, we're coming up on Hamid. Give Gibraltar a call."

Unlike most military aircraft, Air Force One was equipped with both VHF and UHF radios, using the former for communications with civilian installations and the latter, more precise and reliable, for military. Since the president's personal aircraft used almost exclusively civilian airports once outside the United Sates, the seemingly redundant equipment was necessary. Major Patterson's voice filled Hasty's headset. "Good morning, Gibraltar Center, U.S. Air Force One with you at flight level four-two-oh."

The Irish accent was thick enough to be spread with a butter knife. "Top 'o the morning to you, too, Air Force One. We have you radar contact two-eight northwest of Hamid at flight level four-two-oh. Squawk two-zero-one-zero."

"Two-zero-one-zero," Patterson repeated, confirming the new transponder code as he entered it into the beacon-like device.

Hasty stretched in his seat. "I make a little more than 2,500 nautical."

"Confirm that," piped the flight engineer. "2,657 to be exact. If there are no changes in the winds aloft, we need to move the ETA up about forty minutes."

Arriving before the host country had the normal bands, military ranks, and welcoming committee arrayed on the tarmac would create an international incident. More than once, Hasty had had to fly a holding pattern upon an early arrival. The waste of fuel appalled him.

"Major," Hasty said to Patterson, "text our people in Cairo of the new ETA."

"Yes, sir!"

"And make sure they acknowledge."

Hasty hoped the premature ETA would be the biggest glitch the flight had to offer. He enjoyed excitement as much as the next person, just not on the job.

60

Gendarmerie
Timbuktu, Mali
Forty Minutes Earlier

From his recon the day before, Viktor had learned only a few streets had names in Timbuktu. At least not names posted at corners or on buildings like any city he had ever seen. Best he could tell, there was simply "the street where bazar is" or "the street that runs by the police station." Things like that. If one of the narrow, meandering lanes with sand over your ankles didn't pass some landmark, it simply had no name.

That was true of the kilometer of road that went from the police station west to the Sankore Mosque. The police station was also a puzzle. Like many third-world countries, there was no such thing as police in the sense of a civil force whose function it was to preserve order and keep the city safe from crime. These men were militia, soldiers, whose main job, Viktor guessed, was to discourage any number of rebel, separatist, or religious factions from taking over the area.

After his trip to the Sidi Yahya Mosque yesterday, he had come to this street and haggled with a street vendor whose donkey-borne wares had included flashlight batteries, rubber flip-flops made in

China, strips of brightly colored cotton cloth, and plastic bottles full of murky water, the source of which was something Viktor didn't dare speculate upon.

Viktor had been interested in none of the above but the pantomime debate had afforded him an opportunity to observe the police station. Three trucks, two Toyota pickups and a Suzuki with what looked like a .50-caliber machine gun mounted on the bed. Through glassless windows of the station itself, he could see perhaps four or five figures lounging under an overhead fan. There might be more he could not see.

No matter; it was the vehicles that had his interest. That was why he was standing in this sandy road in the predawn darkness. The police station was dark, apparently unused during the night. The important thing was that the three trucks were silhouetted against the darker night sky.

Unslinging a sack from his back, he heard voices and the squeak of footsteps in sand. Hastily picking up his bag, Viktor retreated into the darkest shadows he could find, that given by one of the five million or so trees the World Food Program had planted in and around the city in hopes of slowing the encroaching desert, now one of the few remaining trees that had not been chopped down to make charcoal as soon as the well-meaning but naive WFP representatives had left.

Viktor could hear two voices now, a series of sounds more like clicks and grunts. Certainly not French, the country's official language. Koyra Chiini, Arabic, Bambara, or one of the dozens of dialects indigenous to the city. The only thing he knew was they were getting closer. He guessed no one other than the militia or those early for worship would be out at this hour. And the footsteps were coming from, not toward, the mosque.

A voice in unmistakable English asked, "Kremlin, you online?"

Dermo! Shit! He should have remembered to turn off the little two-way radio Jason had given them all!

The approaching voices stopped. Then resumed. The inflection was certainly a question answered by a single word. Carefully placing his feet, Viktor pressed backward until stopped by a wall. He turned the knob on the device in his pocket. He thought he had turned it off, but he sure wasn't going to chance exposing the lighted dial if he were mistaken.

The footsteps began again, this time much slower. They—whoever "they" were—were searching for the source of the radio broadcast. Viktor was trapped. The slightest move might well give him away.

Wait a minute. What was he hiding from? He had done nothing wrong, not yet.

But what if they looked in the bag?

Why would they? In a city where merchandising was largely a curbside enterprise, a man in Bedouin attire carrying a sack would hardly be worthy of a second look. At least during daylight hours. Well, he couldn't stay where he was and do the task he had been sent to do.

He took a step forward, then another. One hand gripped the bag, another the butt of the Glock under the Bedouin vest.

Suddenly, he was blinded by a flashlight. A voice was demanding answers to questions he could not understand. In the periphery of the light, Viktor could see uniforms. Militia. He shrugged and shook his head as his eyes rolled. In third-world countries the nonviolent mentally disabled are more often left alone than institutionalized. The problem in playing this role was that few would mistake the fair-skinned, clean-shaven Russian for a bearded, desert nomadic Bedouin.

Viktor kept the lower part of his face covered by the flowing ends of his kaffiyeh while he muttered, a man not comprehending.

Now the questions were coming harsher and in another language. Viktor's mumbling became more agitated.

One of the two spoke, this time to his companion. The other man laughed. The light went off, and the two vanished in the direction of the police station.

Viktor stood still for a full minute, making sure they had really gone before he reached into his bag and began the task he had been assigned.

61

Sankore Mosque
Timbuktu, Mali
A Few Minutes Later

If any of the waiting worshipers noticed the sound, they did not comment on it. A rough rumbling that seemed to come from the ground up, from a single minaret, from everywhere and nowhere all at once. It was a noise that came and went there. Updating the electrical work, the imam had explained, although no one had ever seen an electrician coming or going, nor, for that matter, was there an electrician of that level in the city. Except for the few hotels, such work was done by general handymen, for there was not enough of it to support a specialist. Many homes had electric lights and fans, a few even televisions, but none possessed the elaborate schemes of climate control, lighting, cooking, and other electronic systems found in the most humble of American homes.

The paucity of electrical equipment was the reason the facade of the mosque was not illuminated, as would become a World Heritage site. It would be difficult to imagine Notre Dame or Westminster in total darkness, but Sankore, possibly older than either, with its exterior beams jutting from its face, was just that: dark.

At the base of the west-facing minaret, Emphani and Andrews waited, also in Bedouin garb, as the night's darkness began to fade into a dishwater dawn.

Inside the minaret, Moustaph and Abu Bakr also waited.

"Only minutes until the infidel American's plane reaches the target area," Abu Bakr announced.

"How will you know exactly when to fire," the other man asked.

Abu Bakr pointed to the tiny earbud almost obscured by his head-dress. "Our friend who is monitoring both the radio transmissions and radar returns will tell me the instant the plane reaches the designated point, Hamid. Allah willing, the electronic aiming system will deliver kilometer-wide bursts of particles at the plane's altitude and a point just east of Hamid on an intercept of the aircraft's heading."

Moustaph nodded in what he hoped was a knowledgeable manner. He understood few of the devices of the modern world. TV, cell phones, and computers were not specifically condoned in the Holy Book, and were therefore contraptions of the devil. Had not cell phones been perverted by the American devils to serve as a means of pinpointing a number of his former comrades to those devices of Satan himself, drone aircraft? Even now, that thing Abu Bakr had in his ear could be guiding one of those invisible, soundless engines of death. If it was Allah's will, so be it.

Still, the thought gave little comfort.

Hell's contraptions or not, only a fool would deny modern devices were imperative if a modern-day caliphate were to be established, no matter how unholy. The answer was to let the Abu Bakrs of the world use them, thereby saving the true believer from becoming *khawarij*, outside the religion.

He became aware Abu Bakr was saying something.

"Can you assist in moving the machine closer to the window? For our safety, I want the nozzle outside."

Moustaph was reluctant, praying he would be forgiven for touching the machine in a greater cause. He was surprised at how easily the large weapon swiveled, the nozzle now inches across the windowsill.

Below, in the dawn's gray light, Emphani and Andrews saw the protrusion break the plane of the minaret's side.

"Showtime," Andrews muttered as he clicked twice on the transmit button of his radio.

They still had to wait, but this time only for seconds. Then they would be executing a plan that worked only with split-second timing.

62

Colonel Wild Bill Hasty tapped gently on the door before a muffled "Come in."

The "White House" part of the aircraft—the presidential suite, office, and conference room—was located along the starboard of the 747, leaving a hallway along the portside wide enough to accommodate two Secret Service members who were posted there from the time the president entered the plane until the time he left it.

Hasty entered the office section. With its solid wooden desk and heavy leather chairs, there was little to suggest the room was not a normal suite in any office building in the world. Only the muted hum of four General Electric CF6 engines and an occasional tremor of light turbulence suggested otherwise.

As pilot-in-command as well as commanding officer, protocol required that Hasty, not a subordinate, deliver any significant news of the flight.

The president looked up from some papers on the desk, a question on his face. "Yes, Colonel?"

"Looks like we'll be about forty minutes ahead of schedule, sir."

The president smiled, always amused at the precision with which things were done aboard this aircraft. "*About* forty minutes?"

"I'll have the exact time as soon as the flight engineer completes her recalculations of anticipated ground speed, sir."

"You have notified the Egyptians of an early arrival?"

"We have, sir. They acknowledged receipt."

"Sounds as though you and your flight crew have it all under control, Colonel."

"I believe so."

The president gave a dismissive nod as he returned to the papers on the desk before him. "Carry on, then."

Hasty silently slipped back into the hallway.

63

Hotel la Colombe
Rue Askia Mohammed
Timbuktu, Mali
Seconds Later

The double clicks told Jason that Emphani and Chief were in place on the western face of the minaret, the side with the window facing away from him that he could not see. An earlier triple radio click had told him Viktor had completed one phase of his assignment and was ready for the next. It should all be over in less than three minutes, 180 seconds Jason knew would stretch into a lifetime.

There was just enough light by now for him not to need the infrared scope. Jason could see the two men ostensibly in conversation just outside the open doorway of the minaret. Four more were scattered within a few feet. None of them seemed interested in joining their fellows inside the mosque as the last of the electrically enhanced muezzin's chanted *adhan*, the call to prayer, faded from the loudspeakers mounted on each corner of the mosque. Each man's loose garments could—and most likely did—conceal an AK-47, which would be of no use to its owner this morning.

Jason placed the scope's crosshairs on the forehead of the man to the right of the door and took a deep breath, exhaled, took another and held it, held it . . .

The blast of a .50-caliber rifle or machine gun was stunning in loudness, which was why, under ideal circumstances, the shooter would be wearing some sort of ear protection. So great was the reaction to such a powerful shell, without the unique recoil absorption system of the Barrett, a dislocated shoulder might have been the result.

Jason noticed none of this. A pink mist surrounded the target's head as the plain-tipped anti-personnel round removed the top third of the man's skull with near-surgical precision. He was dead seconds before the sound of the shot reached the mosque, and longer than that before his lifeless body hit the ground.

Before Jason could bring the sight to bear again, the remaining guard threw himself into the open doorway of the minaret, fumbling for his weapon as he disappeared behind the mud-brick wall.

Fine with Jason. He had anticipated the move. The next round he had loaded into the Barrett's clip was silver-tipped armor-piercing incendiary. Focusing the Leupold scope on the edge of the doorway, he could make out the muzzle of an AK-47 poking past the left side. He moved the scope's sight a few hundredths of an inch left, now seeing nothing but the mottled brown of the dirt building material.

Once again the .50 caliber fired. By the time Jason could bring the scope back, there was a hole the size of a manhole cover in the side of the mosque where a large, wet blob of red dripped down the back wall. Whether the bullet, shards of sun-baked mud, or both had done the job mattered little.

The remaining four men had scattered to what meager cover the courtyard of the mosque offered while firing in every direction, the mark of poorly trained troops. Two were cowering behind the fountain, occasionally taking a shot at imaginary targets. One or two actually hit the hotel's facade, doing little more than chipping away crumbs of mud. Another, uncertain of the source of the fire, was pressed against the buildings wall in clear sight. The fourth had managed to gain what little shelter the shattered doorway of the minaret provided.

Jason swallowed and withdrew his finger from the trigger. He had to force himself to stop the killing, destroying those people, one man at a time. They had been responsible for 9/11 and Laurin's death.

But he was not here today to indulge himself in the enjoyment of splattering Al Qaeda brains and intestines against the crude mud brick.

Reluctantly, he stepped away from the Barrett.

64

Gendarmerie
Timbuktu, Mali

The shots made Captain Elijah Yahya al Wangam of the National Army of Mali nearly drop his morning coffee. Not that shooting in Timbuktu was that rare. Bandits, FNLA, Tuaregs, Islamic Maghreb, all had made an effort at seizing power in the ethnically diverse and, in al Wangam's opinion, ungovernable, northern part of the country within the last twelve months. What these people were fighting over, he could not imagine. Sand, stones, mud buildings, a few sheep and goats with an occasional camel. Hardly worth killing people over. Had the politicians in Bamako the intelligence of a pile of camel dung, they would let these people secede in peace and thank them for it.

Now they were at it again, whoever "they" were; and al Wangam and his woefully small garrison would have to restore the peace. He was reaching for the citizens' band radio just as M'kal, his lieutenant, stuck his head into the room.

"Make sure Paarth is awake and sufficiently sober," he ordered, referring to the third man on duty that morning, if reporting stumbling and reeking of alcohol could be considered on duty. Yes, he would have loved to fire him, but once again, this decision had to be made in faraway Bamako. "Bring the Suzuki around and make sure the .50 caliber is loaded while I try and raise the off-duty men. We may have a full-scale insurrection on hand."

Thornbush hedges were common in Timbuktu. Not only did the prickly plant thrive in arid, semi-desert conditions, its armament of thick spikes of thorns made it one of the few living things a goat couldn't eat, thereby presenting a natural defense of the small gardens the locals cultivate with a great deal more optimism than success.

It was from behind one of these natural barriers that Viktor watched the hurried departure of Timbuktu's finest. Three men, two in the truck's cab and a third clutching onto the machine gun mounted on the bed behind, screeched out of the Gendarmerie's dirt parking lot and slid into a turn toward the sound of occasional gunfire.

The driver either did not see or did not understand the peril presented by the series of spike strips Viktor had laid out in the predawn darkness, a series of plastic strips about four feet in length, each with half a dozen steel spikes sticking six inches above the roadway, the same simple, but effective, tool that had ended so many televised high-speed chases.

What happened next would satisfy a fan of true slapstick. The rock-worn tires of the truck somehow made it past the first row, either avoiding them or showing no effect. The second set of spikes not only punctured the tires, the immediate effect was rubber spaghetti. For a second, the steel rims struck sparks against the rocky sand with a grating sound. Then the lug bolts sheared from the torque and strain and one or more of the wheels went its own way.

The truck skewed like a bronco suddenly running out of rope, launching the man standing on the bed into a less than graceful dive. Reversing ends, the vehicle began a spin, sending both doors flapping like those of an immature bird trying to fly. Instead, what became airborne was the truck itself as it dug its nose into a sand dune and flipped onto its back.

Viktor watched he cab's two upside-down occupants dangling from their seat belts as they struggled to get free. He keyed his radio. "Police not a factor."

65

Sankore Mosque
Timbuktu, Mali

Within seconds of Jason's first shot, Emphani and Andrews shed their Bedouin attire and were scaling the steep slope of the pyramid-like minaret like mountain climbers. A rope was tossed over a beam before each man pulled himself up, retrieved his line, and tossed it over the next protruding wooden log. Slow work, but certainly a better means of attack than the original plan, which had contemplated a frontal assault on the door on the other side of the minaret.

Each man carried only a knife and pistol for armament. Were anything heavier needed, the battle would be lost. Also, weight had to be saved for the other objects they carried in their backpacks. Andrews was standing on tiptoe to throw his rope over the next beam above his head when he felt his footing give way. He just had time to lift himself up when the wood beneath his feet snapped off like a broken matchstick.

"How the hell does wood in the desert rot?" he hissed at Emphani who was being less than successful in hiding his amusement.

"There is a rainy season here. That is why it is not quite desert.

Perhaps one too many servings of *assab* at dinner last night is at fault, not the wood."

Andrews started to retort he had eaten less of the spiced meat poured over boiled, cracked millet than Emphani, then realized the absurdity of arguing out here on the side of the minaret and pulled himself up to the next beam.

Inside the minaret, Moustaph watched uselessly as Abu Bakr entered a series of numbers into a laptop as they came to him through the earbuds. The older man felt purposeless in the face of such technology, but was determined to see this, his greatest victory over the infidels since 9/11, completed. He was mentally reviewing the CD already in the hands of Al Jazeera, Kawthar, and other major Islamic television networks in which he explained to the world at large why Al Qaeda and its allies would fight to the death to remove the Crusaders from the land of the Prophet, may Allah give him peace. Even the stations in America would run translations of parts of his speech, including Fox, the one hated most by the martyred Bin Laden, may Allah raise up his soul.

Speaking of whom, Moustaph . . .

These was a sound from outside the minaret, a sound right outside the window like the snapping of a dry twig but much, much louder.

Abu Bakr had heard it, too. Both men struggled to get past the giant nozzle to the window, but there simply wasn't room for one, let alone two adults. The two men had the same idea at the same time: They swung the machine back away from the window and pressed forward to the opening.

For an instant, Moustaph could not believe what he was seeing: Two men, one white, one black, were standing, no, climbing, on the exposed wooden beams below. That devil Peters! But how . . . ? For the whole past day, the American had not left the hotel according to Moustaph's spies. Moustaph had been certain the president's plane, or what was left of it, would be at the bottom of the Atlantic before Peters could figure out a way to prevent it. But now . . . ?

Reaching into his shirt, Moustaph produced a 9-millimeter Makarov, a souvenir of his service with the mujahideen against the Russian invaders of Afghanistan two and a half decades ago.

Abu Bakr knocked his arm aside. "No time! We fire now or it will take minutes to recompute! Get the nozzle back into position!"

Moustaph complied. He would deal with the man's insubordination later.

Emphani and Andrews were on the row of beams just below those even with the window. Andrews tied his rope to the wood protruding overhead, looped the ends around his belt to free his hands and hung his backpack from it. In seconds, he had attached a short hose to something in the pack. A few feet away, Emphani held a knife in a position where it could be thrown at anyone appearing at the window.

"Fire the thing, you insolent son of a dog, fire!" Moustaph snarled at Abu Bakr.

Hose in his right hand, Andrews used his left to raise his body until his eyes were level with the bottom of the window. He was looking into a narrow room almost completely filled with the machine. Jammed into a corner was a small, low table with two cushions stacked upon it and a pot Andrews guessed was designed to hold tea.

There were two men, one of whom had what looked like a Russian pistol in his hand. No time to take him out, just . . .

Ducking his head below the windowsill, Andrews squeezed the grip in his hand. There was the crack of a pistol and the angry buzz of a bullet past his head a split second before a click of a battery generated a spark and the hiss of escaping gas, and, instantly, the *whoosh* of the expansion of superheated air, a much magnified sound of the burner of a gas stove igniting.

There was a duet of screams from inside as a jet of napalm flames licked the room, hungering for its contents at the same time it was glued to them.

Andrews swung down from the window, making room for Emphani, who was reaching into his own backpack. Was that a red blotch Chief saw on the front of his shirt? No time to ask. Emphani was holding a package the size and shape of a book, a little something the Russian explosive expert, Viktor, had concocted. He snatched a string from the parcel and tossed it into the window. Both men hastily rappelled down the side of the minaret, dodging the beams that had made their ascent possible.

From the hotel window, Jason saw smoke belch from the minaret's entrance, an assurance Andrews and Emphani had at least partially succeeded.

He spoke into the mike of the citizens' band radio. "I need a taxi to the airport."

Viktor's cue. He would be outside the hotel in the Toyota in less than a minute. Jason glanced through the scope and fired two random shots into the mosque's courtyard to freeze the men cowering there.

"Your taxi is here, sir," Viktor's disembodied voice said.

Jason took one last look through the scope. He had hoped, prayed if you could so define his pleas to an uncaring universe, that he would see Moustaph make a break through that door. Likely, the flame-thrower had incinerated the bastard. Still, killing him, putting a bullet into the very face of evil, seeing one of the brains that had plotted 9/11 splattered over desert sands, would be a catharsis, an expurgation of the irrational guilt Jason suffered. Laurin had been on her way to fetch him a cup of coffee that late summer morning. Had it been the other way around . . .

No time for rumination. As much as he wanted to see Moustaph's dark face quartered by the crosshairs of the Leupold, he could not risk the lives of his men on the chance the man had survived the flame-thrower's blast or what was to come next.

66

Knapsack on his back, Jason dashed through the lobby, the Barrett in his hands, wiping the smile from the desk clerk's face to be replaced by astonishment. The camera equipment had become as superfluous as the *National Geographic* charade, both left in the room.

Viktor was in the driver's seat of the Toyota truck parked at the front door. "Taxi? Is set rate for airport!"

Carefully placing the sniper's rifle in the truck's bed, Jason climbed into the cab. "First the mosque. And stand on it!"

Emphani and Andrews had shed their backpacks the instant they could spare a hand to wriggle out of the straps. Emphani took a step before his knees buckled.

Without hesitation, Andrews scooped him up, slinging him across his shoulders in a fireman's carry. He immediately felt the warm fluid soaking through his own shirt. "Goddammit, man, why didn't you say you were hit?"

A faint chuckle. "And you would have done what, call 9-1-1?"

Before Andrews could reply, there was an earth-trembling blast and a hot wind strong enough to nearly knock him down. Turning, Emphani still draped across his shoulders, he gaped at what he saw.

The top half of the minaret had simply vanished, leaving a cloud of gray-brown dust slowly settling around the shattered base like a woman putting on a shawl. Tiny metallic parts, the remains of the machine, were distant stars in the early morning light. Viktor was as skillful with explosives as he proclaimed himself to be.

"Jesus Christ on a . . ."

Apparently, his astonishment at the amount of damage done by a pound and a half of C-4 had rendered him unable to describe the appropriate mode of transportation.

The battered Toyota's worn brakes screeched just outside the mosque's courtyard. Jason was yelling and motioning from the passenger's seat.

Burdened with Emphani, Andrews waddled across the sand. "Gimme a hand here, Artiste."

Jason helped Andrews gently lay Emphani flat in the truck's bed before climbing over the side. "You ride with Viktor. I'll see if there's anything I can do."

Andrews took one last look. "Poor bastard took one meant for me."

Jason was unpleasantly surprised how much blood had accumulated in the truck's bed in the few seconds Emphani had lain there. Kneeling, Jason pulled his knife from its leg scabbard and cut away the blood-drenched shirt. A small tide of crimson was flowing down the right arm. It didn't require a second look to see why: A neat hole just below the armpit was gushing blood like an uncapped oil well. Jason used the knife to cut a strip from Emphani's shirt and then to tighten the rude tourniquet. From what he could see, the brachial artery had taken a direct hit. Without medical help in the immediate future, the man would bleed out. Jason had seen worse deaths. A fatal loss of blood meant the victim drifted quietly off to sleep, never to wake. Relatively painless or not, helplessly watching a comrade die was not an experience to which Jason would ever become accustomed.

"How bad is it?" Emphani was whispering.

"Ah, a scratch. You'll be fine."

It could have been a cough, but more likely it was a weak laugh. "Jason, you cannot lie for *merde*."

Before Jason could reply, Emphani had grabbed his shirt in a remarkably strong grip. There was nothing strong about the voice, though. Jason had to put his ear next to Emphani's lips to hear.

At first, he thought he couldn't hear. Then it dawned on him what the dying man was saying.

"Harvard?"

Emphani smiled, managed a nod, and lay back flat.

Whatever thoughts and emotions Jason had were interrupted by a frantic tapping on the cab's rear windshield. Chief's mouth was open, yelling something that could not be heard over the rumble of an exhaust long without a muffler, the rattle of a chassis loosened by washboard-like roads and the general clatter of loose objects banging around the bed with each gully, ditch, or pothole. What was clear was that he was over Jason's shoulder. One glance answered the unasked question.

Behind them, almost obscured in the Toyota's dust, was another truck, this one mounted a flashing blue light and filled with armed men in uniform. Apparently, Mali's finest had not only managed to survive the damage Viktor had done, but round up reinforcements as well. Worse, they seemed to be gaining.

67

36° 45' 47" N, 3° 3' 2" E
Algeria
42,000 feet
Twenty-Six Minutes Later

Colonel Hasty had never flown in Algerian airspace but he had heard the stories: Strict adherence to ATS routes to avoid endless military airspace, no matter how circuitous, constant fuel consuming changes of altitude and controllers whose English was unintelligible despite the fact the language was the lingua franca of aviation.

That was why he was pleasantly surprised to hear a very American voice in his head phones. "Air Force One, descend to and maintain flight level three-one-oh. You are cleared Cairo International direct. Stay with me. Oh yeah, give my best to your chief passenger."

Though non-aviation-related chatter was discouraged on the airways, the controller had started it, and rank does, in fact, have its privileges, and Air Force One ranks right on up there.

"Uh, I'll do that, Algiers Center. You sound like an American. Midwest, if I'm guessing right."

"Indianapolis originally. Worked Atlanta Center till '82. Listened to the damn union and went on strike in '81. Got fired and been here ever since. Not half bad if you don't mind sand, heat, and couscous with every meal. Good news is there's no retirement age here, not if you have any aviation experience. Sure would like to go home, though. Maybe you could put a word in with your boss."

Hasty had come across the world's most garrulous air-traffic controller. Surprising he hadn't been fired before defying a presidential order to return to work.

As is so often the case for people who work closely together over a long period of time, Patterson knew what his superior was thinking. "Maybe the guy just gets long-winded when he has a chance to chat with a fellow American. '82? That's before my time."

"Maybe so but just our luck to run into an air traffic controller who likes to talk."

Had Hasty any idea of what had happened just more than thirty minutes ago in arguably the most obscure place on Earth, he might have had a different concept of luck.

68

Timbuktu, Mali

With one hand Jason held on to the side of the truck bed while he picked up the Barrett with the other. He had no intent to kill or injure the men behind. They were simply doing a thankless job of trying to keep order in a lawless place in a fourth-world country. On the other hand, he had no intent of spending time in some hellhole of a jail while explaining the destruction of part of the mosque as well as the deaths of several of its occupants, either.

Kneeling, he rested the Barrett's barrel on the truck's tailgate. The precision sight was worse than useless in the bouncing truck. He removed it, clumsily dropping one of the mounting screws. No matter. If he failed in what he was about to attempt he would have to ditch the incriminating rifle anyway. He used his knees to wedge himself into a corner of the bed while one hand held the rifle and the other searched the pockets of his cargo pants until he found what he was looking for. Then he spread out in a position as close to the prone as possible.

Although probably not doing forty miles an hour, the rutted road made the ride bone jarring. Without the scope, there was no rear sight, only the circled post sight well aft of the muzzle. With the following vehicle bouncing above and under his aiming point, a single sight would do. This was an imperative shot, but one that did not require great precision.

Patiently, Jason waited. The front of the truck behind jounced into the air as it hit a rock, something, then dove as its front wheels dug into a pothole or rut. The process repeated itself irregularly. As the bumper came up again, he fired.

For an instant, he thought he had missed. He was already jacking another round into the chamber when the truck disappeared behind a geyser of steam. A .50-caliber armor-piercing bullet into the already overheated radiator will do it every time.

He made his way forward, careful to hold on and tapped on the glass. The response was a thumbs-up from Andrews.

Jason's smile faded as he put down the rifle and knelt beside Emphani. The man's eyes were closed and the slight rise and fall of the chest bespoke shallow breathing. Jason removed, replaced, and tightened the tourniquet, more because it was the only thing he could do than because he thought it would do any good. As if to mock him, the blood seemed to pump even faster than before. Emphani's lips moved slightly although his eyes remained closed. Perhaps a final prayer to Allah before he went to meet the Prophet in person?

The roar of aircraft engines overhead made Jason look up to see a venerable old DeHavilland Twin Otter descending. To Jason's right was the two-story brown terminal building, its sole decoration fading red letters across the front proclaiming AÉROPORT DE TOMBOUCTOU. There was no parking lot per se, but a gaggle of vintage Japanese trucks with varying degrees of body damage was double-parked in front.

Past the terminal, an olive drab Bell UH-1 "Heuy" helicopter sat among rusting remnants of general aviation aircraft. Only the slowly rotating blades and the characteristic *wump-wump* of its jet turbine engine indicated it was not a part of the aviation graveyard. Jason knew the identification numbers along the rear fuselage probably belonged to some long dead plane, possibly one in Vietnam where the model had starred on nightly newscasts into the 1970s.

As Viktor drove the Toyota closer to the left side, the overhead blades whined into a blur. Two men in flying helmets and uniforms without insignia appeared at the open cargo door. They placed what looked like a Browning .50-caliber machine gun into a mount and fed in an ammunition belt.

Viktor screeched to a stop within a few feet of the open door. He and Andrews were on the ground almost before the truck's engine died and began ticking with heat. The two men lowered the truck's tailgate. Viktor climbed in and slid his hands under Emphani's limp arms, started to lift, stopped, and looked at Jason, shaking his head.

Emphani was gone.

Jason jumped to the ground and took each of Emphani's boots in a hand before snapping at Viktor. "Go ahead and lift. We'll put him aboard. We don't leave our dead."

Viktor's face showed that the Russian Spetsnaz did not share that tradition with the U.S. Army's Delta Force. Nonetheless, he did as Jason requested. As gently as possible, Jason and Viktor carried Emphani to the helicopter where the two men inside, faceless behind the shields of their helmets, lifted him aboard.

As Andrews, Viktor, and Jason threw their backpacks aboard and climbed in after them, the intensity of the whine from the rotor blades increased, the aircraft pitched forward, and the ground dropped away. There was no sound of a radio from the headphones inside the helmet one of the crewmen offered Jason. He guessed the 'copter was taking off without clearance from the tower. And why not? The Twin Otter was probably the sole traffic in the area for the next hour or so, and Mali had no air force to enforce order on departures.

But the country did have an army of militia, four or five of whom were gathered on the tarmac in front of the terminal with raised rifles. Although altitude and rotor noise prevented the sound of gunfire from being audible, Jason could hear the occasional rattle of small arms piercing the helicopter's aluminum skin. The odds were the Huey would be out of range before a lucky shot hit an engine, fuel line, or rotor blade.

The ship's crew elected not to take the chance. The .50 caliber rattled, sending a whiff of cordite throughout the cabin. Below, the tarmac erupted in a line of shattered pavement only ten feet or so from the men in uniform, sending them scattering for cover.

At what Jason guessed was about 2,500 feet, the Huey leveled off. Below, the silver ribbon of the silted up Niger River sparkled in the morning sun before the ship changed course. Now the scenery below was uniform, the trackless sands of the world's largest desert.

He shifted his view from the open cargo door to the Chief and Viktor. Both were staring straight ahead, their thoughts no doubt on what had happened, the mission completed, though at the cost of a comrade. Jason knew the feeling well. The adrenaline drained away, leaving an empty shell of weariness. The humor and bravado of the pre-mission minutes were replaced by quiet reflection.

Jason was not looking forward to delivering Emphani's body to his wife and daughter. He could, of course, simply have the remains shipped, but that was the coward's way, a violation of the sacred duty comrades in this line of endeavor owed one another. At the same time, he would turn over Emphani's share of Momma's largess, more money than he guessed the family had ever seen.

Then there was Maria, questions he would find difficult to evade, the issue of where to live next. He sighed. Sometimes combat was easier than the peaceful life. Before he knew what was happening, he fell into a light sleep. Had Andrews or Viktor noticed, they might have wondered why he was smiling. There was no way to know he was dreaming of a large, shaggy dog and a very fat cat with half an ear missing.

69

Eden Rock
St. Barts, French West Indies
The Following December
7:47 p.m. Local Time

The Eden Rock is just that: a rock jutting out into the small bay forming the beach at Saint-Jean. The promontory offers a splendid view from hotel's restaurant, an establishment that thinks nothing of charging the euro equivalent of thirty dollars for a hamburger of stringy, European-style beef. A side is, of course, extra, perhaps because here they are *pommes frites* rather than fries. That is just lunch.

Lobster, the clawless Caribbean variety, is priced by the gram so that a single tail can easily exceed a hundred dollars, which, as Jason had observed during his first visit, was chicken feed compared the price of rooms with a view of the beach. Those overlooking the parking lot or the very busy and noisy road for only slightly less.

Jason had a strong preference for the superior views and closer-to-reasonable prices at the nearby Village Saint-Jean and the quality of food served at Eddy's in Gustavia. But his preference was not what had brought him, Maria, and their just-arrived guest to the Eden Rock. At Maria's insistence, he had politely declined Viktor's invitation to stay at the Russian compound at Gouverneur. She had taken an instant dislike to the man for any number of reasons she enunciated except the real one. He treated women, particularly his wife, rudely; he drank far too much; and was way too loud for her comfort. Jason suspected none of those things really mattered to her. What did was that, with that intuition peculiar to the female sex, she somehow detected the smell of violence and death on him, a stench she only occasionally noted on Jason.

She had deemed the hotel "more appropriate." It was a phrase Jason had learned to simply accept since questioning it usually induced an argument he could neither understand nor win.

They sat at a table illuminated by candles, clothed in white linen, and set for three placed on a niche carved into the rock below the main dining room, watching luminescent waves fill and empty the crescent of the beach. Faint music floated from one of the many seaside bistros, a discordant rap beat as out of place on a French island as a polar bear in a jungle. Jason plucked the slice of lime from his Havana Club and tonic, squeezed it, and dropped it back into the tall glass.

Maria held up a pale glass of Pinot Grigio, sloshed it around, and took a tentative sip as she gazed around. "Simply lovely."

"Very romantic," Jason added, knowing this was small talk, a prelude to the interrogation that would follow.

He was never sure whether Maria's total intolerance of violence of any kind blinded her to the truth or made her unable to accept it. Just as she had brushed off his explanation of the injury to his leg, she had dismissed Timbuktu as the site of his last adventure.

"Timbuktu?" she had sniffed. "Why do you choose such outrageous stories? First, you are attacked by a woman with a knife on a train. Now you expect me to believe you were looking for something in a place I am not sure even exists. Isn't this Timbuktu, what is the word, the one that means the same thing?"

"Synonym?"

"Yes, a synonym for some place that does not exist?"

"I think that would be 'Shangri-La.' "

"Anyway, if you do not want to discuss what you have done, just say so."

He had, many times, uniformly resulting in being presented with her back in bed, if, in fact, she deigned to share the covers with him at all. A stony silence would rule their waking hours until one or the other found an excuse to be gone from the common residence for a few days.

And the same storm clouds were gathering again.

"Good evening, everyone."

Jason looked up to see Margot, her café-au-lait skin golden in the candlelight. She wore a long, diaphanous dress, more illusion than fabric, that was the rage among young women that season, as defined by the displays in the windows of Chanel, Prada, Christian Dior, and the other mavens of fashion that lined Gustavia's main street. Jason had noted that when it came to beach dress, the prices varied in inverse ration to the amount of fabric employed.

A white-jacketed waiter appeared just as Margot sat.

"I will have the same," she said, nodding toward Maria.

Jason chose not to comment on the anomaly of a young French woman drinking a very un-French Italian wine. Instead, he asked, "Did you have a pleasant flight?"

She rewarded him with a dazzling smile. "Other than a being a little late leaving Boston, yes." She knitted her eyebrows in a mock scowl. "But you should not have paid the extra for first class."

"You're worth it," Jason said.

The smile returned "Perhaps, but all the college boys are in coach."

A real sense of intrinsic versus extrinsic value.

"So, how do you like Harvard?" Maria asked.

"I love it. I cannot thank Monsieur Peters enough."

"That's Jason," Jason said. "All I did was pull a string or two."

Actually, a single string: Momma. He had not asked, nor did he dare speculate, what had persuaded the dean of admissions to accept a seventeen-year-old graduate of a French parochial school over the best and brightest the United States had to offer. Knowing Momma's lack of subtlety, it had possibly involved innuendos questioning his (or her) personal safety as well as that of the family, including the dog. Ah well, if the woman had no qualms about tricking Jason into risking his life, a metaphoric arm twisting of an academic would hardly trouble whatever semblance of conscious she had.

After all, she owed Jason far beyond the money. Seeing the joy on Margot's face every time she mentioned her school made him feel well compensated.

"And your mother is OK with you spending part of your holiday with us?" Maria wanted to know.

Her wine arrived and she waited for the waiter to depart before answering. "Mama is. With the money Papa left, she has purchased the restaurant building where we also live and the one next door. She is busy combining the two. It will be the grandest bistro on Marseille's waterfront. She is happy to have me out of the way for a few days."

The conversation turned to matters feminine: the best beaches as defined as to how many college-age boys might be there, when the shops downtown opened tomorrow.

Jason tuned it out. With a smidgen of luck, Maria would be so occupied with her new young friend, she would forget whatever he had been doing in Timbuktu, if, in fact, he had really been there.

Make that a couple of smidgens.

AUTHOR'S NOTE

Yes, Nikola Tesla was a real person and yes, he really does hold the U.S. patent for the radio as well as more than 900 others, including AC current. The oscillator existed as did his relationship with Mark Twain. Whether the death ray was real or not is subject to speculation. His words describing it to a reporter are accurately repeated in the story.

The events of June 30, 1908 also took place, including the dead owl.

There also seems to be some uncertainty as to Tesla's original nationality. The Croatia of the 1850s Austro-Hungarian Empire of Tesla's birth is not the same as today's Croatia. Tesla might well have been born in today's Serbia. The operators of the Tesla Museum in Belgrade certainly think so. I chose Croatia simply because, at the time I wrote the story, I had not been to Serbia.

I think that is what is called literary license.

Was he genius? Surely. A nutcase? A little of that, too. There are a number of biographies on the Internet for those inclined to dig deeper into one of America's lesser-known characters.

When writing fiction for a general audience, there is always a choice to be made when subjects of a scientific nature become part of the story: Burden the non-scientifically inclined reader with details he neither understands nor cares about, or make the scientific mind feel short-changed? As one who would be the nation's oldest high school student had physics been a required course, I'll leave the explicit details of why things work to my science fiction writing friends.

I do make an effort to be correct when dealing with historic events such as the Bosnian-Serb War or whatever one calls the 1990–1991 events in the Balkans, the greatest shedding of blood in Europe since World War II. This was an explosion of ethnic/religious hatreds that had simmered since multiple diverse people had been lumped together as Yugoslavia at the end of World War I. With the fall of the iron rule of Communism, there was nothing to prevent the chaos that followed. I think I got it right but understanding the underlying prejudices and hatreds, some of which go back four centuries, makes understanding the Israeli-Palestinian conflict simple in comparison. If I got it wrong, I'm sure I'll hear from some of you readers.

Yes, I know air-to-air tankers such as those described don't fly out of Andrews Air Force Base. Please see "literary license" above. In the same vein, I'm aware the Niger River is frequently not navigable as far north as to be within a few kilometers of Timbuktu.

In the spring of 2012, while this book was being written, the democratic government of Mali was overthrown by a cadre of young military officers who were dissatisfied with the handling of the latest Tuareg separatist rebellion in the Timbuktu Province. The Tuaregs seized the opportunity to take the city of Timbuktu and declare their long-desired independence. Whether the central government will let them go in peace or seek to reunify the country is anyone's guess. For that reason, I have chosen to not deal with the status of Timbuktu here.

And, finally, thank you:

Thank you, Chris Fortunato, my inventive and hardworking agent who took me on when my previously publisher had folded and my previous agent had retired. His knowledge of both the domestic and foreign publishing businesses have made him invaluable.

AUTHOR'S NOTE

Thank you, Rob Hart, my editor at MysteriousPress.com. Rob sees an extra twist to be had with each tale and improves the story thereby. He also catches the inconsistences that haunt every writer, all of which lends authenticity to the yarn.

GL
June 2012

EBOOKS BY GREGG LOOMIS

FROM MYSTERIOUSPRESS.COM
AND OPEN ROAD MEDIA

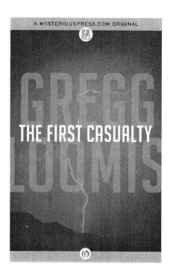

Available wherever ebooks are sold

MYSTERIOUSPRESS.COM

INTEGRATED MEDIA

MYSTERIOUSPRESS.COM

Otto Penzler, owner of the Mysterious Bookshop in Manhattan, founded the Mysterious Press in 1975. Penzler quickly became known for his outstanding selection of mystery, crime, and suspense books, both from his imprint and in his store. The imprint was devoted to printing the best books in these genres, using fine paper and top dust-jacket artists, as well as offering many limited, signed editions.

Now the Mysterious Press has gone digital, publishing ebooks through **MysteriousPress.com**.

MysteriousPress.com offers readers essential noir and suspense fiction, hard-boiled crime novels, and the latest thrillers from both debut authors and mystery masters. Discover classics and new voices, all from one legendary source.

FIND OUT MORE AT

WWW.MYSTERIOUSPRESS.COM

FOLLOW US:

@emysteries and Facebook.com/MysteriousPressCom

MysteriousPress.com is one of a select group of publishing partners of Open Road Integrated Media, Inc.

Open Road Integrated Media is a digital publisher and multimedia content company. Open Road creates connections between authors and their audiences by marketing its ebooks through a new proprietary online platform, which uses premium video content and social media.

CPSIA information can be obtained at www.ICGtesting.com
Printed in the USA
BVOW08s1443251013

334635BV00002B/5/P